What readers are
The Batch Magi

"An **absolutely delightful, a**_____, ____, _____
Priceless characterisation, right down to the lovable dogs, and
descriptions of flora and fauna by someone deeply in love with
the English countryside. It is a stunningly charming tale, one
that becomes a part of your heart."
Henrietta Bellows, Amazon

"I absolutely loved this wonderful book and its colourful
characters!… Kudos for **a fantastic reading experience**.
I just knew I was going to love it from the very first page!"
Jeri S. Connor, Amazon

"I loved this book! It's lyrical and very amusing, with **all the
charm of an old Ealing comedy**…"
Carole Kelcher, Amazon

"You know you love a book when you're a week past finishing
it and you're still savouring the language… **I found myself
often chuckling, sometimes wiping a tear, and on a few
occasions, reading sections aloud to my cat**…"
S. Kay Murphy, On Simply Being True

"I first got this book out of the local library, and then bought
a copy – I wanted to read it again and again. It's **a treasure, a
smashing read, funny and beautifully written**."
Anne James, Amazon

"… a lovely romp through a beautifully described English
(when it is not Welsh) countryside full of hedgerows,
meadows, and misty riverbanks, home to skylarks, peacocks,
and an assortment of beloved mutts. The descriptions are to
be savoured, not skimmed. **I thoroughly enjoyed my visit
to Batch Magna**, and am looking forward to reading the next
book in the series."
*Pamela Grandstaff, author of the Rose Hill Mysteries,
Virginia, USA*

CLOUDS in a SUMMER SKY

THE BATCH MAGNA CHRONICLES, VOLUME FOUR

PETER MAUGHAN

This edition published in 2019 by Farrago,
an imprint of Prelude Books Ltd
13 Carrington Road, Richmond, TW10 5AA, United Kingdom

www.farragobooks.com

ISBN: 978-1-78842-132-4

Have you read them all?

Treat yourself to the whole Batch Magna Chronicles series:

The Cuckoos of Batch Magna
Welcome to Batch Magna, a place where anything might happen. And often does...

Sir Humphrey of Batch Hall
The course of true love never did run smooth – especially not when badger baiters are involved.

The Batch Magna Caper
Sparks fly as a real gun and a real crook find their way into a historical re-enactment at Batch Hall.

Clouds in a Summer Sky
The steam boat *Batch Castle* starts carrying passengers once more, leaving local taxi magnate Sidney Acton with a score to settle.

The Ghost of Artemus Strange
Sir Humphrey's plans to play Father Christmas are thrown into doubt, and ghostly goings-on turn more chaotic than planned.

Turn to the end of this book for more information about Peter Maughan, plus – on the last page – **bonus access to a short story** by the author.

For Henrietta Bellows Lala
My friend across the water

Author's Note

I would like to thank Captain John Megoran, skipper of the PS *Kingswear,* who gave freely – and patiently – of his time and his wide knowledge of a working paddle steamer.

Chapter One

Smoke from the funnel ringed with Trafalgar blue and gold idled in the air above the PS *Batch Castle*. On deck, Sir Humphrey Strange, the 9th baronet and squire of Batch Magna and this March, took the cigar from his mouth and grinned beefily for the cameras of the local press.

"This is an historic occasion, boys!" he boomed, as the Church Myddle Silver Band on the landing stage finished with 'The Drunken Sailor' and started on 'Haul Away, Joe', the polish on their instruments liquid with sunlight, and the boat's whistle screamed three times, at full throttle, letting the village, the valley, know that they had steam.

Humphrey grinned again, looking up, as if the sound were visible, and waited until the notes had died.

"My great uncle, Sir Cosmo Strange, started the Cluny Steamboat Company over seventy years back now. A guy who went to London to sort out the family finances and came back instead with five paddle steamers," he said, sharing it with a grin of pride, as if to say, 'how's *that* for sorting out the family finances'!

"He bought them at a public sale on the old River Thames," Humphrey went on, re-telling a family legend. "And from there he sailed at their head to dry dock at historic Chatham, were they were took apart and hauled over to the railhead for the journey to Shrewsbury and the home waters of the Cluny, carried there on a train pulled by an engine called *Progress*. That's history for you, boys! And today we're gonna make a bit more history when the *Batch Castle* here once more sails under the company's flag. Today, boys – today," he announced, his voice lifting as the steam whistle erupted again, "the Cluny Steamboat Company is back in business! Even if there is only one of 'em," he felt obliged, on a quieter note, to add.

"Sir Humphrey, are there—" one of the reporters started.

"Humph, son, Humph," Humphrey reminded him.

"Humph. Any plans, Humph, for more working boats?"

Humphrey rolled the cigar round his mouth, his eyes narrowed at the river, as if calculating how many he could get on it.

"Well, we couldn't use the other three paddlers, that's for sure, because people, friends, live on them," he said then, reluctant to let go of the idea. "Like the Commander and his wife, Priny, did on this, till last year. But we did a straight swap, see, the *Castle* for one of the old Masters' Cottages on the river here."

He pointed at the deck saloon against inclement weather on the aft deck, with a galley to the stern of it. "Only a few months back the saloon there used to be their living quarters, a lounge, small bedroom and bathroom.

We left the kitchen, the galley, as it was. We're gonna be serving food and drink from it. It took a lot of work and money, converting it back – but luckily, unlike the other paddlers what was left of her engine hadn't been ripped out. That's the problem, see, guys, money. Money," he said again, shaking his head, pestered by that tiresome reality.

Reality, to the man who wanted to bring part of Tower Bridge home with him from his London honeymoon, bought with money he didn't have from a man who hadn't the right to sell it, even if it had been for sale, was a killjoy, a party pooper, a grey, boring presence turning up on the doorstep with a briefcase of facts and figures just as life had started to liven up.

"But you never know, boys, you never know," he added breezily, and winked, determined not to let reality have it quite all its own way.

"Anyway, gotta go now, it's my turn on the steam whistle."

The photographers wanted one more shot, and Humphrey, cigar in mouth, hands gripping the lapels of the Brooks Brothers executive suit his large frame was attired in, worn for the occasion with his best Yankees baseball cap, gazed, eyes narrowed, into the distance for their cameras, a man of destiny sizing up the future.

"And be sure to get a good one of Lady Clem and the babe," he told them then, waving the cigar, a Havana torpedo bought to go with the executive suit, in the direction of his wife with the newly arrived baby in her arms, a son to go with their daughter, Hawis, now playing tag among the crowd on deck with Jasmine Roberts's brood and their friends from the village.

"Ralph Franklin T Strange the Second. Gonna be running the joint one day. And my mom's about somewhere. Hey, and don't forget the Commander, the guy in charge. Get a couple of him in his new uniform. And Sion Owen, the head fireman, and Tom Parr, ship's chief engineer," he said, promoting both of them on the spot.

"We're doing the captain and crew next," one of the reporters said.

"Master, he's called the master. Shipping master. Make sure you get that right, fellas. Help yourselves to a drink. Hey, and don't forget to get that in about it being a historic occasion," he reminded them, already on his way through to the wheelhouse and the steam whistle, glad-handing people and slapping backs en route.

Humphrey was fond of the phrase 'historic occasion', the words used on the notices advertising the event, penned by Phineas Cook, a crime writer off one of the houseboats, the *Cluny Belle*, now wearing his steward's hat, as he put it, happily popping celebratory corks from one of the drinks hampers on a deck bench.

He considered it had a ring to it. And it referred to history, and Humphrey knew about history. It was responsible, through the feudal law of entailment, for where he was now, and he lived with it looking over his shoulder.

It followed him about, like the eyes on the family portraits lining the staircase of Batch Hall, his ancestral home. He carried it about with him in a title which went back to Charles I, and it waited for him each week in St Swithin's, home under its Norman roof to the 17th century alabaster figure of the first baronet, his sword and his Welsh wife Hawis by his side. And in case he needed another reminder, it sat above his head in the form of the Strange family escutcheon, painted in fading dark blue and gold on the wall of the squire's Jacobean box-pew. A box-pew in which this squire, in his Brooks Brothers suit, baseball cap in hand, diffidently, almost apologetically, took his rightful place with his family each Sunday.

Because if history had come to terms with Humphrey, an erstwhile, overweight short-order cook from the South Bronx, with a taste for Hawaiian shirts, baseball caps and cigars, Humphrey had yet to fully come to terns with it. History to Humphrey, a man who had largely been unencumbered by any sort of history, including that of his native USA, was like a parent or teacher he was still trying to prove himself to. Whatever he did as squire, he did with one eye on history.

And if today wasn't history then would somebody kindly tell him what the heck was.

And so Humphrey played on the paddler's whistle bell, varying the flow of steam and thus of pitch, as Tom Parr had taught him, a steamy song of triumph to history and to the man who over seventy years ago had brought the boats home.

The sound sending back for the older villagers there echoes of a past when Batch Magna felt like a little port, exotic with travel as far upstream as Shrewsbury and back, the five paddlers the company had then chugging up and down it like a bus service, carrying passengers and goods, and deck cargoes of livestock from the fields on market days, and crates of chickens, geese and Christmas turkeys.

And now that past had returned, or at any rate one part of it had, the PS *Batch Castle*, about to be put to work again after more than twenty-five years tied up at that landing stage, keeping company with the three other houseboats on the estate's stretch of river, all paddle steamers and all once part of the old Cluny Steamboat Company.

The PS *Sabrina*, the vessel which had made the full complement of that tiny fleet, would be acknowledged with a salute of steam as the *Castle* once more thrashed her way upstream past her wreck, a diving board for generations of village children, and with moorhens nesting in her broken wheels.

The boiler of the paddler had exploded two years into service when her master tried to push more speed out of her than her maximum eight knots safely allowed in an effort to beat a previous time to Water Lacy, the halfway stop on the journey to Shrewsbury.

The master of the PS *Batch Castle* would make no such mistake. If she went out of business then so would the new CSC, with the loss not only of the money invested in her, but of a potential income as much needed as anything else the estate did to keep things together.

It was a responsibility that Commander Cunningham, as master, had not taken lightly.

After lessons on her wheel from Tom Parr, an old CSC hand, paddling up and down to Shrewsbury, practising keeping the shallow-draught vessel on a straight course in the strong midstream current, and in and out of the twists and turns the River Cluny and the Severn were known for, he had applied for his master's licence.

The result of that test was framed on the back wall of the wheelhouse, along with all the other licences and certificates a working boat needed, ready to reassure any passenger who knew the Commander had only one eye and that he liked a drink.

He had one in his hand now, leaning on his badger head stick, talking to the first lieutenant, as he called his wife, Priny, now in charge of the CSC booking office, but today a passenger, one of the forty they were licensed to carry, a mixture of invited guests and first-come-first-served ticket holders.

The Commander was remarking that it was only last week, or a fortnight ago at the most, or so it seemed to him, that he and Tom Parr had been rowing up and down the river, bringing back salvaged bits and pieces from the wreck of the *Sabrina*. And now look at her.

And now look at her. She had been scraped, patched, welded and riveted, and her engine brought to working order. Her upperworks dazzled the eye with sunlight and fresh white paint, while elsewhere she wore the dark gold and Trafalgar blue livery of the old CSC, her name, with its fairground flourishes, touched up along the arches of her two side paddleboxes.

The company's house flag, a castle and lion and otter rampant in gold on a blue field, had been hoisted again on her mast, the red ensign, the flag of St George, the Stars and Stripes and the red dragon of Wales flew from staffs at the stern. And she was dressed in bunting like a tart's handbag, as the Commander had put it, red, white and blue fluttering from the masthead and from the funnel.

It was Tom Parr, one of the few villagers living to have worked for the old CSC, who had largely been responsible for the refitting of her engine. Tom had joined the company in the 1920s, a young motor mechanic who, after one trip on a paddler, happily went backwards, swapping the promising future of the internal combustion engine for the external one of the past.

In Tom's day, the engineer on the boats had also been the fireman. But then, in Tom's day, Tom's arm had been stronger, so Sion Owen, the estate's gamekeeper – or head gamekeeper, as Humphrey described him, ignoring the fact that he only had one of them – now worked on the plate, shovelling on the heat from the wheelbarrow loads of coal he'd pushed up the gangway the day before from John Beecher's yard in the village.

But Tom's real worth was in his head still, and he was once more on the deck of a working paddle steamer, in his white engineer's overalls and the aged company cap with the gold CSC ribbon he'd kept all these years, a castaway rescued from the Cluny's past.

It was then the Commander's turn for the press cameras, in his new navy CSC shipping master's uniform, navy and white cap with its badge of the Strange family coat of arms in a wreath of gold oak leaves, and four gold rings on his sleeves topped with Nelson loops.

He was photographed at the boat's wheel, and with Humphrey and Clem, and then with his two-man crew, and one with Priny on his arm, dressed as if for Ascot and wearing her pearls.

The Commander watched the reporters trooping after Tom to inspect the engine room, and moved his neck as if his collar were too tight.

"I only hope, Number One, that I don't prang her," he muttered in an aside to his wife. "And end up on the front page."

"Nonsense, Cunningham," Priny said briskly. "Of course you won't *prang* her. You haven't yet, and you've taken her up and down enough times."

"Not with forty odd souls on board, I haven't."

"Besides," Priny added, brushing at nothing on his shoulder above his Fleet Air Arm medal ribbons, "Tom wouldn't let you. And if you're good, I'll bring you up something in a glass once we're round the island," she said, referring to Snails Eye, an island they had first to go down to and round to start their journey upriver.

Tom had opened the sea cock and boiler-stop valves earlier to let steam, the lifeblood of the paddler, into her pumps and engines, and when he led the reporters into the small engine room behind the wheelhouse, one of them, finding the engine slowly turning, looked at his watch.

"I thought the departure time was ten o'clock."

"Ah, it is. I'm just warming it through, getting her joints moving. She's an old lady, and like me teks a bit of time to get going of a morning."

He nodded at Sion, shovelling coal into the mouth of the firebox.

"Same as her boiler there. Teks three days, it does, to get it up to a working pressure from cold, so's not to put too much stress on it, see."

"Where d'you get the water from?" one of the reporters asked, looking about him.

"From the river, of course. By a water feed pump, worked off the crankshaft," Tom said, as if that should be obvious.

"Nice engine," another reporter said vaguely.

"Ah, it is," he agreed, looking at it, fond as a parent, the strokes of the copper piston rods carrying light up and down on them from the overhead bulkhead lamps, its enamelled ironwork a shining post-office red. "That's a twin cylinder compound diagonal job, that is."

Tom told them how it worked, a simple tale simply told, of how the boiler turns water to steam, which is fed into pipes, where it expands under pressure to push a piston in the cylinder, which is then passed from the piston to the crankshaft, which turns the paddle wheels.

Tom told it gruffly, looking at them with the glare of age in his eyes, sounding defensive, or protective. This was his world, in the bowels of a late Victorian paddle steamer smelling of engine oil and grease, and the heat of her fire. That other world, beyond the hills of his valley, may do all sorts of clever things, and did, such as landing men on the moon. And let them, that's the way Tom saw it, as long as they left him and his twin cylinder compound diagonal steam engine alone.

"And a compound engine," he went on, pointing a oil-stained finger, "uses the remains of steam after it's pushed

18

the cylinder's piston to repeat the job in that second, low-pressure cylinder there. A twin cylinder job, see."

After they had left, Tom checked the steam pressure gauge on the boiler Sion was still heating up. They needed a working pressure of one hundred and twenty pounds per square inch. Less than that and the boat would move too slowly, if at all. More than that and there was a danger of her sharing the same fate as the PS *Sabrina*.

Not long after that Tom had his steam pressure. She was ready.

Sion, a Welsh bullock in a coal-stained singlet, his dark Elvis quiff flattened with sweat, was leaning on his fireman's shovel thirstily seeing off a pint of cider from a plastic gallon of it. He was done for now, the fire up, its heat burning at its banked heart like a sun around which everything needed to move the boat revolved.

Her fire was up and she breathed steam. She was ready.

The Commander was talking to Humphrey at the bottom of the wheelhouse steps, Humphrey waving his cigar at the river, describing, perhaps, the future of the new CSC.

"Her's ready, Commander," Tom reported.

Humphrey shot an executive cuff on his wrist watch. "And ten minutes before time, Tom!" he congratulated him.

"Thank you, Tom," the Commander said briefly, his good eye saying the rest. On the painted glass of the other, like blood in it, he was showing the flag, flying on this day that had come at last, the Union Jack.

"All ashore what's going ashore!" Sion bellowed, holding his fireman's shovel as if ready to help them on their way with it.

He followed the last of the dawdlers down the gangway and cast off fore and aft from the newly painted iron bollards that had once secured all the vessels of the CSC. He chucked the ropes up on deck to Tom and then hauled the gangway up after him.

He and Tom disappeared back into the engine room and the Commander limped up the wheelhouse steps on his stick, followed by the Cunninghams' Welsh collie, Stringbag.

He checked his watch, took his time lighting a pipe, and then rang down to the engine room on the brass telegraph bell for ahead, his good eye steady.

Tom pushed the ahead lever on the engine and turned the small wheel on the steam valve. And then turned it again, letting more steam into the cylinders, and pushed more speed out of the engine with the ahead lever.

The paddle wheels stirred, and started to turn, and there was cheering from the landing stage and waving from the port rail, as the *Castle* pulled slowly away with a double blast of steam, the Silver Band breaking into 'Hearts of Oak', the bouncy, sea-brisk notes following her out to midstream.

The new Cluny Steamboat Company was underway.

Chapter Two

Seen from the surrounding hills, Batch Magna sits in the palm of its valley as if placed there by a child's hand, a small model world of houses and cottages, manor house, shop, church and pub.

A Marcher village, the flag of St George flying from the Steamer Inn claiming it for England, the red dragon above the entrance to the Pughs' shop and post office for Wales, sheltering under the pinnacled Norman tower of St Swithin's Church and the tall, star-shaped chimneys of Batch Hall, a half-timbered, black and white Elizabethan confection, the ancestral home of Sir Humphrey and his family, and all that history.

The portraits of past squires and their families lining the wall of a Jacobean staircase looking down, or so it seemed to him, on the present squire and his baseball cap and Hawaiian shirts, and on the one-armed bandits, the bingo evenings, and the voice of trade, the business conferences in the servants' hall, the vulgar intrusion of Open Days and paying guests, and all the other means employed to keep what was left of the estate together and the Strange family under its patched roofs.

And now the *Batch Castle*, the spirit of Sir Cosmo, the old CSC, riding the river again, leaving behind its past, her sister ships, the three houseboats, and the PS *Sabrina.*

They returned faster than when they went up, coming down on the midstream current as if with a tide up her skirts, as the Commander put it. After the advertised hour and a half break at Shrewsbury, for lunch or shopping, they had sung their way back, led by Phineas Cook with his entertainments officer's cap on, and had come ashore at Batch Magna in a rowdy sort of holiday mood, a kiss-me-quick sort of air, as if returning from a trip round the bay.

It had been, everyone agreed, a great success, and they were now in the village pub drinking to it. They were at a table in the saloon bar, the larger of the pub's two bars, a room of worn Welsh flags and beams of estate oak, and a fireplace big enough to stable a pony.

Built in 1662, the Steamer Inn, a paddle steamer puffing away on its sign, had then been named the Black Boy in honour of a restored monarch, Charles II, until Sir Cosmo brought the boats home.

Framed photographs and other memorabilia of that time looked out silently now from a wall of the bar. Copies of sailing bills and freight charges, advertisements, tickets, local press reports, and photographs of the paddlers and the shipping masters and their crews, Sir Cosmo in a silk topper among the passengers in their best bonnets and bowlers, and the first herd of sheep being loaded, dog low at their heels.

The present day CSC shipping master was sitting with his crew and his wife Priny, and the river contingent, or the water gipsies, as Mr Pugh, village shopkeeper and rigid Methodist, disparagingly called them. Annie and Owain Owen, Sion's parents, who lived on what was once the flagship, the *Felicity H*, and Phineas Cook, pint of cider to hand, beaming pleasure at the occasion from under his Gent's Superior Panama, and Jasmine Roberts off the *Cluny Queen*, the next boat down from his, her brood a small riot in the room.

Humphrey and Clem were also there of course; Clem, who'd tripped up and down the river enough times on the practice runs, rejoining them there with Hawis and the baby, and Shelly, Humphrey's mother, chatting with Miss Wyndham. Miss Wyndham, a villager who had sailed as a passenger many times with the old CSC, had been one of the invited guests on the inaugural trip of the new CSC, and had dressed for it in her best summer frock and garden party hat, her face flushed with the sheer excitement of it all, and another schooner of sherry.

The Commander regarded them fondly with his good eye.

Lieutenant-Commander James Cunningham, DSO, DSC and Bar, RN (ret.), a wartime Fleet Air Arm pilot, had lost an eye in the same incident that had shattered his leg, and had commissioned a miniaturist to paint seven plain glass ones, six depicting scenes from his favourite paintings, famous sea battles and landscapes that spoke of England, the seventh flying the flag, usually worn when a bit of swank, a bit of defiance in the face of whatever, was called for, which in their rackety past lives had over the years covered a lot. Today he wore it in celebration.

He lifted his drink. "I give you Sir Cosmo. A man who had the great good sense not to listen to accountants. And to the PS *Batch Castle*, the old duck, and her future."

Chapter Three

A month after that someone else also had in mind the future of the Cluny Steamboat Company, and he did not wish it well.

Sidney Acton, the owner of what was once Globe Cars and was now the Kingham Prestige Car Service, was in his first-floor office when Dewi Brice, his bookkeeper and office manager, knocked softly and entered.

Dewi inclined his head. "Good morning, Sidney."

"Morning, Dewi," Sidney said, with something that might have been amusement, or contempt, and placing the teacup down on its saucer dabbed at the corners of his mouth with a paper napkin.

"The monthly returns, Sidney."

Sidney folded his arms, waiting with resigned impatience as the tall, stooped elderly man, bald like a monk, laid out the twelve stapled sets of figures, fresh from his Calcumatic, neatly on the desk in two columns of six, one set for each of the drivers.

This was the way Dewi had always done it and that was the way he continued to do it. Sidney had long given up telling him to just stick 'em on the desk. The old boy had come with the business when Sidney bought it three years before, and he'd kept him on for his local knowledge more than anything else.

Wilf Ellis, the previous owner, used to go through the returns sheet by sheet, finding more than just profit in them. He had built the business up from a single car, his own, and had driven most of the journeys logged there many times himself, knew the clients, had shared their lives from week to week, first schools, funerals, weddings, engagements, new births and the latest medical and dental appointment, until his own success isolated him in the first-floor office.

The only figure Sidney was interested in, as Dewi left as quietly as he had entered, was the combined total at the bottom of a single sheet with the twelve individual monthly returns on it in columns. As with business so with life, as far as Sidney was concerned: what's it add up to?

And what it added up to this month caused him, in a sudden spasm of agitation, to snap in half one of the Grosvenor Select biscuits he insisted on to accompany his Earl Grey tea.

He added the columns up, and then did it again, and still came to the same conclusion as Dewi's Calcumatic.

He scribbled the weekly totals down on a piece of paper, totted them up and arrived at the same monthly result for all twelve sets of figures. He then went through the returns sheet by sheet, running his accountant's eye down the weekly columns, adding them up and ending with the same totals.

But it wasn't long before he started to notice what he was looking at – or rather not looking at.

There were scarcely any journeys logged to Shrewsbury and back, the most profitable of the runs, along with his various council contracts. The From and To columns were full for each week on all the sheets, they'd been as busy over the past month as they usually were, now that his was the only taxi firm in town.

But entries for jobs to Shrewsbury were largely missing, the name of the town like a signature on a series of weekly cheques, long, regular runs there and back, with waiting time in between, all adding up to a steady, lucrative monthly total. Until now.

He didn't bother with the intercom.

He scooped up the single sheet of figures and went straight out of his office and across the landing into the office opposite, where he held it up like evidence, diverted for a brief moment by his secretary Shirley Meddins standing at a filing cabinet in white plastic boots and denim hot pants, before getting back to business.

Dewi beat him to it. "Shrewsbury," he said ruefully, looking up from the ledger in front of him and nodding, as if he'd just remembered it. "Yes. Yes, I know. I meant to mention that, Sidney. Completely slipped my mind."

Dewi hadn't meant to do anything of the sort. Let him find out for himself, that was his attitude. It went with calling him Sid behind his back, and the sabotaging of the Fortnum & Mason's biscuit barrel each week, replacing a week's worth of Sidney's Grosvenor Select with a cheaper version, and exchanging the Earl Grey leaf tea in the Wedgewood caddy with the contents emptied out of Cymru teabags, as he had that morning, knowing that Sidney, for all his London airs, wouldn't be able to tell the difference. He's an upstart, a counter jumper, a bloody damned, puffed-up blasted pip-squeak – an Englishman, he'd ended, running out of insults, muttering rebelliously with one ear cocked for the sound of Shirley, in early, coming up the stairs.

This was Dewi having his say, even if it went unheard. Another small act of revenge for Sidney's patronising attitude to him, and for referring to other Welshmen as Taffy, as if they all looked the same to him. He had never yet called him that, not to his face. But Dewi seethed at the thought of it all the same, having no doubt that to his chums in the back bar of the Blenheim and at the golf club, he, if spoken of at all, was reduced to a jocular note in Sidney's life, one called Taffy.

Dewi had found a new interest, along with old time dancing and the outdoor bowling club, the sort of social activities his doctor had suggested to help keep his mind off things: Sidney.

In his flat above a laundrette he regularly planned a more permanent revenge on him, while eating Sidney's Grosvenor Select biscuits after dinner and sipping his Earl Grey tea, without milk, as Sidney did, relaxing in an armchair in a cardigan and slippers, eyes closed to the background strains of Mantovani on the radiogram, and the latest satisfying end to Sidney.

It had started crudely enough, with an axe, which, one morning in Sidney's office, had finished off both Sidney and his antique reproduction desk. That had got things out of his system, but it wasn't really him. He wasn't a man to make an exhibition of himself. And it lacked entertainment value, being over almost as soon as it had begun. He had learned patience after that, and cunning, taking time and pleasure over the preparations, and ending up for the next one wearing gloves and hiding on the links with a silenced sniper rifle, waiting for Sidney, in his Pringle sweater and fancy spats, to appear and then taking him out with a single bullet to the forehead, a hole in one.

He had wired up Sidney's car with a bomb and timer, listening beatifically to the strings of Mantovani swelling in a crescendo as Sidney's life ticked on its way to an explosive finale. He had cut his brake lines with the hill on Sidney's way home in mind, sitting back, eyes closed, head moving gaily to the music, smiling his secret knowledge of the tragic accident waiting for his boss at the bottom. And had given himself up to grief as always afterwards, weeping crocodile tears at the untimely end of a colleague and a young businessman of promise, while clinging to Shirley at his funeral.

He had recently moved on to murder at its most refined and clandestine, involving disguises and false details in the poison books of different chemists' shops both sides of the border, before settling on arsenic. He was killing Sidney off slowly this time, savouring the spiking of his tea, watching Sidney die in instalments.

"You know, Sidney," he said now, with a small conscientious frown, and as if it had just occurred to him, "come to think of it, there was a piece in the *News* a short while back about an old boat, a paddle steamer, that's apparently been refitted and put back on the river again at Batch Magna, a village about six miles or so from here. It said in the paper that they were doing day trips up to Shrewsbury and back. And I wonder now, you know, I wonder if that's got something to do with it…?"

He gazed expectantly at Sidney, as if waiting to be told what he should think about it. While knowing that not only had it got something to do with it – it had *everything* to do with it.

He knew that because he'd recently partnered one of the regular Shrewsbury fares at the old time dancing in the community centre, one of the blue rinse ladies from the leafy part of town. And she'd come straight out with it as he twirled her round in a foxtrot, said that she and her friends were now taking the paddle steamer each week for their hair dressing appointments, and for shopping and lunch, and what's more they intended to keep on doing so. It was such *fun*.

"I *bet* it's got something to bloody well do with it!" Sidney snarled, glaring at him.

"Oh, it's great, that is, that boat!" Shirley put in, wiggling her way back to her desk. "It's like being at the seaside, or something," she shared with them chattily. "It's a scream, honestly! Me and Ronald went on it with my friend Fay and her boyfriend the other Saturday. It's ever so popular. And it's dead easy to get there from here, Batch Magna is, just hop on a bus," she said, naming a second rival to the Kingham Prestige Car Service. "There's one that gets you there just before the sailing…"

Her voice trailed off when she saw Sidney's face.

"It won't last, I'm sure, Mr A," she said, smiling at him in a sympathetic, motherly sort of way. "It's just a bit of a novelty, like, that's all. It won't last."

"A passing fad, Sidney," Dewi echoed reassuringly.

"You'll see," he added, after Sidney had closed the door sharply behind him, a comment on them both, and buried a smile in his accounts ledger.

A short while later, when Dewi came in to collect the monthly returns for the files, Sidney was standing at his office window.

Dewi couldn't see his expression, but he doubted it was a happy one. He was certainly preoccupied. He had neither heard him knock nor turned round when he came in. He closed the door after him as quietly as he could, out of consideration.

Sidney was not only preoccupied he was also unsettled, and with more than thoughts of the month's loss of profit. He was feeling a draught from somewhere else and had no idea from where.

He had built walls around himself since arriving there, and now felt obscurely that they had been breached. He had never felt altogether secure, altogether at home in the persona of Sidney Acton, and the new life he had made for himself here. And now, in a way he didn't begin to understand, felt even less so.

He had come a long way since leaving London, and had to remind himself of that, of who he now was, staring down at the yard below, at a taxi pulling into it, and two of the drivers talking.

Those people, he told himself, work for me.

And while Dewi was chatting away to Shirley in what she considered to be an unusually animated fashion, Sidney was back behind his desk, the large reproduction antique he had bought when first arriving, with a leather-upholstered captain's chair, made for command.

He had started out then as he meant to go on, and he wasn't going to let anyone get in his way now.

He had wobbled briefly. But that was the old Sidney, the way he had been. Now the new one was back.

He picked up the phone and dialled straight through to Councillor Probert's office at the town hall.

Chapter Four

The morning was waiting for Jasmine Roberts when she came out on the deck of the *Cluny Queen,* the climbing sun finding the river through the trees in an explosion of white light, its surface throwing back its brightness like a shattered mirror.

She was in a dressing gown, and sat with a tray of toast and tea at a white plastic deck table and matching chairs from the Patio Living pages of one of Bryony Owen's catalogues, regarding the scene with an air of complacent ownership. Her family were still asleep in the uptops, as the two children's bedrooms built on top of the deck living quarters were known. When they woke on non-school days they seemed to do so together, and immediately started squabbling or playing, as if switched back on at the same time.

But for now the morning was hers. Like being on holiday, she thought, not for the first time in her years there, and the old weather, as well, like.

But meaning more than the river and the summer shades the birds were calling from, the reflection of trees on its banks a sunlit green water world under the blue of another sky, and the old weather. Meaning all of it, at any time, meaning Batch Magna and the sheltering hills of its valley, meaning all the things she had never quite been able to find other words for.

Jasmine was a psychic, a world-famous one according to her ads in the local papers, with a special rate for pets. She had one to see shortly, a young Siamese cat in Fenton called Itty Mew. The vet hadn't been able to find anything wrong with him, and he's not off his food. But he's been so *listless* lately, the owner had told her fretfully over the phone. Can scarcely be bothered some days to lift a paw, and looks at me with those big soulful eyes as if begging me not to leave him.

I bet! Jasmine had thought tartly. She'd heard it all before. It was typical Siamese. The animal was 'coming it'. All an act to keep his mistress's attention solely on him. That family were known for it.

What he needed was a good talking to. Told that if he didn't buck his ideas up he'd end up in the local cats' home, replaced with a moggy who knows when it's well off. Not that the owner would hear any of it, the communication was silent, but Jasmine had no doubt Itty Mew would get the picture.

A while later she was dressed for work in voluminous purple silk printed with stars and moons, rainbows and comets, and wearing her crescent-and-hand necklace and Egyptian charm bracelets, her plump hands heavy with fish and abraxas rings. She charged extra for home visits, and extra again for a Sunday call-out, and liked to give value for money.

She left her eldest daughter, Meredith, who was thinking of a career as a social worker, and who found plenty of material to be going on with in her own home, in charge of things, with vague, hurried instructions on her way down the gangway to make sure she behaved herself, and to make sure everybody else behaved themselves. And to remember it was a Sunday.

It was a Sunday. Batch Magna's High Street, with the shop closed and the pub not yet open, was almost deserted, the quiet disturbed only by the din that came from Upper Ham and the *Cluny Queen*. With Jasmine out of the way, her clan and their friends, eagerly escaping village homes out into the weather and the freedom of the river, had taken over the boat as if they had just boarded it, and had the crew, the adults, below in irons.

They were running, whooping and yelling, round the deck and up and down the companionways to the uptops. They were out on the moorings and on the river, packed precariously on a pram dinghy like survivors on the last lifeboat, the older ones swimming in it, splashing enthusiastically about or earnestly showing off crawls and breaststrokes, and jumping in from the deck and then coming ashore and running back up to do it again.

Further downstream Ffion Owen, Annie and Owain's middle daughter, on their boat the *Felicity H,* was also in a swimming costume, shallow diving from the starboard paddlebox in a gorse-yellow silk bikini, slipping with no more disturbance than a fish rising into water she'd been swimming in since she was five. While Annie, her mother, happy to do anything on the river except swim in it, with the number of dead sheep she'd seen floating down it over the years, was feeding the livestock.

The *Felicity H* was tied up where Upper Ham turns into Lower Ham, with the pub's terrace and slipway in between them. The land went out there on a meander before coming in again, giving the Owens the largest moorings of the houseboats.

When Home Farm still belonged to the estate it had been used as a spare field, and after the last war an ailing Fordson tractor had been driven onto it, and had stayed, half buried now under grass and rosebay willow herb, keeping a gamekeeper's field hut from the same period company, the hut rotting in an amiable sort of way under a crab apple tree. And there were a few old wooden railway containers, bought by the estate when the local branch line at Nether Myddle closed, and used now as sheds and a house for the deep-freeze, and stove logs weathering under wraps, coils of old mooring cable and the bones of a beached sculling boat with grass growing through it.

Annie was scattering mixed corn and pellets for the fowl, ducks, geese and chickens, watched with a sort of know-all, snooty amusement by Megan, a long-eared Anglo Nubian milking goat chewing the cud in the long grass, tethered well away from the temptations of the washing line.

Annie was due at the Hall to help with the cream teas for Open Day, and after that the fun of a family jolly on the lawns to look forward to. Her husband Owain, now a ghillie for the estate, had been a head gamekeeper at the time of another Sir Humphrey, the late squire and great uncle of the present one, and Annie had been a housekeeper then at the Hall. She was now back there, as a friend and factotum, helping Clem and Shelly with whatever needed to be done.

Although a non-sailing day, Tom Parr was also on the river, on the deck of the *Castle* as if on the beach, in a white cotton sun hat and flannel vest, his trousers rolled up. Sion was working with his father on the pheasant pens in Cutterbach Wood above the village, and Tom was nursing the fire with the coal Sion had humped aboard yesterday, warming things through in readiness for the first trip of the week in the morning.

He was taking a break now, sitting in one of the two deckchairs from the engine room with the *News of the World*, a flask of tea and a pipe on, more at home there than in his own kitchen.

He had picked up the newspaper from the bin outside the shop, delivered there by the newsagent from Church Myddle, the Pughs refusing to taint their hands with commerce on a Sabbath. The Commander was on his way back from there, ready for breakfast in their new home in the terrace of five Masters' Cottages in Upper Ham facing the river, newspaper propped up against a bottle of Lea & Perrins, tucking into a mixed fry-up, his usual start to any day, reading the odd piece of interest out to Priny – 'Here's a thing!'

He'd step out again later, after changing with Priny for church, the bells of Matins ringing out over the village. A village which on a Sunday gave praise from both ends of its High Street. From its church and the 19th century

Methodist chapel, tucked away on a small plot of land squeezed between an alley running down to Lower Ham and the river, and a small terrace of black and white cottages that were once alms houses, holding close to its walls the weathered gravestones of chapel notables.

Today, the Pughs, along with most of the congregation, sat listening with awed incomprehension to a visiting lay preacher, a Welsh speaker come among the English, as he regarded the place, no matter which side of the border it was on, a man with sweat in his hair, bringing them like hot coals news of damnation from north Wales.

While in St Swithin's at the other end of the High Street, within singing distance of the pub, its door open to summer, Miss Wyndham was on her feet, hymnal in hand, her wide-brimmed peach straw hat, dressed with chiffon and silk roses, quivering to the words of *New Every Morning*, Humphrey's bass baritone booming from the box-pew, his Bronx accent promising new mercies like a threat.

Chapter Five

Phineas Cook usually attended church on a Sunday, turning up for it as if summoned.

God to Phineas was at one with his bank manager, various school masters and several wives since. He entered that building with the air of a man who had knocked politely first, his expression, as he took his pew, suggestive of both contrition and reasonableness. The air of a man who knew he was in the wrong, whatever it was about, and who was not only prepared to listen, but to go away and jolly well do something about it.

But this morning he had slept through the call of the Sunday bells, and the telephone ringing, and woke to hymns and the sun on his face like a benediction. He heard the voices as if from some celestial distance, a heavenly choir singing him on his way as the river carried him home, his eyelids fluttering as if seeking a last view of the world as he surfaced from a hangover.

He was half-cocooned in a hammock on the deck of the *Belle*, his usual bed in hot weather, and something else from the Patio Living pages of one of Bryony Owen's catalogues.

He was fully dressed and had been there since two o'clock that morning, not long after Patrick, the landlord of the Steamer Inn, had finally called time on a lock-in and the barrel of cider Phineas had been helping to empty, doing so enthusiastically and with extended largesse, putting back over the bar a good deal of the much-needed royalty cheque Patrick had cashed earlier.

Sheepsnout cider, from Dotty Snape's smallholding, made from apples such as Sweet Coppin, Dabinett and Michelin, left behind, along with the church, by the Norman French, pulped and then fermented in their own juices in the cider shed, the name stencilled on the wooden barrels like a warning.

He was squinting at his wrist watch, wondering what part of the day it referred to, when the telephone extension bell on the sitting room roof rang, as it had been ringing off and on for the past couple of hours.

But by the time he had untangled himself from the hammock, and had lurched, as if hitting a rough sea, down the deck to the sitting room, it had rung off. But he knew who it was. It was Sally, his girlfriend, wanting understandably to know what had happened to Aberystwyth.

That had been the plan yesterday, his plan. A trip to the seaside, with a picnic hamper strapped in on the back of the Frogeye, his Austin Healey Sprite, for breakfast on the sands after a paddle.

He stood staring at it, its silence a louder rebuke, and a rather sad one, he was in the mood to think, seeing her, dressed for summer and the beach, with salad and cold meats waiting in the fridge, quietly putting down the phone, more in sorrow than anger.

He did not, he told himself, deserve her, and wondered if he had time for coffee.

There was no sorrow in evidence when he turned up at her flat, only anger, of the silent, handle-with-care sort. One wrong word from him, he knew, and up it would go.

Not at his sharpest this morning, he hadn't been able to think of an excuse that didn't, even to his ears, sound feeble, or that he couldn't be sure she hadn't heard before. And by the time he'd reached Kingham and parked the Frogeye, he'd decided that he would simply tell her the truth, making a virtue of the decision, even though it was either that or turn round and go back to bed.

And after all, honesty is the best policy, he reminded himself reassuringly, and with a certain prim resolution, a man who had undergone some sort of transformation already, between the car and the foot of her stairs.

He put up a hand immediately she opened the door, his expression suggesting that he understood perfectly, and owned up there and then, on the doorstep, because that's as far as he got. She stood blocking the way, one arm up on the doorpost as if to stop him slipping past, waiting with stony detached interest to hear what he had to say this time.

Holding his Gent's Superior Panama to his chest, he confessed all, shared it with her, as he thought of it. Starting with the royalty cheque in the morning post and ending up in the hammock, shaking his head over it and looking almost as grim as she did, suggesting that from this sorry tale a lesson had been learned, that out of it a new Phineas was emerging.

He added that he had not even stopped first for a much-needed coffee, as if offering proof of the new Phineas, and made a face, indicating just how much needed it had been.

She regarded him, sucking on a corner of her lower lip, while he waited, looking haggardly back at her.

She dropped her arm from the doorpost, and still without speaking walked back into the flat. And as she hadn't closed the door after her, let alone slammed it on him, he followed, diffidently, hat in hand.

She went into the kitchen, and he peered round the door in case she was collecting ammunition. She'd thrown things before, and her aim was unerring. Sally played a strong game of tennis, and when she lost her temper it showed.

He watched with relief as she picked up the kettle and started to fill it.

On the way back to Batch Magna, it being too late for Aberystwyth, he detected that there was a certain reserve still, a suggestion of distance that his cheery comments about this and that hadn't entirely managed to reach, but he considered that normal service had more or less been resumed.

After stopping off first at the *Belle* at Sally's insistence, for Phineas to wash and shave, and change his clothes, and then the pub, coming away with supplies for the jolly at the Hall, they sat in the smoky shade of one of the horse chestnuts on the lawns, with Bill Sikes, Phineas's large white boxer dog, dozing next to them.

They were listening to Jasmine singing. Her brood, their village friends back in the custody of home and Sunday lunch, were on the loose in the grounds, and she was taking time off with her guitar, hunched over it on a garden bench, her long black hair shining.

An enthusiastic singer himself, if with a limited repertoire, all of it enthusiastically out of tune, Phineas's expression, as she soared on a high note, suggested he feared she'd lose it, while knowing she wouldn't, her voice balancing faultlessly on the top of it, before swooping down again with a dramatic clash of chords.

"She's very good," Sally murmured.

"Singing," Phineas said, having finished a second pint of Sheepsnout and in the mood to be sententious, "is a place Jasmine escapes to. It's where she turns her untidy life into an audience. Her… her umpteen kids," he finished vaguely, not sure, as many weren't – as even Jasmine seemed not to be sometimes – quite how many, "squeezed into that boat like the old woman's shoe. The bills filed in the back of a kitchen drawer," he went on, touching on his own filing system for bills. "And the romances which always set out in the fairest of weather and always end up on the rocks. It's where she says never mind all that, look at me, this is who I am. Singing is where Jasmine *always* has the last word."

Sally laughed. "Well, why ever she's doing it, I like it."

"Thank you," Phineas said solemnly, and dipped his head, as if taking a bow for Jasmine. "Have another drink," he added, and replenishing her wine glass and his own with cider, leaned back against the trunk of the tree as Jasmine took off on the wings of another song.

Drinks were also being taken in the shade of table parasols, which earlier had shaded the Open Day visitors and their orders of cream teas, after a tour of the Hall's history given by the ninth baronet in a shirt with native dancers in grass skirts on it, the garden furniture, green wooden tables and chairs, all from another catalogue of Bryony Owen's, the woman who had introduced the village to life on the never-never.

And the smell of lunch was on the air, from the large barbecue recently bought second-hand from a county show caterer. The Hall had music on the lawns in mind, rock and roll, rather then Glyndebourne, music to go with hotdogs and chips. Humphrey, that erstwhile short-order cook and burger flipper, was sweating over it now, wearing what was said on the front to be a Master Chef's hat and an apron with Food Dude written on it over his ample front, aided by Owain Owen who had experience of outdoor cookers and their erratic fuel.

Home-made beef burgers were on the menu, along with Conies, Coney Island Specials, hotdogs turned into the stuff of local legend by a pickle relish garnish, the recipe for which Shelly had brought across the Atlantic with her, and baked spuds, and chips, and cowboy drumsticks at Humphrey's insistence, and which were now giving him trouble.

Two trestle tables bore festive loads of paper plates, napkins and cutlery, bowls of salad, some of it from Tom

Parr's garden in another of the Masters' Cottages, now the *Castle's* fire was up and well banked, and plastic gallons of cider, and beer and wine, including Annie's home-made contribution, the fruits of fields and hedgerows, the bottles innocently labelled, like jam.

Miss Wyndham was on her second glass of dandelion wine, the sparkle of spring sunshine in it, sitting at one of the tables with Clem, and Priny and the Commander, and Annie and her eldest daughter Bryony, who was having her new baby cooed over, while Shelly sat on the grass with Ralph Franklin T Strange II, and his sibling, Hawis.

The *Castle's* first successful month on the river was being celebrated under summer skies innocent of the weather awaiting the new CSC, the storm clouds that were gathering elsewhere.

Chapter Six

Sidney didn't call Councillor Mervyn Probert Taffy, at least not to his face. He couldn't afford to. And Councillor Probert, who had held decided views on the English when living in Swansea, before irregularities in the local planning department he'd presided over there caused him to migrate, had also to compromise.

They shared a sort of guarded friendliness, each knowing the other's secrets, equals in conspiracy. Mervyn the more assured of the two, and the more experienced in venality, carried it off rather better, expressing it, with jocular cynicism, in the language of a press release, as the meeting of two business minds across borders.

And those two business minds met again across the border the following day, in the pub in Rhos-Tiwyn, and again on a livestock market day, the bustle in the streets and the pub's surge in trade a cover for their meetings.

Councillor Probert had got there first, and waited for Sidney to find him at a small table next to a tiled fireplace with a cardboard Babycham ad on the mantelshelf and the remains of the last fire in it. They went through a charade of bumping into each other there, both Rotarians and members of the same golf club, Sidney, at Mervyn's invitation, then sitting on the other chair at the table with his half of bitter and a newspaper, a small, harried-looking figure in a pinstriped suit, bringing his business worries in with him.

Mervyn leaned back, and putting his arms out as if stretching, glanced casually around, his councillor's smile, the public face he was hardly aware of these days, oiled by what he knew was taped in an envelope to the inside pages of the newspaper.

In the bar, men with the weather of the hills in their faces were tucking into one of the dishes chalked up on a blackboard, or rowdy with talk over pints of Red Dragon bitter or cider from the barrel, finding their voices again after the silence of the fields, and with cheques from the sales pens in their pockets. And Sidney still found himself trying for a few sentences to make sense in English of what he then recognised to be Welsh. A language which irritated him when he heard it spoken in public, considering it bad manners, something that should only be done in private. Between consenting adults, he'd add in one of his rare jokes, lumping it with a vice the rural Welsh male, with only sheep for company, was rumoured to indulge in.

Mervyn cleared his throat sharply, twice, as if calling a meeting to order, and Sidney waited while he removed several folded and stapled sheets of A4 paper from a breast pocket of his lovat-green suit and put them on the table between them.

He took a pair of gold-framed reading glasses from another breast pocket and settled them on his nose. He pulled at the lapels of his jacket, and at the knees of his trousers, and fluffed out the yellow silk of a handkerchief which bloomed in his top pocket like a buttonhole. And then peered at Sidney over the half-moon spectacles.

"Had to go to the third floor in the town hall for this, Sidney. To a contact of mine in the Public Transport Office, meaning Odgar Llewellyn-Jenkins, the department's head."

"Welsh, is he?" Sidney said.

Mervyn smiled a little at it. "Yes, and luckily for you, Sidney, he owed me one from last month, when I got a planning application from his wife's cousin in through the back door. And it helps of course that we're both chapel and in the same choir. Do you sing, Sidney?"

"Only in the bath."

Mervyn smiled again. "Odgar sings bass. I'm a baritone, ranging from second F below middle C to the F above middle C."

"Very interesting."

Mervyn put back his head. "*Myfanwy boed yr holl o'th fywyd Dan heulwen ddisglair canol dydd. A boed i rosyn gwridog iechyd I ddawnsio ganmlwydd ar dy rudd,*" he crooned, and raised a hand in acknowledgement as one of the men at a nearby table called something approvingly to him, and then joined in, followed by his friends, as Mervyn sang on, arms out, lifting the sound, while Sidney sat with his folded, staring at the table.

"Mervyn," he said then, when a few others in the room took it up, fearing in this Welsh bar a communal sing-song. "*Mervyn* – do you think we could get on!"

48

"Yes, yes, of course. Sorry, boy. Got carried away. What we call the hwyl. A thing of the emotions. A Celtic thing. Something the Saxon is unburdened with. The song's a favourite with us. She was a Welsh princess of legend, Myfanwy, with a beauty that broke the giving, tender heart of a young bard," he said, the song dying around the bar, the impromptu choir simply returning to whatever they'd been talking about, song for the Welsh male being just another sort of conversation.

"Yes, very interesting, I'm sure. But if you don't mind," Sidney complained, "I've got a business to run."

"Quite right, Sidney, and that is the purpose of this meeting. Business. Meaning yours," he said, tapping the A4 sheets.

He pulled them to him, and then looked up. "Odgar didn't deal personally with the application in question, mind, one of his staff did. But he dug out all the relevant paperwork and copied it for me himself." Mervyn's voice took on a hushed tone. "Odgar Llewellyn-Jenkins, Sidney, is a principal officer of the council. One grade below a director. And rumour has it that that's next. He is the man whose thumb yearly decides the fate of any company plying for hire within the county council's jurisdiction. He has the ultimate say when licences are due for renewal whether or not that company stays on the road." Mervyn shook his head admiringly. "He must be raking it in."

"What, passengers on rivers as well as roads?" Sidney asked alertly.

"The Public Transport Office, Sidney," Mervyn had him know, "covers highways, byways and waterways."

"Right, I see, Mervyn," Sidney said expectantly.

"Issuing licences for hire and pleasure boats carrying no more than twelve passengers."

"Twelve passengers?" Sidney echoed.

"That is the maximum," Mervyn said firmly.

"Is that all it carries – *twelve*?" He was beginning to think that this might not be too bad after all, seeing the PS *Batch Castle* as something not much bigger than the one that goes round the boating pool at Margate.

Mervyn smiled. "No, no. That is a reference to the licensing remit of the relevant local navigation authority, meaning the third floor at the town hall. No, the vessel in question, according to the records, is licensed to carry forty."

"Forty passengers?"

"Forty passengers."

"Well, what—?"

Mervyn held up a hand as if stopping the traffic. This was town hall business, even if he was selling it, and town hall business was not to be rushed, and especially not by a member of the public.

"For those boats carrying more than twelve passengers, and/or for those whose movements of travel take them outside those categorised waters under the county council's jurisdiction, meaning in both cases the subject of this meeting, then the proper navigation authority is the Marine and Coastguard Agency."

"The Marine and…?"

"In Milford Haven."

"Where the hell is Milford Haven…?" Sidney asked wonderingly.

"Wales," Sidney," Mervyn said with a laugh. "The country we're sitting in now. Land of hill and stream, of the bard and the sweet harp. In Pembrokeshire, to be exact. Historical, it is, Milford."

"And what use is that to me?"

"Aberdaugleddau," Mervyn said, as if cursing him, and smiled. "That's Welsh, Sidney, for Milford Haven, meaning the mouth of the two rivers called Cleddau. Goes right back, it does, that town. The French landed there to give support to Owain Glyndwr in his attempt to overthrow the yoke of tyranny, meaning the English. Present company excepted, of course."

"And is that it? Is that all I get for my money? A history lesson?"

Mervyn took a sip of his gin and tonic and twinkled another smile over the glass.

"Not quite, Sidney." He tapped the sheets of A4 again. "You wanted the full SP, a full report on the Cluny Steamboat Company, meaning the PS *Batch Castle,* and that is what I have here. From the office of Odgar Llewellyn-Jenkins. And that office, Sidney, acts when required in liaison with the Marine and Coastguard Agency in historical Milford Haven."

Sidney shifted on the chair. "Go on…"

"It is the function of the PTO in a case of this nature to collate the various information appertaining to a licence application. And then the relevant documentation, along with the PTO's recommendation, is exchanged between the offices by telecopier. It behoves local government, Sidney, to keep pace with modern business methods. We have the latest Xerox Magnafax machines."

"Yeah, yeah – and *what*, Mervyn?" Sidney said impatiently.

"Well, for a start we learn things like the skipper of the boat, a certain Commander James Arthur Cunningham, only having one eye." Mervyn chuckled. "A one-eyed captain! Who does he think he is, Long John Silver?"

"Right," Sidney said, chuckling with him.

"No, he only had one leg, didn't he. Still, I wouldn't like to be a passenger on Commander James Arthur Cunningham's boat."

"Nor me. And what – they didn't know about his eye at the time, or something, is that it?" Sidney said, grinning and nodding hopefully at him.

"No."

Sidney's grin dried. "No?"

"No. No, apparently whoever issued the licence did know."

"What? And he was still given—?"

"That's what I thought when I read it, Sidney. Odgar Llewellyn-Jenkins had his hand out there, I said to myself."

"Well, that's a bloody disgrace! Means people's lives are at risk."

"Now, I don't know that, mind."

"What's it say about it?" Sidney demanded, jabbing a finger at the A4 sheets.

"Just that the applicant has monocular vision but that his good eye is healthy and adequately compensates. Eye test passed."

"That's a bloody disgrace!" Sidney said again, his face flushed with it.

"Well, I agree with you, Sidney. But there you are, what could they do? And people do drive with one eye, I suppose."

"Not for me, they bleedin' well don't," Sidney said, the accent that went with his new persona as businessman roughened with emotion. "I've never heard anything like it! What else you got?"

"His medical examination…" Mervyn said, seeming to find something interesting about it.

Sidney moved again on his seat. "What about it?"

"Hmm? Oh, professional interest, Sidney, that's all. First time I've seen form M L Five stroke Seven A. It appertains to rivers, canals and estuaries. There's a facsimile of one here with the results of his medical."

"And…? And what about his medical!"

"He passed it."

"Mervyn! is there *anything* in there for me?" Sidney snarled. "*Anything* I can use!"

"I don't know, Sidney, I haven't read it all yet." He smiled sympathetically. "Let's see, shall we," he said, flipping over a page.

"British Inland Waterways Licensing," he read, giving full weight to the words. "Appertains to vessels in categorised waters under the jurisdiction of the county council, and in accordance with that body's recommendations and regulations. Or in accordance with the recommendations and regulations of a competent navigation authority. And where Articles ten or fourteen of the Public Health Act does not appertain to the local authority, then the relevant certification for operations in categorised waters, i.e.

non-tidal waters, is the responsibility of the transferred competent navigation authority under Article ten, section ninety-four, of the Public Health Acts Amendment Act nineteen-o-seven. As amended," he added fondly.

This was Mervyn's first love, despite his years and acquired gloss, the tailored tweeds and his expensive barbering and brown suede brogues, and it stirred him still. This was the language he had first embraced as a young clerk from a pit village working in the local council offices, another distance, along with the handful of pens worn like a badge in his top pocket, put between him and the pithead.

"Milford issued his boatmaster's licence," Mervyn translated, seeing Sidney trying to keep up, hope winded but staggering on in his eyes.

"Grade three, for inland passenger operations within categorised waters of more than twelve passengers but no more than two hundred and fifty. Issued on…" He flipped over another sheet of A4 "… the recommendation of the County Council Public Transport Office and in receipt of a liability insurance certificate and safety certificate."

He made a disappointed face. "Both duly certificated, Sidney, I'm afraid. Got the facsimiles here. Along with the company passenger licence, premises licence, and copies of his other certifications – local knowledge, passenger control, seamanship, emergency situations," he read, turning pages and shaking his head regretfully over the results.

"The marine surveyor's report…" he said then, and something in his tone brought Sidney's head up from his bleak contemplation of the table. He looked from the sheet to Mervyn and back.

"What?" he said carefully.

"Hmm? No, it's just that I was thinking, Sidney, that this surveyor never uses one word when twenty will do."

"And what does it say, Mervyn!" he snapped. "What does it *say*?"

"What doesn't it say? He must charge by the word," Mervyn said with a chuckle, and then sobered. "But I'm afraid as far as you are concerned, Sidney, the bottom line is that the Cluny Steamboat Company, meaning the PS *Batch Castle,* was found to be sound and a certificate of river worthiness was duly signed and issued. And that, I'm afraid, is that," he said, taking off his glasses.

Sidney stared at him. "What," he said, spreading his hands. "That's it?"

"I'm afraid so, Sidney." He folded the sheets of A4 and stuffed them back into his breast pocket. "Sorry," he added, composing his face for it, a mourner's face, taking a last and deeply hypocritical look at the deceased.

Sidney looked away, looked about him, his eyes sour, aggrieved at his surroundings and at the thought of what he'd paid for the privilege. The men at the nearby table had their heads together, and then laughed. Some joke, he thought, no doubt involving sheep.

"Not a lot for my money, is it," he said, reluctant to leave it there.

Mervyn drew the newspaper to his side of the table. "Sidney, you got what you paid for, you know that. You asked for all we had on the Cluny Steamboat Company,

55

and that's what you got. It's not my fault that it's not what you wanted to hear." He glanced at his watch. "And now I have to go."

He finished his gin and tonic and picked up the newspaper. "No rest for the wicked. Got a big planning application waiting," he said, winking, and grinned, showing Sidney a mouthful of polished teeth.

And was then reluctant to leave him like that, staring down again at the table, feeding on resentment. There was enough spite in the man to bring them both down if he thought he had been short-changed, thought he'd been done in some way. He felt that like the scorpion in the fable, Sidney would strike even if it meant them both going under. That, he had come to understand, was also Sidney's nature.

And besides, it had occurred to him that there might be a little extra in it for him.

"You know, Sidney," he said, sitting down again, "you could always take things into your own hands."

"What's that mean?" Sidney said sulkily.

Mervyn learnt towards him, a Welsh intriguer. "I could always on your behalf pay another visit to the boyos."

Sidney looked blank for a moment, and then said, "Yeah... *Yeah*, I see what you mean. I see what you *mean*, Mervyn. Right, yes. End of problem. Like before. And even if they—"

"I didn't mean that!" Mervyn hissed. "Are you *mad*!"

"Well—?"

"Duw, man! you can't do that. How long do you think it would be before they put two and two together?"

"Well, what, then?"

"You got away with it last time because—"

"We," Sidney cut in, the single word both a reminder and a warning. "*We* got away with it last time, Mervyn."

Mervyn shrugged. "All right, we got away with it. And we got away with it because it was the first time, and we were lucky with the rest of it. This time, they'd be looking straight at you, bound to. I think we can rely on even our constabulary getting round to that one. And then my doorstep next," he added, knowing Sidney would make sure of that, the thought of it for a moment at bay in his eyes.

And then he chuckled. "No, I was thinking of something a little less drastic. Something along the lines of the boyos and a few of their mates causing a bit of mayhem on the boat. A punch up, that sort of thing. During which," he added, coming up with a bit more colour, "one of the passengers goes overboard. It would then be a matter of what's called the interests of the public, as set out in the provisions of section ninety-four of the Public Health Acts Amendment Act nineteen-o-seven. And the interests of the public, Sidney, will not be considered best served by one of them going over the side. Whatever a licence is for, that licence, at any time, may be suspended or revoked if it's felt to be in the interests of the public to so do. The public would be surprised sometimes, Sidney, the things done in its interest."

"Go on," Sidney said.

"Milford issued the paperwork, but it's the town hall, the Licensing Committee, that has the last say, convened in accordance with the County Council Constitution under the Local Government Act nineteen fifty-eight, meaning the proper democratic process. But there's the Local Government Act and the proper democratic process, Sidney, and then there's the Chair of the licensing Committee – Odgar Llewellyn-Jenkins."

"What's that mean?"

"Passenger licence suspended for a year. Next please! That's what it could mean, Sidney, when Odgar Llewellyn-Jenkins has your best business interests at heart."

"And what then, what happens after that?"

"They have to apply for a new licence, of course. Go up before the Licensing Committee. In front of your pal Odgar Llewellyn-Jenkins. And if they do get it back – and even Odgar can't be too blatant – I'll have another word with the boyos. A second occurrence would give Odgar strong grounds to move for revoking it, meaning the business's finished, and you get Shrewsbury back. But the thing is to make sure that it gets a good airing. Report it to the police. It will get passed on to us officially then. Get one of your drivers on board, it's in his interest. Get a family man, one with young kids. And get his wife to write to the local papers, saying they were terrified – *terrified*, they were. The kids screaming their heads off, and little Blodwen off her food and having nightmares about it. Give Odgar Llewellyn-Jenkins something to get worked up about. He's good at that, the old moral outrage. Like a preacher, he is." Mervyn chuckled. "Conscience, no doubt."

Sidney looked unconvinced. "And what's all this going to cost me? Would I be chucking good money after bad, that's what I have to ask myself now," he said, and gnawed on his bottom lip.

"Well, I understand that, Sidney. As a businessman you have to consider return on investment. I see that, of course. But perhaps I can be of some help there. Now, you'd have to give the boyos a drink of course, but their mates will probably do it for the sport. They do it all the time at football matches. And as far as Odgar's concerned, well, I'll see what I can do for you. See it doesn't come to an arm and a leg. No, no, that's what pals are for," he said, putting up a hand as if to cut off Sidney's gratitude.

"And what would they want, the boyos?"

"Well, there again, I think I could get them to do whatever it takes for, say, two hundred – two fifty, each, plus of course expenses, their fares, you know. Look, between you and me, let's call it four hundred quid for cash. And I can get them at that price, Sidney," he hurried on, "because I put plenty of work their way. Otherwise, for a reliable job elsewhere, you'd have to add a few hundred, believe you me."

Sidney sat digesting it and looking as if he didn't much like the taste.

Mervyn came up with something else. "He's an American, you know, the owner of the boat, this Sir Humphrey. Oh, yes," he said, when that got Sidney's attention. He knew how Sidney felt about foreigners. He felt the same, but in the American's case he was prepared to give him credit for at least not being an English one.

"An American?"

"An American," Mervyn said, nodding at it. An American, a foreigner, coming in here and helping himself to the cream.

"How's he get a title like that if he's an American?" Sidney said suspiciously, as if the town hall might have had something to do with it.

Mervyn chuckled. "Nothing to do with us, boy, more's the pity. Be a London job, that would. Office of Heralds, that sort of thing. Over a glass of Amontillado."

"That's a liberty!" Sidney said indignantly. "A diabolical bloody liberty!"

He had no more time for the aristocracy than he had for foreigners, but they belonged in a story of England he carried about with him like a passport. An England of stately homes and thatched cottages, rolling green acres and London pomp, and the Queen in her house at the end of The Mall. An England that, as an Englishman, he felt belonged as much to him as it did to anyone else.

Mervyn shrugged. "Goes on all the time down there. No doubt he wanted it to go with the rest of the stuff he'd bought. The manor house, lands, village. That boat be like a toy to him, what with the river on his doorstep. Something to play with in his bath, like."

Sidney was further outraged. "Well, it might be a toy to him, but that run's bread and bleeding butter to me!"

"More like jam, Sidney, that Shrewsbury," Mervyn reminded him. "Nothing to someone like him, of course. He's a multi-millionaire, by all accounts. Started out as a short-order cook, as they call them over there," he said, quoting his contact on the *Kingham News*, before returning to his own version of the story, "and ended up owning a chain of such places, right across the continent of America. The Burger King, they call him there. That's the sort of man we're talking about. Well, I ask you, is he likely to leave it like that? That's what you have to ask yourself, Sidney. Would it stop there – *could* he stop there. A man with conquest in his blood?"

He looked at Sidney, his expression grave with doubt.

"Or, bored with paddling up and down the river, would he then cast his eye landwards, to new horizons? That's what I'm thinking, Sidney. Will we end up calling him the Transport King? Well, I wouldn't be surprised, not with this boyo!" he said, shaking his head and chuckling over the outlandish possibilities, while wondering if he needed to add that those possibilities might well include a take-over of local taxi firms.

But Sidney looked as if he had got there on his own.

The draught he had felt earlier in the day was now a chill wind blowing where once walls had been, leaving the life he'd made for himself exposed to the marauding gaze of the American. He had arrived at the pub with a single business concern, one that after paying the money Mervyn was clutching to him in the newspaper, he had reasonable hopes of having resolved, and now found himself faced with the possibility of not having a business to be concerned about.

Mervyn got to his feet and stood regarding him, head cocked, and smiling sympathetically, as if leaving a sickbed.

"You have a think about it, Sidney," he said, as if telling him to get well soon. "You know my number… Well, no peace for the wicked, is it. Lechyd da," he added cheerily by way of goodbye.

Chapter Seven

Batch Magna's Lower Ham went up one side of the pub, turned into the High Street along the front of it, and then ran back down to the river on the other side as Upper Ham.

Jasmine's boat was tied up there, and Phineas's paddler the *Cluny Belle*, along with of course with the newly commissioned flagship, as Humphrey had optimistically described her, of the Cluny Steamboat Company. And as with the *Felicity H* in Lower Ham, the moorings there had once belonged to Home Farm, one long meadow used for pasture, hedged off from the lane by the same sort of plain iron fencing that had once marked the boundaries of the Hall's park, broken now, fallen to rust, holed by time and half buried in the bushes between trees.

Outside the entrance to the PS *Batch Castle,* a board advertised sailing times and the number of places available after those booked in advance. Clem, keeping a watching brief, ready to bring Phineas back to historical fact when he wandered off into dramatic fiction, had roped him in to write the words for a brochure outlining the story of both the old and new CSC, copies of which now sat in hotels, guest houses and tourist offices both sides of the border. The new Cluny Steamboat Company was flourishing.

The ticket office and waiting room had been repainted in Trafalgar blue, the company's house flag flying again above their roofs. The door which everyone used to get to and from the paddler when it was a houseboat, now had a stern notice on it stating that it was for Staff Only, and the path which no one used because it was taken up with Priny's flower pots and tubs, was now the public entrance.

And once more passengers went through the wrought-iron gate which, after Humphrey's great uncle's triumphant return from London, had replaced a wooden field gate for the pasture and the hay wharf, a berth for the barges from Shrewsbury. The gate, painted white, stood between the office and a goat willow which, as it had done for the past three hundred years, flowered with a new lemon freshness in spring as if for the first time, and in a circle at the gate's centre, picked out in the company colours of blue and gold, it held the old CSC's initials under the iron outline of a paddle steamer making smoke.

Ffion Owen, with her boyfriend Gareth, led the two other couples with them through the gate to take their place in a small queue at the booking office window, as the *Batch Castle*'s whistle gave three blasts of steam to hurry along any dawdlers. Gareth imitated the sound, and grinned at the others. The girls smiled politely. The two other young men seemed to find it as amusing at he did.

"I hope the rain keeps off," one of the girls said, glancing at the sky.

"There's a deck saloon if it doesn't," Ffion told her.

It had rained earlier, sudden, fat summer showers with the warmth of the sun in them, the sky patched now with a fresh blue among blossom-white clouds brittle with sunlight.

When it was their turn at the ticket office window, Priny peered out at them over a pair of fuchsia pink, diamante-studded reading glasses, swept up at the corners like cat's ears, on loops of purple beaded chain, beaming approval at a party of young things on a jolly. She was in full make-up and wearing her pearls, her hairdo carefully preserved from her visit to the hairdresser's yesterday, a superior cashier down on her luck at a South Kensington Odeon.

She wanted to give them complimentary tickets, but Ffion insisted that they pay, pointing out that otherwise she wouldn't feel free to bring friends again, not without feeling she was taking advantage. Priny said with an air of mild surprise that she was quite right, of course, and always ready to admire common sense in others, beamed in a fond, proud sort of way at a show of it from Ffion, a young woman she had watched toddle off with her mother for her first day at the village primary school.

Ffion led the way to the landing stage, chattering brightly about the new CSC, pretending she hadn't noticed Gareth's arm going around her waist. Her arm, which only last week, when they had arranged the trip, booking lieu days off together, would immediately have gone round his, making them a couple, now just hanging there between them, awkwardly, at a loose end.

It must be love, she had told herself after their first date not quite a month back, when she woke the next morning thinking about him, as if teasing herself about it, a worldly eighteen-year-old who knew all about love, while hoping that it was.

He was a vet at the Kingham practice where she had a new job as a receptionist. She had taken to him almost immediately. A tall, well-built young man who gave out a sense of suppressed energy and fun. Which was what had first attracted her to him, his jokey way of looking at the world. A humorousness she had come to see as something else.

Gareth moved carelessly through life, isolated from it by his youth and strength, and by an innate conviction of superiority he didn't always bother to hide. And a quality of indifference which seemed to find almost all of it a joke – a joke which included, Ffion had lately come to suspect, behind his concerned, professional face, not only the anxiety and sometimes the grief of the animals' owners, but even the suffering of the animals themselves.

Ffion was a female mixture of instinct and realism, and it was realism that had taken charge one night last week when having a drink with him after work. He was telling her about one of the partners in the practice ticking him off about his timekeeping, imitating his voice, something he was good at, mimicking people, when out of the blue, and without losing the smile she was used to wearing when with him, and with about as much interest as if she'd noticed a stain on his tie, she realised that not only did she not love him, she didn't even like him particularly.

Now all she had to do was to break off the relationship. Something, she suspected, he would not find in the least amusing.

She was glad it was Tom Parr and not Sion collecting the tickets at the top of the gangway as he sometimes did. She suspected that her brother wouldn't like Gareth, and if Sion didn't like someone he didn't bother to hide it. And by the time he emerged from the engine room to cast off and haul the gangway up, and the telegraph bell had sounded for ahead, she was standing with her friends and other passengers at the door of the galley in the stern, the enticing smell of frying onions on the river air.

The day's wares were chalked up on a blackboard one side of the door, headed by Shelly's Coney Island Special Hotdogs ('Served With The Famous Stars And Stripes Extra-Special Relish!!!'), and followed by pork pies, buns, Scotch eggs, Welsh cakes, chocolate bars, crisps, fresh cheese and ham sandwiches and rolls, biscuits to go with the tea and coffee in plastic cups, soft drinks, draught beer and lager from metal kegs, and Sheepsnout cider in a barrel. Best-Lick-On-A-Stick ice lollies, and cones of the Famous Batch Castle ice-cream from a bubblegum-pink machine bought second hand from a stall on the pier at Aberystwyth. And it was a measure of Humphrey's commitment to business, that when it was his turn 'to do the galley', he left the bulk of his mom's Conies and the soft ice-cream, which had honey and brown sugar in it, for the passengers.

Today it was Shelly's turn, and Ffion had to give her speech again when she tried to wave away the money for the Conies and drink they'd ordered.

They carried them down to the bow, where Ffion pointed out her home, the *Felicity H,* pulling away from it as if saying goodbye as they thrashed on downstream to go up, round Snails Eye Island where turtle doves returned every summer to sing of it, and where otters lived under one of the big hawthorns, something else that had returned to the home waters of the Cluny.

She didn't of course add that the late squire of Batch Magna, Sir Humphrey's great uncle, had come back to this world as one of them, appearing first when Batch Magna had been threatened. And then again when the future in this place of the Strange family had been in doubt, to tell them to be of good heart, that all will be well, as it was the last time. And had then made a home on the island to make sure it stayed that way. She couldn't, not without making a joke of it.

She viewed the legend now from the amused distance of her eighteen years, and the modern world which she, if nobody else on the river, now lived in. But in some part of her that had still to catch up, or was perhaps reluctant to do so, she was not quite, not yet, ready to laugh about it with others, nor even to herself.

She told them instead about Mawr Wood when round the island, the nights they camped there as children, listening to the tawny owls calling like ghost stories at bedtime, and the red shadows that broke from the trees at first light, dainty-footed deer, quivering with alertness, their noses finding them on the air.

The paddler beat her way up past the two houseboats on the other side of the river, moving them on the ropes that held them there, tied permanently to the land, leaving behind also the broken *Sabrina* further upstream, with an extra blast of steam for the gang of village children playing on her. Past black and white farms among orchards, a tractor driver on one of the fields, standing in his seat, cap held high, and two glossy hunters, carrying the sun on their coats as they kept leisurely pace with them, before losing interest.

Trailing smoke and ribbons of white water they left the valley behind, out between hills into open country, past grassland and rolling woodland, sheep and cattle on the grazing meadows lurching away from the sudden noisy intrusion of the world where the world shouldn't be, as she puffed her way importantly round the twists and turns up into the Severn, leaving fishermen cursing and lesser craft rocking on her swell.

For Ffion and some of the other passengers it was a landscape seen before, others seeing it for the first time, that other world of the river, of things normally seen from the front, or seen not at all. The back gardens of a hamlet appearing round the next bend, someone putting out the washing, dog walkers on the banks and people waving, players pausing on a tennis court, and life glimpsed on a high street as a village went by.

And then a stretch running straight as a canal to Water Lacy, the halfway stop, the steeple of its church like a marker above the trees. The Commander gave two short blasts of steam, followed by two long, on the approach to let them know that not only had they arrived, they had done so again on schedule.

The paddle steamer slowed to the ringing of bells from the Commander to Tom Parr below, and Ffion found something fascinating to look at on the other side of the river as the *Castle* settled alongside, putting the saloon between herself and the engine room.

Her brother came out on deck and chucked the mooring ropes down to someone Humphrey described as the CSC's Water Lacy agent. He was one of the barmen who nipped down twice a day from the Waterman Arms just up from the landing stage, a service the pub's landlord had agreed to after Clem had offered him free advertising on the back of the CSC's tourist brochures.

Sion was first down the gangway he'd just lowered, heading for the pub with a plastic gallon container for a refill of cider, to replace the sweat he shed in the fierce breath of the firebox, leaving Tom waiting at the top of it with a roll of tickets and a leather bus conductor's satchel, ready for the few extra passengers they always took on there.

The Commander got a fresh pipe going and came stiffly down the wheelhouse steps on his stick, followed by Stringbag, the Cunninghams' Welsh collie, now officially First Mate, with a ship's ration of dog biscuits and a bunk in the wheelhouse. He looked in on Shelly first, who was busy re-stocking, the ice-cream maker rattling away with a new mix, and then took a turn round the deck, answering with unfailing courtesy what he privately regarded as damn fool questions from some of the passengers, and posing with his First Mate for the tourist cameras.

Ffion waited until her brother was back on board, and the telegraph bell had rung down again for ahead, and then had to make a dash for it with the others for the saloon when the morning turned suddenly to dusk midstream and the clouds opened.

"Crikey! Where did that come from?" one of her friends said, brushing the rain from her hair as they watched it lash the deck in a squall, the river corrugated with it.

"Wales," Ffion said.

"And Wales can keep it," her boyfriend said.

"Hey! Watch it, boyo!" Gareth said, grinning and stressing his Cardiff accent like a threat.

"It'll be gone soon, Jerry," Ffion said.

"Great trip though," one of the other men said.

"Whoops!" he said then. "Feel that?" The shallow-draught vessel rolling a little as the wind suddenly switched direction and pushed at it beam on.

"Hope you can swim, Davie," Gareth said. "Remember that wreck we saw on the way up?"

"Take no notice of him," Ffion said. "That was the *Sabrina*. Her boiler blew up when her skipper pushed her too hard. These old boats are as safe as houses, they are. The two paddle wheels see to that…" She left it in the air, her attention suddenly elsewhere, caught by a young man among the other sheltering passengers. He was grinning, joking with a small group she took to be his friends. She watched him, attracted by his grin, or his long hair, or something, and then looked away, before he, or anyone else, noticed.

"I told you," she said a few minutes later. The squall was spent, the clouds moving on like the shadow of something vast passing overhead, leaving sunlight behind, the air washed and sparkling with it.

They were waiting to be served again after that at the galley, when Ffion decided she didn't want anything. She wandered off and was drawn by the sound of singing coming from the saloon.

She recognised 'The Last Thing on my Mind', one of Jasmine's numbers, and singing it was the young man with the grin, sitting with a guitar on the bench which ran round the walls, with his friends and several other passengers for an audience.

He grinned again then, and missed a couple of beats, when he saw her framed in the doorway, in a mini skirt and the leather boots she'd saved up to buy in Pennington's, her dark hair shining with the light behind it.

She smiled back in a polite sort of way, her expression suggesting she was wondering what he thought he had to grin about. He wasn't, she considered, as good as Jasmine.

But then she supposed that, to be fair, Jasmine's version was different, sung on a much higher note, and at a faster pace. And she found that she wasn't sure which one she did prefer, sitting on the bench opposite, frowning like a music critic, and wondering if the girl sitting next to him was his girlfriend.

And felt her critical judgement slipping then, when he smiled at her again, looking at her and singing at her, as if singing for her.

And then Gareth appeared, suddenly, standing in the doorway like an enraged husband.

"*There* you are!" he said, loud enough to immediately get everyone's attention. He was flushed as if he'd been slapped from the lager he'd been drinking, and his accent had again crossed the border.

"Yes, Gareth," Ffion agreed calmly. "Here I am. Well…?"

"Well, I've been *looking* for you," he said, as if it should be obvious.

"Well, you didn't have to look far, did you. We're not exactly on the *Queen Mary*."

"Going off like that!"

The singer struck a couple of resigned chords, and folding his arms on his guitar waited.

"Oh, I'm sorry, I'm sure. Excuse me! I didn't know I had to ask permission."

"Made me look a right fool."

Ffion opened her mouth to come back at that, and was suddenly aware of the audience they'd acquired.

She leapt to her feet, fired by embarrassment and indignation. "I'm not your property, Gareth!"

Gareth's colour flared. "When you're with me, my girl, you're with me," he said, stabbing a finger at his chest, and striding towards her as if to carry her off, or strike her.

"Hey!" the singer said, and looked surprised at his own intervention.

"Hey – come on, man, cool it," he said, as if appealing to Gareth's reason.

Gareth had come to an abrupt halt, his expression quick with something like relief. He hadn't been at all sure how he was going to handle Ffion, what he intended doing, but here was something he did know about.

"Or what – *man*? What are you going to do about it, *man*?"

"Gareth!" Ffion snapped.

The singer shrugged. "Well, I mean, don't spoil the party, that's all."

Gareth took in the Doors T-shirt and long hair, and the jeans patched with colour, with baleful relish. "Make peace not war, eh, *man*?"

"Yeah, sure. I mean, who likes being shot at?" the singer said, trying to keep it light. "Unless you *have* to fight, why not?"

"Come on, Gareth," Ffion said. "Let's find the others."

"And you'd fight if you had to then, would you?" Gareth said, and smiled.

"If I *had* to – then, yeah."

"Gareth," Ffion said sharply, touching his arm.

Gareth pulled it away from her. "You keep out of it!"

"What's going on here, then?" someone said, and Ffion didn't have to turn round to see who had said it.

"Never you mind," Gareth told him as Sion walked into the room. "It's nothing to do with you."

"Is that right?" Sion said, and then saw Ffion. "Hello, Fee. Didn't know you were aboard."

"Well, no, I – er—"

"So what's it about then?"

"What's it got to do with you?" Gareth demanded.

"Well, for a start, boy, she's my sister. And I also happen to be a crew member."

"It's all right, Si," Ffion said.

"So who are you?" Sion wanted to know.

Gareth opened his mouth to tell him, but Ffion got there first.

"He's a friend. He's a friend of mine. There's other friends here of ours as well," she said brightly."We're going up for a meal in that new Wimpy bar in Shrewsbury."

"I see," Sion said.

"Well, we'd better go and find the others then, Gareth," she said then, putting a hand on his arm to get him moving, and smiling at her brother. "See you later, Si."

"All right, sis… Have fun," he added doubtfully.

"You might want to know, if you're her brother," a women passenger on the bench put in then, "that he was going to clock her one."

"We don't know that!" the man with her said. "You can't say that."

"No, he *wasn't*," Ffion said with a little amused laugh.

"That's what it looked like to me, love. And that young man over there," the woman said, pointing to the singer, "stopped him. And was about to get thumped himself for his pains."

"It was nothing like that, Si," Ffion said, shaking her head over the misunderstanding.

Sion ignored her. "Were you going to hit my sister?" he asked conversationally, politely even, all the heat in the question there in his tone and expression, something banked down and waiting for the wrong answer.

Gareth appeared to consider it.

"No, of course he wasn't, Sion!" Ffion said, as if about to stamp her foot.

"Hasn't he got a tongue in his head?"

"No, I wasn't," Gareth said then. "I thought she made me look a fool and I was annoyed with her, that's all."

"I *told* you," Ffion put in.

"Because if I thought that lady was right," Sion said, nodding at the woman, "you'd be leaving this boat before we docked. Understand?"

Gareth didn't feel intimidated. He'd had a few fights at school and a couple since and had won. And fear was something else he had yet to experience.

His was an intelligence which, unencumbered by emotion, his own or anyone else's, went straight to what was or wasn't good for him. Sion was shorter by several inches, but broader, a muscular Welsh bullock in a sweat- and coal-stained singlet, a muscular Welsh bullock with a calmness and confidence which told him that fighting was a sport he was good at.

Gareth looked over at the singer, putting the blame for this where he considered it belonged, and with the air of a man who suddenly found the whole thing beneath him, turned and walked out.

She didn't see Gareth again until they reached Shrewsbury, and didn't see the singer again even then.

She and Gareth put on a social front for their friends, bridging the new distance between them with the politeness of strangers when it came to passing the tomato ketchup at their table in the Wimpy bar, and their comments on the décor and the meal.

And neither as far as she could see was the singer aboard when it was time for the boat to leave. Which just as well, she thought with sudden irritation, as if she'd intended giving him a piece of her mind, as if, like Gareth, blaming him for the way their trip had ended.

She stood at the stern rail as the *Castle* pulled away, a solitary figure in an attitude of looking back, of saying goodbye, as if at the end of some story with love in it. A drama in which she was the audience, as well as its star. She was, she had decided, finished with men.

Chapter Eight

Councillor Probert turned into one of the streets off Claypit Lane, the road that bisected the red-brick pre-war council housing estate and gave it its unofficial name. On documents referring to it in the housing department of the town hall, usually complaints from neighbours about neighbours, or copies of police reports on disturbances, it was the Julian Culpepper Estate.

The small market town of Kingham had in a history which went back to the 13th century only two known citizens of note.

One was Edwin Preedy-Jones, an obscure backroom scientist who, in the 1920s, read a paper to the Royal Society on something he'd termed The Special Hierarchy of Applied Theoretical Structures in Science. The ideas in it fired off with the heat of long neglect, and the impatience of genius for lesser minds. Ideas, even for that learned audience, of such bewildering, arcane complexity that when it was later proposed that he be awarded the Society's medal for Innovation in Scientific Theory, the few uncertain, questioning voices were quickly overruled by the rest of the sitting committee anxious to move on to matters they did understand. The other was Julian Culpepper.

Culpepper was an early 19ᵗʰ century composer of works for voice and piano, and a favourite of Queen Victoria, frequently joining the Queen and her consort for soirees in Prince Albert's music room at Buckingham Palace, where they took turns at piano and song duets, while the servants whispered and giggled in the corridor with the Prince's parrot, removed on these occasions because it liked to join in. Favourites such as The 'Spring Song', and 'Schöner und Schöner Schmückt Sich', Culpepper giving a selection of his compositions, and his party piece, the Austrian national anthem played with one hand and 'Rule Britannia' as the bass with the other, a nod to both his hosts.

And then the Queen attacking a few arias from her favourite operas in the soprano that could be heard, it was said, perfectly by her guard in their sentry boxes and the audience of loiterers at the gates, their young Queen singing in her new home lit like an opera house at the end of The Mall.

Edwin Preedy-Jones's Royal Society medal excited the front pages of the local papers at the time, and the mayor mentioned him in a speech, and although even today, thirty years after his death, his paper on The Special Hierarchy of Applied Theoretical Structures in Science remains stubbornly resistant to lesser minds, a recent, newly-built science block added to the secondary modern school was solemnly opened in his name.

But it was Julian Culpepper that Kingham had lavished civic love on. There was a bust and a full oil of him posed with a piano in the lobby of the town hall, and another portrait, if a smaller one, and bust in the town's museum, along with framed copies of his compositions (including a piano duet arrangement written for the royal couple to play, with a note of appreciation accompanying it), letters to his mother telling of the royal visits, and an illustration from a life of Queen Victoria showing Culpeper and his hosts, Culpepper seated, coat tails swept back, at the royal piano.

There was a Julian Culpepper bust in the public library, in the entrance of the swimming baths, and in the casualty department of Kingham General. There was also an observation ward there named after him, a municipal park, three streets, a secretarial school, and the Culpepper Arms pub on the Claypit Estate, as it was otherwise known.

Councillor Probert turned into another road on the estate and pulled up outside the house he wanted, behind an overgrown privet hedge. Walking up the path he saw that the front garden had acquired a fridge since he was last there.

He was about to lift the knocker when the door was opened by a woman, middle aged and embattled looking, making a fight of it with extra make-up and a chiffon dress halfway up her thigh.

She took in Mervyn's bespoke tweed suit with a glance like a pawnbroker, before recognising him.

"Hello, Paula."

"Hello, Mr P," she said in a low voice, making it sound like an invitation. "Fancy seeing you here."

"I tried ringing beforehand, but…" He shrugged.

"Yes, well, I was a bit late paying the bill, wasn't I," she said waspishly, and then made a face for a man with town hall influence. "You've no idea what it's like sometimes, Mr P, for a single mother of two, honest you haven't."

"I see you're growing fridges now, Paula," was all Mervyn said, nodding at the one half buried in the grass.

"Can't afford to have it collected since they started charging for it. Dunno what we pay rates for."

Mervyn was able to tell her. "For services and the maintenance of the civic infrastructure under the Act, Paula, that's what. For roads, the repair, cleaning and lighting of, for schools to educate us, social services to ease our way through this vale, crematoria and cemeteries when our day is done, and sports and leisure amenities, arts, heritage and cultural facilities while we're waiting."

"Yeah, well," Paula said.

"He smiled on her like a Witness at the door, selling her his vision of the world as the town hall sees it. "Allow me, Paula, to get you a copy of the latest publication on domestic rates, meaning the costings and distribution of. It's all in there, including a new structure of exemptions, statutory discounts and discretionary reductions and appeals. And in this issue, in the interests of further clarity, there's an addendum concerning itself solely with past valuations, the current *re*valuations, and a forecast of future valuations, with diagrams and tables. Very interesting, it is."

"Yes, I'd like that," Paula confided in a low voice, looking up at him from under her eyelashes, as if he'd suggested that they read it together, and long past being surprised at what turned the male sex on. "What, you'll drop it in for me, will you then?" she added with a throb in her voice, and ran the tip of her tongue along her upper lip.

"No – I'll have it sent, Paula," he said with a chuckle, indulging her notion that he'd actually have to do the delivering. "Along with the latest effort from my department. Planning and Strategic Development – the Future for Kingham."

"Thanks a lot," she said sarcastically.

Mervyn inclined his head modestly in acknowledgement. "It behoves us at the town hall, Paula, to remember that we are only stewards of the public purse and servants of the community. And we are committed, in the modern way of things, to transparency, our affairs, like our financial accounts, an open book."

"Yes, well, I can't stand here nattering to you all day. Leonard's not here, but Victor's in the kitchen, picking out today's losers. Have you got something for them? It's about time they brought something in, apart from trouble."

"I might have, Paula, yes."

"*Vic-tor*!" she bawled back along the passage, genteelly separating the syllables for the sake of the neighbours. "You've got a visitor. From the town hall," she let it be known at the same volume. "Shut the door after you," she added to Mervyn, and waving a hand as if dismissing him wiggled off trailing perfume down the path.

Victor was sitting at the kitchen table with the racing pages of a tabloid in front of him, in a short-sleeved check shirt and Union Jack braces, his scrawny arms decorated with knuckled fists with 'hate' picked out on the fingers, death's heads, daggers, snakes and swastikas, a heart tattoo with the word love on it like a flower among them.

He was rolling a cigarette and when Mervyn came in he leaned back in the chair with interest. The appearance of the councillor meant the promise of money.

"Hello, Victor. Mind if I sit down?" Mervyn said, sitting down.

"What's this then? Bit of biz?"

"Might be, Victor, might be."

"Another late payer?"

"No, not today. But you'll still need to let Lennie off his lead for it," he said, and chuckled, a reference to a joke of his that his brother Lennie ought to require a licence.

"Bit of agro then, is it?"

"That's right. And if we agree terms you'll be causing it, boyo."

Victor flicked a lighter at his roll-up, and looking at Mervyn hooked an arm over the back of his chair, a tough attitude that had the effect of making him seem somehow smaller and much younger than his seventeen years.

"Somebody trying to muscle in on yer here, are they?" he said, an avid follower of the South London gangland case currently in the news, and referring to Mervyn's unlicensed money lending business on the estate. Victor saw himself as the brains behind a small gang of skinheads, with Lennie, his half-brother and the much bigger of the two, the gang's blunt instrument. It was Lennie who Mervyn's customers found on their doorstep when they were late with repayments.

"No, no, it's nothing to do with me. I'm here simply in an agency capacity. Acting for somebody else," he explained.

"Who's that then?"

Mervyn shook his head. "Client confidentially, Victor. You should know that."

"Yeah, right," Victor said, looking impressed. "Well, what's it about then?"

Mervyn told him.

And then digging into a breast pocket he brought out an envelope and said portentously, "I am authorised to pay you in total, Victor, two hundred pounds. Half now, seventy-five pounds, plus twenty-five for expenses, for the boat fares."

Victor watched him spread the notes out on the table. Like coloured beads before natives, Mervyn thought. "One hundred pounds. To tell you the truth, I felt obliged to tell my client it was too much, but there you go," he said, shrugging off his client's unnecessary generosity, one eye on Victor who was still looking at the money.

Victor hooked an arm again over the back of his chair, and found his cigarette had gone out. He relit it and blew out smoke. "Not much, is it."

Mervyn gave a little laugh. "Not much. Well, as I say, Victor, I think it's too much for what's involved – especially as you'll no doubt be keeping most of it. Still, if that's what you think," he said, gathering up the notes.

"Hold on, hold on. I didn't say I wouldn't, did I…"

"Yes or no, boyo. I haven't got all day."

"Yeah, all right, all right."

"Spoken like a businessman, Victor. An executive decision needed to be made and you made it."

"Yeah, well," Victor said vaguely.

Sidney finished off what purported to be a Grosvenor Select biscuit, bought by Dewi in the discount shop across the border in Penycwn, took a sip at what he believed was tea cultivated by monks in a monastery garden, and touched at his mouth with a paper napkin, his eyes sour with his thoughts.

He didn't like Mervyn. For one thing he was Welsh – or rather wasn't English. And the other thing he'd never quite been able to put a finger on. But he was sure it was more than simply that he, Sidney, was English and therefore superior and resented. He'd encountered that attitude more than once since coming to the Marches and had always tried to live up to it. And until he'd met Mervyn considered he had succeeded. But Mervyn gave him the unsettling feeling that it was he, Mervyn, who considered himself to be superior, and that he, Sidney, was being looked down on – when, that is, the Welshman wasn't going through his wallet.

Well Sidney had news for him.

Perfidious Albion, Mervyn had said of him once, not long after that first meeting, with that chuckle of his, as if he admired the quality. Sidney had laughed with him, feeling complimented, and then afterwards had looked it up in Kingham library and learned that, 'Perfidious Albion is a pejorative phrase used within the context of international relations and diplomacy to refer to acts of duplicity, treachery and hence infidelity, with respect to promises made to or alliances formed with other nation states by monarchs or governments of England.' He then looked up 'pejorative' and 'duplicity'.

He had never forgotten it, and with some satisfaction brought it out again now from the ample store of aggrievement life had supplied him with. Well, the Welshman had no idea about him, about his past before Kingham. But if he and his boyos of his didn't pull off the job he was paying them to do, he would find out just how perfidious this particular Albion could be. He would learn then to his cost just who he was really dealing with.

Chapter Nine

He phoned Ffion on the Saturday evening after the boat trip. Cadi, her thirteen-year-old sister, answered like the receptionist of a grand hotel she'd seen on television and now wanted to be.

"Whom shall I say is speaking…? Thank you. Hold the line, please, caller," she said, and taking her time went down the deck to the kitchen in the stern, where Ffion was helping her mother with the evening meal.

"What are we eating?" she asked.

"Food," Ffion said, cleaning vegetables in the sink.

Cadi ignored her. "What are we eating, Mam?"

"Chicken casserole."

"With chips? Can we have chips?"

"No, we're having spuds."

"I don't like spuds."

"Too bad," Ffion said.

"Why can't we have chips?"

"Because we're having spuds," Ffion said. "You've just been told."

"But I want chips."

"What you want and what you get, Cadi, are two different things."

"Not always, Ffion," Cadi was able to tell her in her receptionist's voice. "Last Christmas, for example, I asked Father—"

"Have you finished tidying the room?" her mother cut in.

"No. Not yet!" Cadi said indignantly.

"Well, go and finish it, Cadi."

"Yes, I'm going to."

"Well you won't do it standing there, will you. And your da will be home soon."

"I was trying to finish it, and then I had to stop and answer the telephone."

"Who was it?" her mother asked.

"Dunno. Can we have ice-cream then afterwards?"

"Well, what did they want, Cadi?"

"Dunno. It was for her," she said, nodding at her sister.

"Her's got a name!" Ffion said. "You're so *rude*. And who was it?"

"Some *boy*," Cadi sneered.

"Well, why didn't you tell me!"

"I am telling you."

"At the *time*, I meant, Cadi!"

"I am telling you at the time, *actually*. The caller is holding."

"You little—! Who is it?" Ffion said, drying her hands.

"I have told you. I do not know."

"You should ask their name, Cadi, when you answer the phone!"

"I'm not your servant," Cadi told her, running back down the deck, and having heard Ffion say it to her mother enough times.

The caller was still holding. Ffion expected it to be Gareth and heard with relief that it wasn't.

"Ffion? Hello, this is Tim, Tim Brown. I was on the boat the other day. The one playing the guitar...?"

"Oh, yes, I remember," she said.

"Great. Look, I hope you don't mind," he hurried on, before she could apologise for the delay in answering, "but I got your number from your brother, Sion, afterwards, when we docked. I hope you don't mind," he said again.

Ffion wondered briefly if she ought to mind or not, and then said no, of course not.

"Well, it was just that I could see on the boat that you were interested in folk music. And it struck me that you might like to go to a folk club with me tomorrow lunchtime in Kingham. You know, as you seemed interested," he said, trying to put a bit of distance between him and any other motive. "It's in a pub there, the Red Lion. In fact," he added with a little laugh, "I've been asked to do a couple of numbers, actually, and thought, you know, as you were interested..."

"Yes, OK. Thank you, yes, I'd like to," she said, not knowing that it *had* been a folk song he'd been singing. It was just a song that Jasmine sang, and more into singers such as Roberta Flack, and songs of sophisticated love and loss, wondered what she had let herself in for.

After he had made arrangements to pick her up, he said, "Oh, by the way, who *was* that who answered the phone?"

The folk club was in an upstairs room of the pub, and they sat with their drinks at a table in front of the stage. She hadn't caught the name of the first act, announced by the friend of Tony's she'd been introduced to when they arrived, but clapped with everyone else, until the performer, marching on in polished black workman's boots and bib overalls, waved an impatient hand at them.

"Leave that to the middle class. *Don't conform!*" she yelled into the microphone, shouting it like a slogan, and then told them that she wouldn't use words for what she had to say. Writing, she went on, emphasising it with a raised finger, is a bourgeois, elitist construct, a tool of oppression and manipulation.

"This is the poetry of the new reality," she cried. "A new living utterance, to use D H Lawrence's phrase. Read his *Fantasia of the Unconscious* and you'll see where we're coming from. We use non-verbal communication, soul poetry, free of the chains of syntax, of language. We utter as the animals must, our fellow creatures under the same yoke of tyranny. You will know them when they speak," she assured them.

Ffion thought that that sounded interesting, and wondered if she was good as Percy Edwards, who, it was said, could imitate six hundred birds as well as many other animals, including, she'd read the other day, whales and reindeer.

She sat back to listen, and jumped when the performer screamed into the microphone on higher and higher notes. She couldn't place it, unless it was a monkey of some sort, nor the roar which followed, and was wondering if that was a whale, or maybe a sea lion, when Tom leaned towards her and said apologetically.

"I don't know how long this is going on for. I didn't even know she was appearing."

"She's not very good, is she," Ffion felt able to say.

He looked both surprised and impressed. "Do you understand it then, this non-verbal poetry stuff?"

"Ohhh… Oh, *that's* what it is," she said, laughing.

She told him what she thought it was going to be, and he laughed with her, until they saw the performer staring at them, the growling she had switched to, which Ffion did recognise, seeming to be directed at them.

They sat dutifully through another twenty minutes of it, before the performer marched off again, followed briefly by scattered applause, before it was remembered that they weren't supposed to do that.

Tom's friend called him up next, and Ffion found herself holding his canvas guitar case as if his coat, watching him mount the steps to the stage with a fixed smile of vague anxiety, like a parent at a school show.

He said without looking at her that he'd like to sing a Pete Seeger number. He had started vigorously on 'If I Had a Hammer', putting everything he had into it for, as far as he was concerned, an audience of one, when the group of skinheads who had just come in let him know what they thought of it, and shouted something about punk rock before noisily leaving.

Tim grinned at her when he rejoined her after finishing his second number. "What is it about you? Whenever I sing, somebody appears and starts shouting."

After the folk pub the Claypit Firm, as they thought of themselves, Victor and his brother Lennie and their friends, moved on to one of the town's cider houses. There was no punk rock to be heard there either, nor any other sort of diversion, apart from the cider and the fruit machine a woman was lethargically feeding coins to, but the drink was much cheaper.

It was poured from a brown plastic barrel on the counter by the landlord, an untidy, shambling figure, who detached himself from the gloom of a recess behind the bar after wondering whether or not to serve them after the trouble last time, before deciding on discretion.

They carried the pint glasses to what looked like a kitchen table, its Formica top scarred with cigarette burns. The pale draught bore little resemblance to cider and tasted less of apples than the chemicals that had given the regulars in the bar complexions the colour of lead. The woman who'd been playing the fruit machine with little expectation of it doing other than taking her money, was one of them, with lank, greying hair and a punished face, her girlish pink duffle coat and decorated bell-bottom jeans like clothes from another wardrobe, another life, someone else's, or perhaps her own.

Victor's brother, Lennie, sprawled, legs out, his Dr Marten boots with the steel toecaps moving restlessly, his eyes surly. He'd been like that all morning, as if looking for something or somebody to kick. And he still wasn't sure that it shouldn't be his brother.

Victor had got the departure time right for the *Batch Castle* from the CSC's advertisement in the *Kingham*

News, but hadn't got as far as the bit which said there was no Sunday sailing. He had to wait for Tom Parr to tell him that, when they arrived in Batch Magna and met Tom on his way in to see how the paddler's fire was doing.

Victor had to pretend that it was Councillor Probert's fault they were returning empty-handed, that he'd said they sailed throughout the week. Otherwise his brother might consider he didn't have to look any further for someone to take it out on.

Lennie, who, simply out of habit, hadn't altogether believed him, now scowled. "So, what – we have to wait now till Saturday, do we?"

"Well, yeah, of course," Victor said complacently. "I mean, you heard the old bloke. The only weekend sailing's on Saturday. And it's their busiest day. So what does that mean, then?" he asked, throwing it open to the table.

They thought about it. "More people?" one of them suggested.

"Yeah, right, more people," Victor said, and smiled, a man with a better answer than that. "More people for maximum disruption," he said, quoting Councillor Probert. "So we'd better do what the old geezer suggested we do, hadn't we. And book tickets for a nice boat ride next Saturday."

Chapter Ten

Mervyn arranged the round of golf that afternoon after morning chapel, suggesting it to Odgar Llewellyn-Jenkins like a code while talking with him and some of the other men, their wives chatting in a separate group of women on the pavement outside.

The golf course, a few miles outside Kingham, was on Mortwardine Hill, the mountains of Wales to the west rising in a mist with eagles in it, the hills and green folds of England tucked neatly away to the east.

Not that the two men showed any interest in the views. They were no longer even interested in the game. They had stopped playing on their way to the next hole, brought to a halt by what Mervyn meant, even though he hadn't said it yet. He had told Odgar between holes what he'd laid on for the Cluny Steamboat Company, and how Odgar could shortly expect a bit of business to come his way. But that was not all he had to say.

Two things lately had been occupying Mervyn – how he might move in on Sidney's business, and what Sidney knew. And it hadn't taken him long to see that the resolving of the second thing would make him a present of the first. A present he was about to share with Odgar.

He'd already talked about the Prestige Car Service, how, as it was now the only taxi firm in Kingham, it was a money spinner. "*Raking* it in, he is," he said, looking at Odgar, a border Welshman, with indignation, as if at the thought of an outsider coming in and helping himself like that. "I wouldn't mind that business, I can tell you. If something happened to him, like."

Odgar looked amused. "Why, left it you in his will, has he?"

"No, no, nothing like that," Mervyn said with a chuckle. "No, I was just saying, you know, if something happened to him. You know…?" he said again, glancing at the other man.

"Well, there's no denying, Mervyn, that we are all at the mercy of time and chance, as Ecclesiastes tells us. The cruel net and the snare, and all that, you know. That ball looks to be further away from the hole than I thought."

"Yes, well, I didn't mean that, Odgar" Mervyn persisted. "I meant if something *happened* to him."

"If something happened to him?"

"Yes, you know…"

"What do you mean if something *happened* to him?"

"You know…" Mervyn said again, softly, the words like a caress, an intimacy between them, Mervyn's elbow lightly jogging his arm.

Odgar came to a halt and turned a face sharp with bones towards him, a face which seemed to have sprung from purer Welsh soil than that of the diluted borders, a Celtic redness high on his cheeks as if painted on, like Punch, his eyes the colour of sloes, eyes seasoned in calculation and alert now with suspicion, and something which might have been alarm.

"What exactly do you mean, Mervyn?"

Mervyn glanced swiftly around. "I mean, Odgar," he said, getting down to business, and lowering his voice to match Odgar's, although the nearest players were on the other side of the fairway, "if he were to meet with an accident. On purpose."

Odgar said nothing, just stared at him. Mervyn was encouraged.

"That building he's in doesn't belong to him, you know," he went on, as if offering it as a justification. "He rents it, off the widow of the original owner of it. Like the chap who had it before him did."

Odgar nodded. "Maurice. Maurice Cottingham. That was the original owner's name," he said, sounding awed, as if recalling some local deed of great infamy. "Then when it became empty Wilf Ellis run his taxi business from it, before falling ill."

"Yes, well, basically all Sidney had to buy off Wilf was the goodwill and the radio equipment. And that's all we'll be called on to fork out. He's living with some woman, but—"

"*Living* with some woman…?" Odgar said, frowning.

"Oh, yes," Mervyn said. "Quite openly, too, apparently. Well – English, see. But anyway, even if she wanted to take it on, you'd have revoked his licence by then, in proper constitutional accordance and under the Act. Quoting evidence of improper purpose and criminal activity. I'll come to that in a minute. And we'll have the paddle steamer licence by then as well, we'll make sure of it. A little goldmine, that is, that run. And Shrewsbury used to be Welsh so we'll just be taking a bit of it back, plunder from under English noses. Be like the old days." Mervyn chuckled. "Perhaps we ought to call it Owain Glyndwr Taxis."

"What are you saying, man?" Odgar said fearfully, and as if asking himself the same question, his own thoughts starting to stray.

Mervyn glanced around again with an impatient movement.

"I am *saying*, Odgar, that we could be the proprietors of a going concern, meaning the Kingham Prestige Car Service. A going concern that would go even further if we were running it, with our contacts. It's called the bigger picture, Odgar. And I see our future there," he said, waving a finger at the sky. "I see us, Odgar, in the *Kingham News* when they do a feature on our expansion into new premises, out on the edge of town somewhere because of the acreage required. I see a fleet of coaches taking our company name to the far corners of these islands and beyond. I hear the applause of our peers in the community, and the after-dinner toasts at the Rotary Club and at the mayor's table. And I see ease and leisure, Odgar, when our work is done, the fruits of the labours of our hands, as the Psalms have it. All this I see, Odgar."

So did Odgar. His tongue flicked out and back again, licking at his lips.

"You'd never get away with it," he said then, looking at him as if in appeal, as if begging him to agree.

"I don't see why not," was all Mervyn said, and chuckled. "The police will be too busy looking elsewhere, meaning Birmingham. I'll ring up beforehand and speak to Sidney's secretary. Tell her in the accents of that city to warn her boss that we run the drugs there and to stay away – unless he'd like to end up in a carpet. Remember that, Odgar, the body in a carpet? Someone else who tried to muscle in, and finished up fly-tipped down an embankment on the M1. That's the way the boyos there do business. Brisk and to the point."

"The Birmingham Carpet Murder," Odgar intoned, seeing the headlines again.

"And poor Sidney just wouldn't listen. That's the way the police will see it, once they've put two and two together. Simple enough arithmetic, even for our constabulary."

"It won't work," Odgar said, as if warning himself, the thought of such a sin wrestling with the promise of riches, standing with his own temptation on another hill with the future he had seen from it. But with a voice at his ear that would not get behind him.

"For a man's ways are in full view of the Lord, and he examines all his paths," he reminded himself anxiously, head bent over his golf club, hands clasping and unclasping on it. "The evil deeds of a wicked man ensnare him, the cords of his sin hold him fast. Proverbs five."

"We have been tested and found wanting before, Odgar," Mervyn said, bowing his head as if joining him in prayer. "And when our day comes we must throw ourselves on His abundant mercy and forgiveness, and ask for one more to be taken into consideration. God is good. Though your sins be scarlet, they shall be as white as snow. Though they be red like crimson, they shall be as wool. Isaiah, one-eighteen."

Odgar, tested, grievously, once more, looked away, the weight of who he was, and was expected to be, on his shoulders. The generations of his forebears, their lives devoted to the public good, the family name a byword in the town for probity and civic duty, his reputation in the chapel and the community, his position at the town hall, and his wife's dream of being the mayoress when he donned the chain of that office, another expectation to be met.

He then seemed to slump, as if exhausted by it.

"Saying that I agreed," he said in a near whisper, "how would you – how would it be – er – you know…?"

"Ah, now you've identified, Odgar, that part of these undertakings that has led many into error and the dock. It is no time to cut corners!" Mervyn said emphatically, suggesting the reason for it. "If we want to stay free to enjoy that future then the job must be done properly. By a professional, meaning what is called a hit man," he said, having read a feature on it while waiting to have his veneers polished at the dentist's. "Someone to whom it's simply a job of work. He will arrive, dispatch Sidney quickly and painlessly – he is not called upon to suffer – and depart as if he had never been. The waters closing again on the deed like those of Avalon, leaving not a trace. It is the modern way of doing things."

"But where would we find such a person?" Odgar said, wondering at the exoticness of it, and not only now agreeing but sharing possible teething problems.

"Northern Ireland," Mervyn said promptly. "I have contacts there among those already holding the English to account. And it is best, Odgar, that that is *all* you do know," he added firmly, Odgar nodding hurried agreement.

"Now, I've made certain enquiries," Mervyn went on like a salesman, "and I can get it done for a round figure of four thousand pounds, including full expenses. Two down, two on completion." He shot up a hand at Odgar's expression. "Yes, I know it *sounds* a lot. But consider the return you'll be getting on investment, Odgar, the sort of future you'll be buying with it. Odgar – Odgar, no names, no pack drill, but this man is a top-flight professional. Top flight. Meaning no clues left behind pointing to us. That's what we'd be paying for. And that was a sum, mark you, now, man, arrived at because I am a friend of a friend. Anyone else, I am reliably informed, would be looking at a few thousand more plus. And of course it helped that Sidney's English."

Shortly after that, two voices were lifted on the summer breezes on Mortwardine Hill, singing softly in harmony 'Lead On O King Eternal' as they moved up the green, as if with one eye on their immortal souls, or that of the soon to be departed Sidney Acton, two voices, one a bass, the other a baritone.

Chapter Eleven

The following morning, Sidney's secretary Shirley Meddins was typing out an overdue account letter, in between admiring the engagement ring she'd acquired over the weekend. Across from her Dewi had his bald head with its short skirt of white hair bent over work on his desk, and she smiled at him unseen.

She was often stirred by thoughts of his life, alone in that flat of his, without even a cat to go home to, and out of goodness, and all she had that he didn't, which today included a ring, was now even more so. They hadn't thought about a wedding guest list yet, but when they did Mr Brice would definitely be on it.

She had paused again, left hand extended, when the phone rang. "Prestige. Good morning!" she sang cheerfully. Today, everybody got a hug from Shirley.

"Would you like me to put you through to him…?" she asked then, admiring the way the diamonds in the heart-shaped ring caught the light. She wondered if she should bear the pale colour, the pale fire, as the jeweller had poetically put it, in mind when she talked wedding dresses with Fay at lunchtime.

"I see. Yes, all right, dear, I'll tell him. Thank you for calling. An Indian gentleman from Birmingham, by the sound of it," she shared with Dewi. "Selling rugs and carpets. I think," she added doubtfully, and leaned forward in her chair. "I couldn't really understand him," she mouthed delicately.

"Did I show you my ring, Mr Brice?" she asked a few minutes later, pausing to look at it again.

Dewi smiled. "Yes, you did Shirley. Twice."

"Ronald did it properly, too. Got down on one knee. I had to stop myself from giggling. But *so* romantic," she sighed, before returning to the world of commerce and somebody's overdue account.

It was a good job, Dewi told himself again on the Friday of that week, when the taxi firm was buzzing with the news about their boss, Sidney, that he been at his desk all day yesterday.

Otherwise he knew he would not have been sure, not to his complete satisfaction, that while looking the other way, as it were, busy thinking about something else, such as buying arsenic for Sidney's tea, arsenic that he wasn't actually buying, because he wasn't actually poisoning Sidney's tea, fantasy hadn't moved on without him and turned into reality on Mortwardine Golf Course.

That he hadn't hidden in a bunker yesterday afternoon, when Sidney was enjoying his regular Thursday afternoon game, and taken a pot-shot at him.

For somebody had. And missed. Perhaps, the latest gossip had it, gossip started by Shirley, influenced by a picture she'd seen last week at the local Odeon about the Mafia, on purpose. Because the shot had brought down a crow which landed, black wings spread, like a message, it was said, at Sidney's feet. Dewi had been reassured by that.

He was not at all certain that he could even hit Sidney, unless perhaps he obligingly stood still long enough, and not more than half a dozen feet away, never mind a bird in flight. And besides, he didn't own a gun.

Which didn't stop him, immediately he arrived home, searching for one, just in case.

Chapter Twelve

Mr and Mrs Tilling were retired civil servants, wore his and hers knitted sweaters and finished each other's sentences. They had resigned their membership of the National Trust in protest at what they saw as a general falling away of standards, both in the buildings it maintained and the sort of people it allowed in these days, and were now founder members of their own historical appreciation society in a Midlands town.

Energetic and earnest, they carried cameras and notebooks and a brisk, impatient air of knowing best and keen to get on with it. And they were here, at the Hall, watched furtively by Clem and Humphrey from behind the curtains of one of the bedrooms.

It had not started well. After making an appointment to view the property, as they had put it, to assess the Hall's suitability for a visit from their society, they had been greeted at the door by Humphrey, all of him, in one of his shirts, behind a cloud of cigar smoke.

Clem, appearing from the kitchen, had known them at a glance, their brand of Englishness under the matching sweaters, the sort of militant snobbery at war largely with itself, a battleground of skirmish and attrition between who they and others were. When she introduced Humphrey she gave him his full title.

Humphrey swept all that, and over three hundred years of history, away with a large hand and told them to call him Humph, for gosh sakes!

The couple were still taking in that this was Sir Humphrey, the 9th baronet of his line and squire of this March, when Humphrey, arms out as if to gather them in an embrace, told them to come on in and take the weight off their plates, as he had learned to call feet, and shepherded them into the kitchen, where they saw two more one-armed bandits to go with the four in the hall, with Jasmine Roberts feeding one of them, and without taking her eyes off the promise of a sudden windfall, yelling now and then at several of her children chasing Hawis round the kitchen.

Clem waved a vague hand at the din as their Jack Russell started yapping again, and smiled an apology.

The Tillings, after an exchange of glances as good as words between them, declined the offer of tea or coffee, and said that they had to get on, that they had three more houses to inspect.

Sharing the sentences with small, brief twin smiles of politeness, they made it clear on their way out to start on this one, that they regarded the properties they visited as belonging not to the current occupants, who were of course merely sitting tenants, but to the nation, and saw their role as being representatives of that nation, of its heritage, its history. They would like, they said, to inspect what they called the elevations first.

They strode busily together far enough out from the entrance to take in the entire front of the building, the two grand end gables either side tilted out of true by age, giving the whole a tipsy look, a foolishly happy, disreputable sort of air, suggestive, in Phineas Cook's phrase, of a down-at-heel aristocrat, ruined but jaunty in a battered silk topper and with a bottle in his pocket, and only a lamppost for support.

Veterans of the Baroque splendours of such stately homes as Chatsworth and Blenheim, the Tillings gazed at it without comment.

Humphrey gave a small defensive laugh. He'd been thrown by having met, as it were, history in person, or rather two persons, its representatives, with notebooks and cameras, and the sort of disapproving air that, when it came to his place in it, he expected history to have.

"Yeah, well, I guess, looking at it, the walls are due a fresh wash of lime. And I can see the timbers need a bit of re-pitching here and there. It's the dry weather we've been having, see, it lifts it on the wood. But it's finding the time," he said, sharing another laugh.

Mrs Tilling scribbled something in a notebook, as if taking down what he'd just said, and Mr Tilling, backing artistically with the camera, took a few shots, as if nailing the evidence.

They then set off at the same brisk pace on a tour of the rest of the exterior, pointing things out to each other, and taking more photographs and making more notes, like landlords building a case of neglect, while the sitting tenants followed on with a vaguely anxious air.

They inspected the interior next, Mr Tilling snapping the hall with its fireplace under the curve of a staircase they told each other was early Jacobean, and familiar with the art collections of all the great houses, which included family portraits by Gainsborough and Reynolds, exchanged glances of amused reserve, noting without having to say so that the past squires and their families lining its wall were merely 'in the manner of'.

When it came to the Hall's grounds, they thanked them and said in tones which threw doubt on the Hall's chances of a visit from their members, that they needn't bother them further, that they'd just take a quick look round themselves.

The moment they were out of the door Clem bolted for the stairs, urging Humphrey, who was frowning after her in the hall, to follow.

"The Garfields' room," she called back, referring to two of their guests. "They're away for the day, doing Ludlow."

He lumbered after her and found her peering down at the forecourt from behind one of the curtains.

Humphrey took the other curtain. "They're just standing there, talking," he said out of the side of his mouth.

"Probably discussing where to start – or if they should just leave. I don't think they—"

"They're off! Heading for the yard. Everything OK there?" he asked, narrowing his eyes at her.

"Yes!" Clem said indignantly. "I swept through it only the other day. Or the day before that," she added in the arithmetic of Batch Magna, and already on her way to an unoccupied bedroom overlooking the stable yard. "Come on!"

They tracked them from there, losing them briefly in the kitchen garden which led to the rest of the grounds, and picking them up again from the tall landing window overlooking the terrace when they wandered out on to the lawns.

"Good job I gave the grass a cut last week… I bet I know where they're heading," Humphrey said then, as if he'd been warning something like this would happen, as the Tillings seemed to gather purpose and moved off in the direction of the glasshouses that were largely no longer used, and the two tennis courts, one of which was now a chicken run.

"Yes. Really must get round to doing something about them," Clem muttered vaguely, meaning the small jungles in the glasshouses, something she said every time she went near them, and ignoring now the chicken run which had been her idea.

"We should have closed both of the damn things. Hardly anyone plays on the other one," Humphrey said, taking the opportunity to get it in. He had wanted to turn the two courts into a piggery, but Clem and Shelly's argument about being able to offer tennis and fresh eggs for the guests had won the debate.

"They've stopped," he said then, tightly. "What are they doing…?"

"Discussing where to go. Home, I hope."

"They're off again!"

"Back to the car, please, like good little Tillings," Clem said, shooing them along with her hands.

"They're looking over here… They're coming this way!" Humphrey warned, jerking his head back behind the curtain as the Tillings turned and started marching in step towards the house.

"Have you noticed how they never move far from each other?" Clem said. "His and hers. He's mine and I'm his. Have they got his and hers children, I wonder? And his and hers house doors, and his and hers cups and plates, and his and hers lavatories, and—"

"They're coming in again…!"

"To have another sneer at the portraits, I suppose. I've a good mind to—!"

"They've stopped… Uh-oh, they're-looking-at-the-flowerbeds," Humphrey said, almost singing it, a song of the state of the beds below the terrace that only the only day, or the day before that, Clem had said, again, that she really must do something about.

"We can't be expected to do everything! Not now Tom's working on the boat," Clem said, which prompted her husband to snatch a glance at his watch.

"Jeeze! Look at the time. I'll be late and it's a Saturday. I better drive down."

And then he looked at his wife and lost a few more minutes. "Come here," he said.

He took her face in his meaty hands, his eyes busy, moving over it carefully, as if checking it was all there, and then he kissed her, on the lips, in the middle of the big window, in full view of the Tillings and anyone else who cared to look.

And history, as far as he was concerned, could put that in its pipe and smoke it.

The Claypit Firm were also running late. The car belonging to one of them, which they normally would have used, wouldn't start, and another gang member, Glyn, had to persuade his father, a builder off sick, to lend him his van.

Once out of Kingham Glyn took to the lanes and kept his foot down. Victor and another skinhead squatted in the back, among bags of cement, tools and lengths of timber. Big Lennie, legs out, sat next to the driver, not saying much, not even when the talk was of their team's chances at that day's away game.

Just sitting there, like a tool himself, a lump hammer perhaps that is not fully a lump hammer until it's bashing away at something, one Dr Marten bother boot tapping steadily, staring ahead, waiting to be fully Lennie again.

Chapter Thirteen

The Commander included Humphrey in the steam-whistle warning to any latecomers, and added an extra one just for him, as galley crew for the day.

"Yeah, yeah, I'm coming, I'm coming," he said, waving complacently in that direction as he took his time climbing into Henrietta in the forecourt, the large, ancient wooden-framed Bentley shooting brake, a wedding present from Clem's parents, mutton dressed as lamb now in her original British racing green paintwork, the days of safely doing more than forty on the road long behind her.

But the pace suited him, as did its ample room. He left zooming about the lanes to Clem in her Mini, the colour of a fire engine. Humphrey liked to take his time with life, liked looking at things, often, when it came to those dear and familiar to him, with an expression suggestive of surprised pleasure, as if seeing, or appreciating them, for the first time. Humphrey was a benign observer of this world, and wished it only well, regarding it from a sort of kindly, tolerant distance, curious, in a mild sort of way, about almost all its doings. And if he found at times the people in it both puzzling and their endeavours amusing, he had the good manners to keep it to himself.

He started off down the drive, windows wound right down to summer, breaking into song, or rather several songs, taking a few words from each, before forgetting what came after that and moving on to the next one, singing lustily at the morning, and was about to go through the gates when the car coughed and spluttered to a halt.

He tried the ignition a few times, and then looked at the fuel gauge.

"Empty. I'm out of petrol," he told himself, tapping the glass. "I'm outa gas *here!*" he growled, looking back in the direction of the house, addressing himself to whoever used her last.

He sat for a few moments chewing on nothing, before remembering the can in the coach house. He calculated that it would be quicker to fetch that rather than walk down to the boat.

He set off back up the drive, another steamy reminder from the *Castle*, exclusively for him this time, prodding a bit more speed out of him, round the side of the Hall and into the stable yard for the coach house. The petrol can was sitting where he'd left it, in a wheelbarrow, and he remembered then that after the mowing he'd used what was left to burn the undergrowth he'd spent a day clearing with his young helper, George.

He rejected the idea of their other car, Clem's Mini, almost as soon as he thought of it, remembering the last time. He wasn't built for a Mini. He'd just have to walk down. Run, you mean, he told himself, checking his watch on his way back into the house first to ring Priny, to let the Commander know he was on his way.

Following the route the Tillings had taken, he trotted with the gait of a Shire horse up the yard, through the kitchen garden, across the lawns, up the terrace steps, and in through the drawing room to the hall, where Clem and their visitors were talking. It came as no surprise to find the Tillings still there. It went with the sort of morning he was having.

He paused in the doorway to get his breath, hand on his chest as if having a heart attack, letting them know what he'd been put through. The Tillings looked at him in alarm.

"I thought you'd gone, darling," was all his wife said, mildly.

"Henrietta. Outa gas," he got out, as if delivering a message before expiring. "Petrol," he translated. "No petrol!"

Shelly, who'd emerged from the kitchen to herd a couple of the children back in as Clem and the visitors were talking, clasped a hand to her mouth. "Aw, gee, honey, I'm sorry. I did a sandwich run with Annie on Thursday and meant to fill her up on the way back. Then we got talking…"

He nodded. He'd thought as much.

"I'm *sorry!*" she wailed at him.

He put up his hands as if in surrender. "All right, Mom. OK."

"Isn't there any in the coach house?" Clem said.

"No, I used it for the mower."

"I'm sorry, Humphie," his mother said again.

"It's all right, Mom. Don't worry about it," he said, as if amused at her concern. "I'm not. I'll walk down. No problem. Nice day like this, birds singing and all that.

What's a few minutes here and there? I'll ring Priny and she can tell the Commander I'm on my way. It's OK," he said again, lifting the phone on the hall table, dialling and acknowledging the Tillings then, smiling on at them while listening to the engaged tone.

He put down the receiver. "Priny," he said, was all he needed to say. Priny could answer the phone to a straightforward passenger enquiry and come away an hour later with somebody's life story.

"I gotta go. You could try again in a few minutes, honey," he said to Clem. "But she'll probably still be talking when I get there. Probably still be talking when we dock. Probably—"

"Darling, I could—" Clem started.

"No, no, no, it's all right. You're busy. It's OK, it's *OK*. There's no problem here. What's the problem?" he asked with a little laugh. "I mean, whose company it is, huh…? Huh?" he said again, pointedly, in the direction of the river and the Commander, and then snorting a laugh in answer on his way out.

He asked himself it again then, jogging back down the drive, nagged along by more screaming of steam from the *Castle*. "That's what I'd like to know. Whose goddam company is it?" he muttered breathlessly, coming on Henrietta round the last bend in the drive, sitting in front the gates, blocking the entrance.

He threw his hands in the air. "I can't just *leave* her there!" he cried, as if to anyone who would listen.

He decided it would be easier to push her out, rather than push her further in, to take advantage of the slight incline in the drive and manoeuvre her through the gates and up onto the verge opposite.

He opened the driver's door, released the handbrake, and with one hand on the steering wheel and the other on the doorframe, pushed. The low-slung, heavy six seater, with generous room at the rear for loaders, guns, dogs, lunch hampers and game, moved a little as if straining forward with him, as if trying her best, and then seemed to give up, and sat back, creaking with age.

He went round the front, with the idea, in that case, of pushing her further in, to open up enough room for other cars to pass. He put two hands on the nose of the bonnet, braced himself and bent to it, the coloured brass radiator mascot, a monocled fox in hunting pink mounted on a hound, grinning at finding itself with the upper hand for once, gleefully bared its teeth at him.

He gave up, and stood breathing hard and glaring at her, his ears burning. He tried the rear then, returning to his first idea, hoping to get her moving and then nip round and steer her out.

He put two meaty hands on the roof, and pushed, mouth clamped shut, grunting with the strain. She just sat there, obstinately, it seemed to him now, as if sulking. He gave her a good shake out of sheer temper, shaking and rocking her on her axles, and then stumbled and almost fell when she moved abruptly forward, and rolled like a tank towards the open gates and the road.

He caught up with her just as she was about to leave the grounds, and with nothing coming on the road decided to steer her across it and up onto the verge opposite. They were almost there when she wanted to go right, to follow the road down, and he'd started correcting her with the steering wheel when she swung suddenly towards him, as if to shake him off, almost knocking him over, and took off again. He hung on to the wheel and tried to get in, making tentative little hopping movements, before being forced to let go.

He stood in the middle of the road, watching like an anxious parent as she went her own way, picking up speed on the incline, driver's door flapping as if waving goodbye, heading for the crossroads and the village, before swinging suddenly right again and mounting the verge that side.

He closed his eyes on what he knew was coming next, and heard it then, when she ran into the Hall's bed and breakfast sign.

Broken glass fell on metal like a full stop in the silence as he trotted after her. She had hit one of the sign's uprights wing on, its headlight smashed and the wing and the bumper that side buckled, stove in.

He looked up hopefully at the approach of a car, and lifted his hands with a rueful smile, sharing it with them as the Tillings went by, two heads turning as one, taking in the new addition to the bed and breakfast sign, topped with a wooden pair of cowboy boots, that they'd agreed on the way in would have been better suited to a holiday camp. And from the river the steam whistle shrieked furiously again.

Chapter Fourteen

Priny was still talking when he got there – and he had no doubt that it was the same call. She had that settled-in look, phone in one hand, cigarette holder trailing smoke in the other, head back on a laugh as if at some goddam cocktail party.

He looked straight at her going past her window, showed her his face, heated and sweating after his jog there, a silent reproof. She smiled absently in his direction, waggled her cigarette holder at him as if getting rid of ash, and went on with her conversation.

The Commander was waiting for him on deck with Sion. On his way up the gangway Humphrey silently indicated first Priny and the ticket office, and then Henrietta and the Hall, a short, breathless story of the trouble he'd had getting there, before giving up and coming to a halt, hands on knees.

He looked up them, his face haggard.

The Commander was unmoved. He consulted the fob watch in his hand.

"Allow me to point out," he said, "that the advertised time of departure is o-ten-thirty."

Humphrey was nodding. "Commander – Commander, you would *not* believe—"

"It is now," the Commander was able to tell him, "o-ten-forty-seven."

"Right, well, first of all we had the Tillings," Humphrey said, as if referring to some domestic problem that anyone might have. "And then—"

"Yes, well you're here now," the Commander cut in briskly, "so I suggest we oblige our passengers by doing what they've paid us to do. Sion, cast off please."

"Yeah, well, it wasn't my fault, that's all I'm saying here. It wasn't my fault," Humphrey muttered mutinously, edging round him.

"Whose goddam company is it, anyway?" he wanted to know again, on his way to the galley, where his first customer, a small boy, was waiting impatiently for him to open up.

Could he please have, the boy said avidly, the money for it clutched in a hand, a double chocolate ice-cream?

Good idea, Humphrey immediately approved, and said he'd join him, the sort of day he was having.

He was telling his customer about the sort of day he was having, starting with the Tillings, while donning his Master Chef's hat and Food Dude apron, and was about to open the fridge door for the chocolate mix, when he saw that the ice-cream machine wasn't where it should have been, sitting with the plastic display stands on a table next to the fridge. It was on the other side of the room, near the stove, where the cartons of crisps and pork scratchings now sitting with the plastic display stands should be. And he knew who was responsible. It was one of the women. They were always moving things around.

He glared at the machine, hands balled on hips, and then looked at his customer.

"*That*," he said, aiming a rigid finger at it, "shouldn't be there. That should not *be* there, near the stove like that. It says that plain as anything in the user manual," he went on, pointing then at where he had no doubt the manual was now, buried under the cartons of crisps and pork scratchings. "Not of course," he added with a short laugh, "that women ever *read* a user manual. Or put gas in the tank. Oh, no, that would be asking too much. This ice-cream machine," he quoted, a man who'd had reason to do so before, "should be kept away from grease-producing cooking equipment like stoves and chip-fryers. Otherwise, what happens…? Huh?" he asked, hands spread, one male to another.

"I dunno," the boy said, shifting fretfully, waiting for his ice-cream.

"Well, I'll tell you what happens. Little by little," Humphrey said, his fingers moving in the air like insects, "bit by bit, slowly, slowly, the grease gets on the condenser, gets on the coils at the back, see, wrapping itself around them. And then more and more grease comes, and more and more, until it's suffocating them. Until the coils are covered with it and they can't *breathe*. Can't get rid of the heat the ice-cream machine makes. And what does that mean? I'll tell you what that means. It means the compressor inside has to work harder and harder and harder. And then, not only is there less and less ice produced, and the ice-cream turns to goo, and not only does it take more electricity, running the batteries down quicker. Not only all that – it can lead," he said, leaving the worst till last, and emphasising it with a finger, "to premature compressor failure. That's what that means."

He was about to share what premature compressor failure meant, when he was suddenly busy with a queue forming at the door. And with nothing prepared, found he needed, as he grumbled to himself, as he'd heard Annie grumble when doing the cream teas, four pair of hands.

He was beset by customers, dishing out more ice-cream, making tea and coffee, pouring soft drinks, beer and cider, in-between chopping onions for the Conies, buttering rolls for the fillings and bread for the sandwiches, a harried figure, Master Chef's hat askew, sweat dribbling from under it in the heat from the stove, blatting at the smoke with a spatula when he burnt the onions again.

And then, thirty minutes out from Batch Magna, what he'd told his first customer could happen, what he'd been telling himself *would* happen – especially as he hadn't had time to move the ice-cream machine from the stove, back to where it shouldn't have been moved from in the first place – happened. Its compressor started to make that noise it made when it was asking for its condenser coils to be cleaned if somebody didn't want the ice-cream turned to slop.

And on the busiest day of the week, as he told himself, or rather told the Hall, those responsible, as he put the kettle on for the water and got the detergent out.

He set about it with an air of martyred resignation, expecting to be constantly interrupted by customers who didn't let him down, apologising yet again in that ice-cream weather for the temporary lack of any, and meaning it, as he hadn't had time yet to help himself to one.

And a short while later, hearing a commotion on deck, and a woman screaming, he left the galley to investigate with the same air of resignation. It would not have surprised him greatly the way things were going to discover that they were sinking.

Victor, with Mervyn's maximum disruption in mind, knew he'd found what he'd been hoping to find when back at the galley with the others for more drinks. They were behind them in the queue, around the same age as them, loud with the exuberant accents of the Valleys, and with a boisterousness that was a wrong word or look away from violence.

Afterwards, when they'd finished their drinks, Victor stood with the others at the rail, trying to reach the bank with the empty glasses, leaving them bobbling in the churned wake of the *Castle* then, when they wandered off, ready for another sort of game.

They found it in the stern, the Valley lads larking about there. There were six of them, two more than Victor's lot. But then Victor's lot had Lennie.

Victor started it off. He was small but fierce inside, a fierceness worn in ink on his knuckles and scrawny arms, and one otherwise usually tempered by discretion when Lennie wasn't there.

He bumped into one of them. "Hey – watch it!" he snarled.

The horseplay stopped as if to a whistle sounded in a playground.

"Or what, boyo?" the Welsh youth said, not expecting an answer, and not getting one. No more needed to be said. The rest of it was in the stillness between them.

And then they moved, suddenly and together, as if to another whistle. Victor, leaving it too late to get out of the way, went down first, fists flailing under the youth he'd warned to watch it. His brother threw himself into it, as if reminded what he was for and making up for lost time, becoming fully Lennie again with his fists, head and the steel toecaps of his boots, the air shrill when they hit bone. The fight spread, knocking into people, a couple of the younger men with families trying to stop it and getting caught up in it, somebody shouting and the woman Humphrey had heard screaming.

And when he came on the scene he was outraged, in the mood to take personally the sight of passengers doing anything other than admiring the scenery or forming an orderly queue.

"Hey!" he bawled, dashing at them, making herding movements with his hands, and yelled again then, when running into one of Lennie's boots.

Humphrey clutched at his wounded shin and the punch that followed hit air. He grabbed Lennie round the legs to stop him kicking again, and lifted him out of sheer temper, hoisting the six-foot-two skinhead high enough to give him, had Lennie cared to take advantage of it, views not normally accessible to passengers. But Lennie was busy trying not to fall, sending Humphrey's Master Chef's hat flying as he clutched at his head, getting in a few blows at it when Humphrey, with no particular plan in mind, ran with him, swaying and threatening to topple, up the deck, in and out of the figures struggling on it, as if looking for somewhere to put him, before, blinded by Lennie's bulk, running straight into the stern rail.

As far as the Commander was concerned, facing the other way in his wheelhouse all was as it should be, and Sion, tending the firebox and with the engine hammering a few feet away, had only now picked up that something was going on.

Leaving Tom, who was half deaf, reading his newspaper, he came out to find the stern deck turned into Saturday night in a Kingham cider house, and the even more remarkable sight of what seemed to be Humphrey tossing a passenger over the side.

"*Man overboard!*" he bellowed, hoping to alert both Tom and the Commander, and dashing for the nearest lifebelt saw Humphrey flinging off his Food Dude apron and leaving the same way as the passenger.

At the end of that day, when Humphrey got home, he found Clem having tea at one of the tables on the lawns. When she was pouring him a cup she told him that Henrietta was in Cwmdach, the garage run by Tom's nephew, Nigel.

"Yeah, right," Humphrey said sheepishly, getting his finger back from the podgy grip of Ralph Franklin T Strange II, reclining like a small lord of things in the fringed shade of his pram.

He'd forgotten about Henrietta. He hadn't even given her a thought when walking back up past the bed and breakfast sign. He had other things on his mind. "I was trying to get her out of the way," he explained. "She was blocking the entrance. And she just kinda took off."

"A bolter. Naughty girl. Anyway, Nigel said he'd have it done in time for the Tuesday sandwich run."

"Another darned expense," Humphrey said, glumly picking up a biscuit.

"Well, it's Nigel. We can always stagger the payments again."

"Yeah…" he said, sitting with the biscuit untouched in his hand. He was watching Hawis toddling along with her grandmother Shelly down by the river, finding things together in the grass. He felt obscurely that he had let everyone down.

"Anyway, it's not all bad news," Clem went on brightly, and Humphrey, about to give her more bad news, opened and closed his mouth. "To my utter astonishment, the Tillings, bless 'em, deemed us – *just*, one very much had the impression – a suitable place to be viewed, as they put it, by their members. They agreed the entrance fee *and* they want us to lay on a tea," she finished, beaming it at him.

He nodded. "That's good," he said, trying to look pleased about it, and then got it over with "We had a passenger go overboard today. There was a fight, some skinheads and Welsh lads."

"Serve him right!" she said, dismissing Lennie, when he got to the bit about him ending up in the river. "But are *you* all right?"

"Yeah. My head's a bit sore, that's all, where he got a couple of shots in," he said, rubbing it.

"And what happened then? I mean, I take it he didn't drown."

"No, but he would have done. I had to go in for him. These boots they wear, they were dragging him down."

"Darling!" Clem said, her eyes wide with thoughts of how it might have ended.

"Then Sion chucked a lifebelt down and they dropped the deck anchor. We spent the rest of the time to Water Lacy sitting in the emergency blankets in the engine room while our clothes dried. Then we put both parties off when we docked. Let them finish the fight there if they wanted."

He hesitated, and then reluctantly went on, "But this guy, one of the other passengers, complained. Said his wife and kids were upset and that we hadn't heard the last of it."

"Well, that was bound to happen, I suppose. We'll probably be lucky if there's just the one. They weren't drunk, were they, these lads?"

"Not unless they brought it with them. I wouldn't have served them if I thought they were drunk."

"No, of course you wouldn't. Well, in that case, darling, we can't be held responsible."

"Yeah, but you can see what he means."

"Oh, yes, indeed. But—"

"He was really fired up about it. Even said that I was fighting with them. That I was just as bad." Humphrey looked at his wife as if she might be able to explain it.

"You were trying to stop them!" she said indignantly. "How else were you supposed to do it? And you risked your—"

"Yeah, I know, I know. But he said – he said that it was my fault he went overboard in the first place."

"Rubbish!" Clem said briskly.

"Yeah, that's what they said, Sion and the Commander."

"And they were right."

"But the thing is," Humphrey persisted, shaking his head, pestered by his thoughts, "the thing is, honey—" He glanced at his daughter with her grandmother, their backs to them, looking at something on the river, and lowered his voice as if they could hear. "The thing is, that the council is hot on this sort of thing. We know that. They laid it out in the stuff that came with the passenger licence. We could end up here getting our licence suspended here. Or maybe even losing it altogether. I dunno…"

"Well, I do know," Clem said firmly, pulling rank as someone born there. "For one thing we provide a tourist attraction. Something that this place, which hardly anyone elsewhere seems to have heard of, is badly short of. And for another – well, for another we're a new company. If we have a punch-up on board every time we sail, then yes, that would be it. But—"

"That's what the Commander said."

"Well, there you are then!" she said.

Said one thing, her eyes another, sharing with him for a brief, unguarded moment what it could mean.

And that was more than the threatened loss of revenue, as necessary as that was. It had never been about money. Revenue from it was for them a bonus. It was who they were and the place they lived in, that's what had set sail on that inaugural voyage. It was more than the PS *Batch Castle* pulling for midstream on those bright mornings to the ringing of a telegraph and the sound of fun, it was the PS *Batch Magna*.

Chapter Fifteen

Mervyn and Sidney never phoned each other at home. Their relationship was strictly one of business, conducted during office hours, And so, on the following Monday morning, immediately after Victor had phoned Mervyn at the town hall, Mervyn phoned Sidney at his office – had reason to phone him after Victor's call, cover, for a man of habitual secrecy, for the conversation he really wanted to have.

And he expected that conversation to start almost as soon as Sidney picked up the phone. Sidney was the sort of man who, even when life was at its sunniest, perhaps especially when life was at its sunniest, carried with him the suspicion that it was only a matter of time. As if some dire prognosis he was keeping to himself, he knew that life was out to get him, and that one day it would succeed. And on Thursday last, at the ninth hole on Mortwardine Hill, life had tried not to let him down. Sidney had been proved right. And apart from anything else, would not keep that to himself for long.

When he answered the phone Mervyn didn't greet him in Welsh as he usually did, and then remark on the weather, also in Welsh, knowing how much it annoyed him. He simply said hello, and asked him how he was, in English.

Sidney, he considered, had enough on his plate.

But all Sidney said was that he was fine thanks, in that whiny tone of his that was itself a complaint, the suggestion in it that he wasn't short of things to complain about but what was the point, as no one ever listened? And Mervyn, about to prompt him, to remind him about the latest thing he had to complain about, wondered then obscurely if it was some sort of trap, and instead said, breezily, "Well, I hope you had your witness on board for the Saturday trip, Sidney. Couldn't have gone better, I'm told."

"Well, they got the day right this time, if that's what you mean."

"Yes, well, that's Victor for you. One of the reasons he's so cheap. I told him it was important to ring me when he had it set up. Still, the deed's done now. And come on, Sidney, they got more than the day right. You got the full card, boy. A scrum of a punch-up and a man going over the side. Very much *not* in the interests of the public as per the Act. Wait till Odgar Llewellyn-Jenkins hears about it."

"Yeah, but the thing is, Mervyn," Sidney said with some satisfaction, "it was one of them doing the fighting that went overboard. A big skinhead from the Claypit Estate called Lennie. Ring any bells?"

"Lennie…?" Mervyn said, digesting it. "Big Lennie? Victor's brother?"

"That's the one."

"Where did you hear this?"

"From one of my drivers. He was the witness. He was there with his family."

"Well, Victor didn't say anything about it… You *sure*, Sidney?"

"My driver is. He knows the brothers well. They turned him over for a fare once."

"Well, I'll be… He didn't say a word about it. *Not* a word. I see now why he moved quickly on to asking about his money. The little—"

"Yeah, well, I was coming to that, Mervyn, about the money. I don't think they should get the rest of it now."

"Not a good idea," Mervyn said immediately.

"Well, I didn't get what I paid for, did I. There's a difference between a yob going over the side and a respectable member of—"

"Sidney – Sidney, listen to me," Mervyn said firmly, sitting on it. "It is *not* a good idea. I know Victor, and believe you me, you do *not* want him on the loose with a grievance. He might decide to share it with somebody – and I'm not talking about a punch-up on a boat, neither. This driver—"

"You said you'd left my name out of that."

"And so I did. But even Victor can count. Even he could work out that two minus one leaves the Kingham Prestige Car Company, if you take my meaning." Sidney said nothing, and Mervyn knew he was sulking. "This driver of yours—"

"I paid for him and his family to go. Like you suggested."

"What, wife and kids?"

"Yeah. Six of them altogether. Cost me another packet. Just hope it's worth it."

"And he was there when it happened, was he? On the spot. An eye witness?"

"Yeah, saw it all."

"Good. And has he reported it? To the police?"

"Rang them soon as they got to Shrewsbury."

"Good, good… He's a big boy, our Lennie," Mervyn said then. "How—"

"There's always somebody bigger," Sidney said, a small man with a mantra he had long consoled himself with. "And in this case it was the boat owner. The Yank."

"The Yank…?"

"Yeah, the American. The so-called Sir Humphrey. He was on board, and got involved."

"Something else Victor forgot to mention," Mervyn said absently, his mind moving on. "What, so he… ?"

"Well, he tried to stop them, didn't he. Then he and Lennie had a go and Lennie went over the side."

"What, the Yank threw him over, do you mean?" Mervyn said, more a statement than a question, and then rushed on with the possibilities as if getting them in first. "Well, that's attempted manslaughter, that is – attempted *murder*, even!"

"Yeah, well, don't get too excited. That's what I thought. But it was an accident, my driver said. And the Yank went in after him then, jumped in and pulled him out. Lennie was in trouble, it seems."

"Witnesses," Mervyn said almost immediately, getting his version back. "His temper got the better of him.

Then the red mist cleared and he realised that there were witnesses to the deed, and he panicked. Simple as that, boy. If there had been no witnesses he'd have left Lennie to get on with it. That's attempted manslaughter – at least!"

"'Cept it's not what happened, Mervyn, is it," Sidney pointed out, but Mervyn wasn't listening.

"This driver of yours," he said then, "could he be – has he seen the police yet? Been interviewed?"

"No, not yet. He's seeing them this afternoon. He's got a busy morning. He needs the money. And so do I."

"Which is what we are addressing, Sidney. What we are in pursuit of. And so to that end perhaps he could be persuaded to say something a little different when he does make his statement. Hmm?"

"I dunno. I suppose so. I mean, he knows the score. I told him when I put the boat trip to him, I said, if the Yank carries on like he's doing I'm going to have to start laying drivers off. He soon got the picture. Like in where else would he go now, round here?"

"Where else indeed, Sidney," Mervyn said, sharing what he meant with a chuckle. "No, it's straightforward enough. All he's got to say is that – er – is that he saw the American, deliberately and with malice aforethought, chuck Leonard over the side. Simple as that."

"And what about the other passengers? What about the other people who saw it? He wasn't the only one there."

"All right, *heard* then," Mervyn said with barely a pause. "He heard him. He was trying to stop the fight, your driver, fearing for the safety of his family, and found himself near them, see, in the melee. And he clearly heard the Yank's stated intention to murder Lennie. Heard him say it. Heard him snarl drown you English bastard! No. No, wait – drown you *limey* bastard. Much better. Get them going both sides of the border, that will. Should get a nice bit of media coverage out of that. Nationally, too, I wouldn't be surprised. The special relationship goes overboard, that sort of thing."

"Yeah, but—"

"Yeah, but nothing, Sidney. We've got him, boy. We've *got* him. Sir Humphrey or no Sir Humphrey, he's finished on that river. By the time we've done with him he'll be lucky to get a fishing licence."

"What I was going to say, Mervyn," Sidney said with heavy patience, "was about the geezer he's supposed to have said it to? What about Lennie?"

"What about him?"

"Well, is he going to say the same thing? I mean, it won't matter what my driver tells them if this Lennie says different, will it."

Mervyn chuckled. "I can see you don't know our Lennie. Lennie will say what Lennie's told to say. In fact, boy, you *have* to tell Lennie what to say. If he can't kick it or punch it he's at a loss. And his pride would have been badly dented. No, Lennie will not be a problem. They'll need a bit of a drink on top, of course," he remembered to add.

"Yeah, I thought they might. And how much will that bleeding well cost me?"

Mervyn hesitated, wondering how much the market would bear. "Fifty apiece," he decided. "If I emphasise that it's part of the same job, I think I could get it done for that. Get Victor to back it up, to say that's what his brother told him afterwards. And I'll waive my usual fee, as a gesture of goodwill. And I can*not* say fairer than that."

There was silence on the other end, the sound, Mervyn knew, of Sidney counting his money.

"Sidney," he said, impassioned, "we'd be asking the boys to commit perjury – in my name, as we've kept yours out of it. Asking them, and me, to risk considerable custodial sentences. And all that is asked of you is a mere one hundred pounds. Think like a businessman, Sidney," he urged. "Think return on investment. Think of the future, the years of steady monthly profit, all for a small down payment now."

There was another silence, and then Sidney said from that unsure place that was his true home, a place Mervyn had recognised as such almost immediately after first meeting him, "And you think that will do the trick, do you?"

"Do the trick? Of *course* it will do the bloody trick, man! The only connection this Sir Humphrey would have then with Shrewsbury would be the dock of the crown court. Goodbye the Burger King and the Cluny Steamboat Company, and his dreams of another crown on this soil of ours. And ta-ta your problem, Sidney! Now and in the future. Believe you me, boy, the days of this interloper would be numbered. Even onto the hairs on his head!" he cried, bringing the chapel pulpit into it in his fervour, the heat of thoughts of his own future and the bigger picture.

"Yeah, all right, Mervyn," Sidney said, impressed. "All right. I'm in."

He'd heard it before of course, that sort of dramatic emphasis, the sudden flaring of passion when the talk was of rugby, or of something else dear to the Welsh male heart, talk turned then into an opera, lapsing into their own language when English couldn't contain them, leaving him feeling even more foreign, more excluded, looking on again. And now he was part of it. Now it was on his side.

He leaned back in his captain's chair, expansive with something he barely recognised, it had been so long.

"'Ere, Mervyn, I was thinking, how about meeting for a drink or three after work?" he said, awkwardly jovial, his accent losing some of its acquired polish in a remembered, unguarded rush of friendship, the old Sid back again, from a time when he had a different name and had found a friend in the playground. "Nothing to do with business. Just, you know, socially. We could meet in the Blenheim if you like," he said, naming Kingham's top hotel, its back bar a meeting place for the worthies of the town.

"Mervyn…?" he prompted.

"Yes. Yes, good idea, boy," Mervyn said absently, and then, having decided on the approach, said, "But – er – but tell me, Sidney, while I think of it, what's this I heard in the clubhouse on Saturday about somebody taking a pot-shot at you. Surely not!" he said with a chuckle, and pressed his ear avidly to the receiver.

"It's me now, is it? Last time I heard it was Tudor Johns, the bloke I was partnering," Sidney said, referring to a Kingham dentist. "Some joker said it was one of his patients."

"Well, as long as someone wasn't trying to kill you, eh, Sidney?" Mervyn said with another chuckle, and nodded furiously away at him on the other end, urging him to say more, his grin, meant vaguely to be sympathetic, manic looking.

"Why should anyone want to kill me?" was all Sidney said.

"The very question I asked myself, Sidney, when I heard about it," Mervyn said quickly, thinking he might have gone too far. "It does *not* make sense, I said. Not Sidney. Tudor, yes, the way he drinks. Botching another job the morning after, and some poor soul, demented with pain—"

"Mervyn – Mervyn, he wasn't shooting at me or Tudor."

"*He…?*" Mervyn said alertly, feeling it move nearly home. "You saw someone then, did you, Sidney? Saw—?"

"No, no, nothing like that. We didn't see a thing. We heard it though. Almost gave us a bleeding heart attack. The police think it was a gamekeeper, off one of the hill shoots. Bringing his pheasants on and getting a bit too keen about it. He got a crow."

"A crow?"

"Dropped at our feet. They found a shell in the big sand bunker there, from a rifle. He bagged the bird and then legged it."

"Nobody said anything about a crow," Mervyn said, sounding aggrieved. "And that's all there is to it then, is it?" If Sidney didn't feel a sense of anti-climax, then he did.

"Yes, but the point is, Mervyn," Sidney said querulously, spurred by a reminder of another bit of clubhouse banter, "as I said to the secretary, it could have been one of us that was killed. It's no laughing matter."

"Indeed it's not. Sidney. Not in the least. And nobody *saw* anything, is that right?"

"Not a thing, apparently. There were no greenkeepers about and the few other players out then were coming up well behind us. They heard the shot, all right, but that's all."

"And the police – what, they have no leads at all?"

"Apart from knowing it was a rifle. That's why they reckon it was a gamekeeper. They told the Secretary they'd make enquiries and get back to him. But he's not holding his breath of course."

They arranged to meet outside Sidney's bank before Mervyn went on to the estate, and when they ended the call Mervyn assured him again, with another burst of Welsh emphasis, that Sir Humphrey was done for, *finished*, boy, and Sidney thanked him again and, with Shrewsbury in mind, meant it. Which didn't stop his expression of gratitude souring to one of disdain when he put down the phone. The expression of a man who hadn't really expected anything else and who hadn't been disappointed. Mervyn had had his chance, and would not be given another.

He had not referred again to the suggestion of drinks at the Blenheim, and he, Sidney, certainly did not intend repeating the invitation. He had offered, as he saw it now, the hand of friendship across borders, and it had been ignored. It would not be offered again.

While Mervyn meanwhile sat at his desk in the town hall and, as Dewi had taken to doing rather more frequently of late, briefly questioned reality, before assuring himself that he *had* phoned Sidney's office that day.

And listening to the conversation again in his head with the detachment of distance, hearing in it more than the audacity of his own words, the risk he had embarked on, he was struck for the first time by how casual his secretary had sounded. Either, he decided, she'd thought it was a joke call, or had misunderstood it. Or he had overdone the Birmingham accent and she hadn't understood it at all, and hadn't liked to say so. What *was* certain, was that Sidney had *not* got the message.

He had never been to Sidney's office, nor Sidney to his. But Sidney, as if he spent his leisure time in the Kingham library, had talked dismissively about how Shirley his secretary spent hers, how she always seemed to be at the pictures, and he'd been relying on her. He thought she'd recognise the scenario immediately, just like something that she's seen only the other night at the Odeon.

There was of course no IRA hit man. He was paying himself to do the job, with Odgar's half of the fee, waiting behind the small cliff at the deep end of the sand bunker with a rifle, waiting to make a start on the bigger picture.

He'd watched their game draw nearer to the ninth hole, watched the ball dribble to halt, followed by the two men. Tudor stood over it, frowning at it and then at where he expected it to go, and no argument, taking his time adjusting his stance as he always did, as if he were playing in the Ryder Cup, instead of having a handicap of twenty-five.

He had lifted a weapon with history in its solid weight, a Lee Enfield, the last rifle of the British Empire, and with a last-minute, vague request to God for forgiveness, closed one eye over the iron sights and lined them up on Sidney's Pringle sweater.

He squeezed the trigger slowly as he had read somewhere it should be done, and yelled with pain as he was flung backwards, the recoil from the hardwood stock striking him like a hammer blow.

He'd hit something, he had now learned, but all he saw then, peering cautiously over the lip of the bunker, batting away smoke, his ears ringing, was that he'd put Tudor off his swing and that Sidney was still standing.

He thought the shot must have been heard all over the course, including the clubhouse, and he'd scrambled back across the sand on his knees, dragging the rifle after him, and then ran with it, crouching like an infantryman, across the patch of rough behind it, through the stand of trees, and down the hill to the lane where he'd parked the car.

He had never fired a Lee Enfield, or any other sort of gun before, his war spent behind a desk in various supply depots around the country, fiddling invoices and helping to keep the local black market buoyant. His uncle had fired one, that same one, many times, in another world war, and could have warned him that the rifle was now aged and a model known for its powerful recoil even when new.

But his uncle was dead, which is how he came by the rifle and ammunition, among the other bits and pieces, and the volumes of books on steam engines and the history of the South Wales coalfields that were still in his attic, things left to him because there'd been nothing else to leave. He had read about rifles being identified by their spent shells, and remembering the one he'd left behind in his panic, disposed of the weapon and spare bullets that day, the Lee Enfield ending its long history in the downstream waters of the Cluny.

And he saw now that it was a good job the shot had gone wild. Without Sidney's secretary to point them in the direction of a Birmingham drugs gang it would have meant the police looking nearer home.

Whether she liked it or not Shirley was now a part of his plans. Next time he would make sure that she understood that, that she, and the police, got the message.

Next time, Shirley would go to the pictures.

Chapter Sixteen

The grin that Gareth shared with Poppy Cadwallender's parents after her bay mare had effortlessly cleared what he had learned to call an oxer jump, congratulated himself as much as the horse and rider.

Gareth not only had a new girlfriend and a new job, he had a new future. He was presently working at a surgery on the other side of the border, quoting a gap year on the application form to account for the time since leaving veterinary school. He'd been sacked from the Kingham practice shortly after breaking up with Ffion Owen, for losing his temper with a client who thought she knew best. He hadn't seen out his notice, but had left the surgery there and then, under the nose of Ffion Owen on reception busily pretending not to notice, a consideration he took to be pity adding to his humiliation.

And then he had met Poppy. Horses were the Cadwallenders' thing, and now they were his. He was going to specialise in them, studying the subject as he'd studied for the exams he was good at passing, with a single-mindedness that was almost an end in itself. When Gareth had achieved what he set out to achieve, got to where he wanted to be, it wasn't long before he was back in a sense to where he'd started, wondering what came next. Because it was never enough for Gareth, whatever it was. Never exciting or interesting or stimulating enough, or something enough. For Gareth, after a while, there would *always* be something missing.

He'd been wondering what came next since leaving the grammar school his parents had gone without to allow him to attend, rewarding them by leaving with top grades. He'd had two management trainee jobs after that, and had worked as an estate agent, before applying for veterinary school. He had no interest in animals, but he had the right grades in maths and sciences and he was taken with the professional standing the job conferred.

And it promised escape, from the home he brought his career failings back to each time, and the city he had almost managed to convince himself was in some way the cause of them. He'd swopped the streets of Cardiff for a bucolic dream lit in his imagination like a TV ad, a life vaguely imagined, with animals in the background somewhere, and reality intruding no further than a pair of muddied wellingtons left outside a cottage door.

And then he had met Poppy, and found what came next. Marriage and, with the weight of the Cadwallenders as in-laws behind him, private practice as a bloodstock vet. Earlier that day he had made his first visit to the Cadwallenders' stud farm, and had seen the future. And it did not involve tiresome people and their pets, their language of love and concern a foreign one to him, or standing in a stone barn letting in winter, rummaging elbow deep in a cow's pelvic region.

141

Gareth was on his way, carefully, the steps he was taking to get there as well judged as the interest he was showing listening to Mrs Cadwallender.

They were watching Poppy taking part in a local show-jumping event. Poppy's father was rather stiff, rather standoffish, but her mother, he knew, was quite taken with him. She had told him about the technique needed before taking a jump and she was recounting an anecdote about a time she had got it wrong when she was in the ring, when he spotted, on the other side of the field, Ffion Owen, and then saw who she was with. It was the hippie with the guitar on the boat that day. He was walking behind her as they made their way through the spectators, and he saw her turn and say something to him, saw him laugh, and Gareth was suddenly no longer careful.

He turned what was left of his amused smile on Mrs Cadwallender and excused himself, muttering something about not being long, his attention already fixed, rigidly, elsewhere. They were leaving, on their way through a field gate into the lane there, the verges of it used as a car park. He made his way urgently round the course to the other side of the field. He had no idea what he was going to say, or do, and didn't care. That he was angry was enough. Gareth never looked much, or for long, further than himself.

But by the time he had reached the lane he knew he had lost them, knew that they must be in the car pulling away further along it.

He came up with the story on his way back, about spotting a friend who, he had learned only the other day, had recently lost his wife in, he'd decided, a boating accident. He'd wanted to say something to him, offer a few words, but had been too late.

He imagined his audience's reaction to it, saw Mrs Cadwallender's face, aghast and sympathetic, and perhaps even her husband bending a little, beginning to see him in a new light.

Chapter Seventeen

At the beginning of that same week, the day after Mervyn had rung Sidney, eager for news, he rang him, or rather his general office, again, from a phone box this time, and almost dropped the receiver when, expecting his secretary, Sidney answered.

"The Kingham Prestige Car Service. Sidney Acton the proprietor speaking. How may I help you?" Sidney intoned, one eye on Shirley's back at the filing cabinets, making sure she heard how the phone *should* be answered, which wasn't as if it were some friend ringing up for a chat, while Mervyn dithered on the other end and thought about bolting.

Sidney frowned. "Hello…?"

"We run the drugs in Birmingham so stay away!" Mervyn got out then.

"What?" Sidney barked.

"Or you'll end up in a carpet," Mervyn remembered to add.

"It's no good you coming that nonsense with me," Sidney said, and found himself listening to the dialling tone.

He'd answered the phone on Shirley's desk, and putting the receiver down looked at Dewi, and then at Shirley, on her way back with the file he'd asked for.

"Do I," he wanted to know, "sound like a Welshman to either of you?"

Shirley handed him the file, and having thought about it, considering him with her head on one side, told him that no, he didn't, and Dewi agreed. "You could not sound *less* Welsh, Sidney. It is obvious that, not only are you English, you are from the *capital* of that country," he said, as if complimenting him on it, on an accent that Sidney, for all the private elocution lessons Dewi wasn't supposed to know about, hadn't managed entirely to uproot.

"So what does Dai, carpet salesman of the year, do when someone who's clearly an Englishman answers the phone?" Sidney wanted to know next. "Delivers his patter in Welsh, that's what."

"Oh, I know who that was," Shirley said. "He rang before. I thought he was an Indian. From Birmingham."

"Yes, that was the other word I got, Birmingham. He's not an Indian, Shirley, he's Welsh," Sidney said, as if it were something he'd had to put up with before. "He's a Welshman from Birmingham. A Welsh carpet salesman based in England and barely able to speak two words of the language." He shook his head unbelievingly at it.

"Or he could have been a Persian from there, Mr A," it occurred to Shirley, feeding a new sheet of carbon paper into her typewriter, "seeing as it's carpets."

"Or Turkish," Dewi put in. "They're known for their carpets as well, the Turks. And there's a shop on the Hagley road there. Big double-fronted place, it is. All carpets, Turkish carpets. You can see them hung up outside, weather permitting, you know."

"The Chinese do them as well, Mr Brice," Shirley told him, "which is something I didn't know."

"Nor me, Shirley. Now that is interesting."

"Yes, we saw some on Saturday, me and Ronald, in Pennington's. Very pretty, if you like that sort of thing. Dragons and willows and flowers, and that, all in delicate, pale, pretty colours," she said, smiling prettily, sharing it with them.

Sidney, standing at the door, regarded his staff, one a woman the other a Welshman.

"He was *not*," he made clear, "an Indian. He was not Turkish, or Chinese, or from Timbuk-bloody-tu. He was from there," he said, dismissing Wales with an abrupt movement of his head in its direction. "A Welshman, in England, trying to sell a carpet to me, an Englishman, in Welsh," he said, including all his fellow countrymen in the look he gave Dewi before leaving.

On Monday, the day before that, after Mervyn had picked up the money from Sidney, he'd carried on to the Claypit Estate to see the brothers. When he could get no answer at the house, and after looking in the pub, he found Victor on his own in the local bookmaker's, the floor of the shop littered with the dashed hopes of betting slips, including Victor's by the look of his face.

While the attention of the men in the room was fixed on the wall television, watching chance line up again in the starting gate, he slipped Victor what was owed, and then leaned into him.

"My client, boy, was reluctant to pay you that. And who could blame him? I mean, it wasn't just another passenger that went over the side, was it, Victor…? Eh, boyo?"

"Yeah, I know. Sorry about that, Mr P," Victor mumbled. "Forgot to tell you."

"I'm sure you did," Mervyn snarled, and flicked a finger at his face. "But it means that our friend did not get what he paid for, does it not?" he said, emphasising it with more flicks of his finger.

"Yeah. Yeah, well, it wasn't our fault—"

"Which is a great pity, boy, because hitherto he'd been talking about regulating the situation."

"Eh?"

"Putting you permanently on the strength. Someone he can call on regularly – meaning jobs paying proper money. Meaning the big time, you might say."

"Yeah, well, like I said—" Victor started miserably.

"So you can consider yourself bloody lucky I was able to persuade him to give you another chance, can't you, boy!" Mervyn said, delivering the good news into his face.

"Oh, right… Yeah, thanks, Mr P."

"Well, just make sure you get it right this time. Opportunities like this, Victor, knock only once. And if you're not at home, they've gone – for good!" he said with sudden passion. "So make sure you open the bloody door, boy. Open the door to your future, Victor, before it becomes your past. Before you become just another bloody loser."

"Right, Mr P."

Mervyn paused, as if catching his breath, and then laid a fatherly hand on Victor's shoulder. "Life can do that to you, bach. Move on before you know where you are, taking your dreams with it. Leaving you with a lifetime of regret. The saddest words in the English language, Victor, are "'if only'". And after all, the job is simple enough," he went on briskly, getting back to business. "He just wants you to tell a few untruths, that's all."

The next day Victor was on his own again when Mervyn called after the bungled phone call to Sidney's office. He'd answered the door after Mervyn had been banging away on the knocker, hearing the sound of a radio or television inside.

It was Paula, Victor's mother, watching a game show in the sitting room, the sound of it through the closed door following them on a wave of laughter down the hall to the kitchen.

"Is Paula deaf?" Mervyn said.

"Nah, she always does that. To shut things out, she says."

"Meaning you two, no doubt."

Victor closed the kitchen door and Mervyn pulled back a chair. Victor had been studying form again, a tabloid newspaper open on the table to the racing page.

"Bit of biz, Mr P?" he said hopefully.

"Yes, of the unfinished sort. The statement to the police."

"Oh, yeah. I've been thinking about that." He hooked an arm cockily over the back of the chair. "And I think we ought to get a drink out of it. With half upfront, as usual."

Mervyn studied him. "Do you ever learn, I am driven to wondering, Victor? What did I say to you only yesterday? I said," he went on without waiting, "my client very generously offered to keep you on his books if you made good the cock-up on the boat. He is a man all for giving the young their head and a second chance."

"Yeah, but as I said, it—"

"Well, wouldn't you say that was generous of him?"

"Well, yeah, I would. But—"

"And now you're trying to put the arm on him. I'd call that greedy, Victor. I'd also call it very stupid. My client is a powerful man, what is called a big wheel, and will not take kindly to such ingratitude. He would see it, Victor, as you taking the mickey. And believe you me, you do *not* want that. You do not want that at all," he said, shaking his head gravely, as if remembering past examples. "Do you understand me, Victor?"

Victor did, or at least had a good idea, after following the trial of the South London mob on the television each evening like a soap opera.

He sat up straight. "I didn't mean anything. I just thought…"

"You have to consider the bigger picture, Victor," Mervyn said earnestly. "Consider the future. There is a tide in the affairs of men, which taken at the flood, leads on to fortune. Omitted, all the voyage of their life is bound in shallows and in miseries."

"I get you."

"But tide and time, Victor, wait for no man."

"Right," Victor said, nodding determinedly at it.

"So let's get to work. Where's Lennie?"

"Worcester," Victor said obligingly.

"Worcester…?"

"Yeah. Went yesterday."

"What for?"

Victor shrugged. "See some bird."

"And when's he coming back?"

"I dunno," Victor said, and as the conversation appeared to be at an end, Mervyn obviously busy thinking about something, went back to the page of runners.

Mervyn looked across at him, at his scrawny neck, his head bent over the newspaper, and restraining himself, made do with lifting his fist and bringing it down hard on the table.

"Where's your manners, boyo? You don't read when you have company."

"Sorry, Mr P. I thought you—"

"I don't have to do this for this for you, you know, Victor."

"No, I know that, Mr P."

"Then you might show a little more interest. So, you've no idea when he's coming back. Is that right?"

"Yeah. I mean, he never said, did he."

"Who is she? Does she have a name, an address?"

"Who?"

Mervyn sighed. "I hope, Victor, that my client has not erred in his opinion of your potential. This girl in Worcester. Who'd you think I'm talking about?"

"I don't know, do I. I don't know her. She's just some bird."

"And he didn't leave a phone number. Where he could be contacted?"

Victor looked at him with curiosity, this visitor from a world where they did such things. "Course not. Why would he do that?"

"Well, did you tell him what he had to say, in his statement?"

"Didn't get a chance, did I. He came in, grabbed his bread, and shot off again. Had a train to catch."

Mervyn shook his head. "You cannot afford to be this slack, Victor. It's your future under discussion. Meaning the difference between a few quid now and then and an executive lifestyle."

That got Victor's attention, brought his straying thoughts back from the first race at Doncaster tomorrow. He'd seen an executive lifestyle. In a large detached house sitting in a garden as big it seemed to him as Culpepper Park. He'd tumbled into it head first through a small bathroom window as if down a rabbit hole, into another world, a world smelling like the Elegant Living department in Pennington's. It was the home, he'd learned afterwards, reading not without pride a report of his visit in a local paper, of a top business executive.

He'd seen an executive lifestyle. He had even come away with some of it. And now he could have the lot.

He looked up as Mervyn pushed back his chair, his eyes wide with it.

"There's a phone box on the main road down there," Mervyn said, stabbing a finger in that direction. "As soon as Lennie gets back, you phone me. Understand?"

Victor nodded slowly. "Yeah… Yeah, right, Mr P."

On the Thursday of that week, uniformed inspector of police Petunia Cholmondley-Jones, or Pet, to her friends, among whom, for the past year, she counted those in Batch Hall and on its river, moved unhappily on her chair in the Hall's kitchen.

She had just arrived and had declined an offer of coffee and a Coney. "I can't stay long. But, well, I thought I should tell you this in person," she said, and hesitated.

"If this is about our passenger licence, Pet," Clem said, "we know about it. We had a letter first post this morning. Temporary suspension while it's looked into. And it's thanks to you that it wasn't the shock it might have been."

"Some guy complained and they had to do something about it!" Humphrey told the others in the room as if, angrily, defending the council.

"It would have been nice if they had heard our side of the story as well, but there you are," Clem said, and waited with a smile which held in it a suggestion of bracing herself, as if suspecting that whatever Petunia had come to tell them it wasn't about that, and whatever it was about they weren't going to like it.

The Inspector hesitated again. "I'm afraid it's worse than that now, Clem. Our prosecuting solicitor's office—"

"Lawyers!" Phineas Cook broke in explosively, as if, after three divorces, he might have known they'd be in there somewhere. Phineas, who'd dropped in to see if there was any news, had stopped for a coffee and Coney.

He then gave Petunia a quick smile to let her know that he didn't lump her in with the lawyers. Their recent past had collided and she had, briefly, been unofficially engaged to him. Flown with wine from the party in Kingham that had introduced them, and out of the romanticism that had long complicated his life, and caused upheaval in the lives of those on the receiving end, he had proposed in the back garden, and she, out of unhappiness, and at a loose end, had accepted.

She had survived her entanglement with him and had then met someone else, and wore a ring to prove it. Her wedding reception was booked at the Hall for later that summer. Phineas would be among the guests.

"Be quiet, Phineas," Clem told him. "Go on, Pet."

The Inspector, who looked as if she'd been perfectly willing for Phineas to take over, did so reluctantly, sitting up straight for it.

"The prosecuting solicitor's office have decided that there are prima facie grounds for bringing a charge of attempted murder, or, failing that, manslaughter, against Humph," she said, and looked at them aghast.

"*Wha* – at!" Clem said on a laugh.

"I'm sorry," the Inspector added miserably.

"And who is he supposed to have attempted to murder?" Clem asked, haughty with concern, and thought with a sort of panic of Hawis and her busy little ears, before remembering with relief that she was playing on the *Cluny Queen* for the morning.

"Or attempted to manslaughter," the Inspector said, and offered a small smile, as if inviting her to look on the bright side. "The chap who went into the river."

"But, Petunia, he *saved* the man's life…"

"And that, if need be, Clem, will be used in mitigation," the Inspector went on, as if pleading with her to understand. "But the decision was based on the signed statement of the witness I mentioned on Tuesday, who claimed in it that that was what Humph *intended*. That he heard him say it. And it's the *intention*, malice aforethought, in English law, that matters in these cases… I'm sorry," she said again.

"Heard him say what?" Clem asked.

The Inspector's shoulders slumped as if she'd holding something in. "He claimed that Humph chucked him over the rail, saying drown you limey…" She made a small embarrassed movement on her chair. "Well, bastard, actually. Drown you limey bastard, that's what Humph is supposed to have said."

"That's a *lie*. A goddam lie! I never said anything. Who is this guy?" Humphrey had shot to his feet, his meaty hands lifted into fists, as if waiting to have the witness pointed out to him.

"She's not allowed to tell us that, darling," Clem said calmly, everything gathered in again. "But of course it's a lie. Especially the limey bit. He wouldn't dare say that. He's married to one."

"Of *course* it is! That's not my son," Shelly said, after loudly blowing what they had learned was called a Bronx cheer at the accusation, and then glancing over at the pram, checking to see that she hadn't disturbed Ralph Franklin T Strange II at his lordly slumbers.

"It's absurd! An out*rageous* suggestion!" Miss Wyndham, who'd been frozen in disbelief, put her tea down, a mug kept for her use alone, its delicate fine bone china printed with strawberry vines and butterflies.

"He should be arrested, for – er – for lying," she told the Inspector, pointing a finger as if in the direction of the witness. "It's outrageous! Out*rageous*!" Miss Wyndham's jowls danced with fresh indignation.

"Gwallgof!" Annie Owen put in furiously in Welsh, her first language, the language nearest to her feelings, before turning to English. "It's bloody crazy, is it! Ridiculous! That's not our Humph."

"That's not at *all* our Humph," Phineas agreed, looking at Humphrey and shaking his head over what he saw, as if at a bit of casting that simply would not do, while Humphrey sat staring down at his Yankees coffee mug, his ears burning with injustice.

"And what does *he* have to say about it, the bloke Humph tried to drown?" it occurred to Clem to ask then. "My husband doesn't exactly whisper at the best of times, so I think we can take it that his intended victim would have had no trouble hearing his malice aforethought – especially as it would have concerned him rather."

"I was coming to that. That's really what they meant by prima facie. It seems that any charges depend on his collaboration of what Humph was alleged to have said, and his version of the incident. But we haven't been able to contact him yet. Their phone's not working and we've been unable to get an answer at the door. He lives in Kingham, on the Julian Culpepper Estate."

"What I don't understand is why he didn't say anything afterwards – to anyone. You'd think he'd have said *something*," Clem said.

Humphrey shrugged. "Didn't say a word."

"I find that funny," Clem said. "I find that *very* funny," she decided.

"Exceeding so," Miss Wyndham agreed loyally.

"Just sat there," Humphrey added, "in his blanket."

"He'd turned thoughtful," Phineas said. "Running into Humph can do that to people. But why is this fellow lying, and making such a job of it? Doesn't run boat trips up and down the river, does he? Or… Haven't made any enemies lately, Humph, have you?" it occurred to him then. "No, of course you haven't," he answered for him, as Humphrey frowned dutifully, considering it.

"Could be simply that he doesn't like Americans," Shelly suggested. "Some people just gotta have somebody to hate."

"Yes, there's that I suppose, Shelly," Phineas said, his own acceptance of others drawing the line only at such people as tax inspectors and lawyers. "And is this chap the only witness? On a normal Saturday there'd have been a boatload of them."

"Yes, odd that, isn't it," Clem said.

"*Very*," Miss Wyndham emphasised.

The Inspector didn't find it in the least odd. "People don't like to get involved. Or have their own reasons for not doing so. But it should be in the today's late editions of the local newspapers, both in Kingham and Shrewsbury, and Border Radio are running the story tomorrow morning," she said, delivering more news with a small smile of apology, "and through them we've appealed for witnesses."

There seemed to be no more to be said after that. For once that room, usually loud with talk and laughter, even with just two in it, was silent.

Chapter Eighteen

Mervyn was sitting at his desk in the spare bedroom, the room he called his study, typing in leather gloves made for winter, and the cause of him frequently hitting the wrong key or several together and having to untangle them.

He was writing to Sidney, getting the death threat this time down on paper. He'd given up on telephones.

He was wearing gloves when handling the writing paper and envelope to be on the safe side, and later the portable typewriter would go the way of the Lee Enfield for the same reason, replacing it afterwards with a similar model, just in case. And tomorrow he would drive the seventy odd miles to Birmingham and post the letter there. He could hardly give the police a stronger lead.

And this time Sidney *would* get the message, the Royal Mail would see to that. He was sending it recorded delivery.

The constable, parked a few doors up from the house on the Claypit Estate, had been about to drive off when Paula walked past carrying a bag of shopping.

He grabbed his uniform cap and stopping only to lock the car, on an estate where any unlocked vehicle, even one with Police written on it, was considered to be the property of whoever got to it first, caught up with her.

"Mrs Knowles…" he said, following her through the gate.

Paula looked round unsurprised.

"You know it is, dear," she said, not unkindly, as if reminding him, given his age. She thought he'd retired ages ago. "Which one is it this time?"

"Lennie."

"*Leonard*," she corrected him, "is not here at present."

"Where is he then? We've been trying to get hold of him all week."

"Leonard," she said, "has gone to Worcester."

"What, moved there, d'you mean?"

"Well, if he has he hasn't told me. But then I'm only his mother. According to our Victor he's gone to see some girl."

"Any idea when he'll be back?"

"Not the foggiest."

"Well, what about contact details – have you got an address there, or phone number?"

"Don't be silly – look, what's this about? What's he done?"

"He hasn't done anything. He had it done to him, apparently. Some bloke tried to murder him. Tried to drown him."

Paula looked startled. "Our Lennie…?" she said, forgetting Leonard in her surprise. "You sure you've got that the right way round?"

He chuckled. "That's what we thought. Makes a change, we said. The bloke concerned is an American, apparently," he added, as if that might explain it.

"Was Victor involved?" Paula asked.

"Well, I suppose so, yes. I mean, he's never far away, is he. So we'll want to speak to him as well. Where can I get hold of him?"

"No idea. Where was this, where did it happen?" she said, wondering at this insight into her sons' lives.

"On a boat trip. An old paddle steamer. On Saturday last."

"An old paddle steamer?" Paula looked amused.

"That what's on the sheet. They're running one up and down the river from Batch Magna now. Anyway, perhaps you'd pass the message on when you do see them. We've got to talk to them and you don't want us turning up every five minutes, Paula, do you."

"Oh, I don't know. It's about the only excitement I get these days," she said, weighing him up with a smile. He wasn't bad looking for a man his age, and she never could resist a uniform.

"Fancy a cuppa before you go back?" she asked hopefully.

Chapter Nineteen

On the following Tuesday Dewi arrived at the office more than an hour early, a couple of plastic shopping bags in his leather briefcase with replacement biscuits and the decanted contents of Cymru teabags in them, along with his usual lunchtime sandwiches with the crusts cut off and his copy of the *Daily Mail*.

A furtive figure, glancing casually about him like a bad actor as he crossed the yard to the offices, moving with the stealth of an intruder past the drivers' and the control room on the ground floor, and up the stairs in the same film, a film in which he, for once, was the star.

He tried the door of Sidney's office first, even called his name, his voice like a squeak, just in case, and then unlocked the one he shared with Shirley directly across from it, and headed for the cubbyhole where they made drinks. Yesterday, Shirley had restocked the teabags and biscuits. Today, it was his turn to do some restocking.

The teabags he and Shirley used were still in their Imperial Stores box, their elevenses biscuits in a tin Shirley had emptied of Cadbury's Roses chocolates one Christmas. Sidney's kept their proper distance on the top shelf of the cupboard over the sink, his Grosvenor Select biscuits transferred to an emblazoned Fortnum & Mason barrel, his loose Earl Grey tea in a caddy of elegant blue and white Wedgewood design. Dewi got to work.

He'd made the switch, a week's supply of Sidney's superior goods packed away in the plastic shopping bags in his briefcase, and was about to plug the electric kettle in for a cup of Earl Grey to sooth his nerves, when he jumped at the sound of the yard doorbell.

He went downstairs, telling himself, without alarm, and for no particular reason, that it was probably the police, and that he'd been expecting them, and found Evans the Post on the doorstep.

"Morning, Dewi! You're in early, boy," he said, hearty with a problem solved.

Dewi showed his teeth in a grin, as if for inspection. "Yes, well, what it is, John, is—"

"About the only one who is, by the look of it."

"Yes, well, what—"

"Have to get this signed for, see," the postman said, handing him the post and indicating a white envelope on top. "Recorded delivery, that is. Recorded delivery," he emphasised, tapping it with an official finger. "Meaning it requires a recorded signature of receipt. Otherwise, under the terms and conditions of that service, her Majesty's mail can*not* be delivered. Until then it remains officially in transit. Neither here nor there. Neither fish nor fowl. In limbo," he added, handing Dewi a receipts pad and a biro.

"If you hadn't answered I'd have had to come back."

"Ah, I see. Right, well, must get on now, John. I've—"

"They can be a nuisance, these recorded, especially for businesses at the start of the round. Then I have to go all the way back again, see, when somebody's there. Mind you, most are for private addresses. And that mainly means the council estate."

"Oh, yes," Dewi said vaguely, his thoughts upstairs with the kettle.

"Debt, usually, or court papers. And then this uniform I wear is anathema to me. Anathema!" he cried, rebuking the navy serge with a hand, striking his chest.

"And then, Dewi, I stand as a turncoat on their doorstep. A capitalist lackey. A class traitor. An agent of subjugation. A tool of the oppressors of the poor and downtrodden," he went on, as if addressing a public meeting, and Dewi said he could hear one of the office phones ringing.

"No peace for the wicked," he said, showing his full set of teeth again while closing the door, slowly, as if reluctant to do so, leaving Evans the Post, who was also Evans the Communist to anyone who would listen, promising the comeuppance of capitalism, including his own part in it, on the doorstep.

There was no stealth this time as Dewi went up the stairs, clutching at his heart when getting his breath back at the top. Curiosity, he thought, plugging in the kettle, would be the death of him one of these days.

Dewi had steamed open Sidney's personal mail before – it's how he knew he'd taken elocution lessons. It's how he also knew that he subscribed to *Health & Efficiency* and *Risqué* magazines, and that he bought shoes with lifts in them from a range called, until Dewi got to work with the kettle, The Best Kept Secret. And how, in his fight against what the latest invoice had termed follicle regression, Sidney had enlisted such nostrums as a purported extract from the testicles of the sexually rapacious Brazilian screamer monkey, guaranteed to excite regeneration in the active hair growth cycle.

Dewi, largely indifferent to his own hair loss years ago, having, as he had regarded it, no longer any particular use for a full head of it, had watched progress with the interest of a friend confided in, hoping almost as much as Sidney must have for success, and shared over time what was surely the same bitter disappointment at failure.

He was almost giddy with his morning, heady with the guilt of more stolen goods and the thrill of another envelope with its flap ungummed, another invitation into Sidney's private life, a door open and waiting. And one this time not only with two Royal Mail recorded delivery stickers on it, but marked 'Strictly Private and Confidential'.

It was not to be rushed. He made himself a pot of Earl Grey first from the store in his briefcase, using Sidney's Royal Albert teapot, and letting it stand for precisely three minutes, as insisted on by Sidney, and then using Sidney's English bone china cup and saucer, with a few Grosvenor Select coffee creams on a side plate with Buckingham Palace on it, fussing about as if in his carpet slippers, as if at home, listening to Mantovani, humming softly to himself, to the music of the moment.

And then he was ready. He took another sip of tea, patted his mouth with one of Sidney's paper napkins, and picking up the envelope with an air of surprised, pleasurable anticipation, as if it had just been delivered to his desk, carefully removed the single sheet of writing paper from the envelope.

And after reading it stared into space as if in shock.

He felt as if he had strayed into someone else's fantasy – or rather that they had strayed into his, as he didn't remember writing it. Didn't remember coming up with a new way of disposing of Sidney, taking him out, as it was put, with a knife, and then fly-tipping him off the M1 with a carpet for a shroud.

Whatever next! Like something out of some detective novel, he thought, as if disparaging it, as if above that sort of thing, while slyly admiring the style and detail and allowing himself to wonder if, after all, he might have written it.

He could have done so. He had once considered joining a local writing circle when they advertised for members. And he had a typewriter at home, from a time life had carried him briefly on its shoulders wearing the blazer badge of secretary of the bowling club, when that official had been temporarily indisposed. And there were all sorts of things he didn't remember these days. He could have written it. The mention of drugs meant nothing, but that of Birmingham and a carpet definitely rang bells.

And then he remembered the phone call from a carpet salesman from that city. And now he came to think of it, he also remembered making a journey to Birmingham by train. Or was that one of his trips to visit his younger sister who lived there? He found he couldn't be sure.

There wasn't a lot these days that he did feel sure about. Life, his life, a life he lived as if it were someone else's and he didn't like to intrude, had become rather too busy lately, had had rather too much of him in it. And now this. First thinking about it, then writing it, and then…

And then would he one day forget about doing that as well? Would he wake, as it were, to reality one evening in his flat, wondering where all the blood on him had come from, and hear the police hammering on the door, there to arrest him for the brutal slaying of Sidney Acton?

He was almost breathless with it, as if with the asthma the doctor told him, along with the other ailments he turned up with each week, he didn't have. He was shakily trying to get the letter back into the envelope to stick it down again before he had a heart attack, to send it on way to Sidney, to warn Sidney with, as it were, his last gasp, when his head shot up at the sound of footsteps on the landing outside the offices.

Asthma and heart attack forgotten, he had shoved the tea things into the top drawer of his desk, and was sitting pen poised as if working, waiting for Shirley, in early, to appear, when the door opened on Sidney.

"Ah, there you are, Sidney!" he was startled into saying, and laughed on a couple of stray high notes.

"You're in early," Sidney said, frowning about suspiciously.

Dewi went into the excuse he'd prepared for these early mornings, and which he practised each time going up the stairs and while waiting for the kettle to boil. "Yes, well, what it is, see, Sidney, is that I had some letters I wanted to get out first post to regular cash customers, pointing out the benefits of an account with us," he said, and scribbled busily on a sheet of paper as if adding a few final words to one.

"I see…" Sidney said, as if giving him the benefit of the doubt.

Dewi grinned. "But you're in early yourself, Sidney," he said, as if teasing him with it, as if Sidney had also been caught putting in extra effort.

"Yeah, well, the wife had a train to catch, didn't she. And we were busy, so I had to give her a lift in."

"Ah…" Dewi said, as if light had dawned. "Birmingham, is it?"

Sidney frowned. "Birmingham? Why should she go to Birmingham?"

Dewi, stuck for an answer, stared at him.

"Well – well, no reason, you know, I just – er… I have a sister who lives there with her family, see. In the district of Edgbaston. And well, not having a car, I take the train myself there when I visit her. I don't have a car because I never learned to drive," he felt obliged to explain. "I did try to learn once, but I just couldn't get the hang of the gears. And the footbrake, and that. Not while keeping my eye on the road at the same time. Anyway, that's by the by. So my sister, she picks me up at the station, see, usually in time for afternoon tea. And takes me back of course, afterwards, to catch my train. I get a return ticket, see. So, anyway, I thought, you know…"

"No, Norwich," was all Sidney said. He was used to Dewi wandering off, and besides he was Welsh. "She went to Norwich. To a school reunion do."

"Ah, I see."

"They have it in a different place each time. And this year it's Norwich. A sit down meal and a good natter. Well, you know women."

Dewi didn't know women. He'd been engaged once, when young, but his nerves in the end weren't up to it, and had never married. And now, in place of what might have been, he had curiosity and killing Sidney.

But he chuckled knowingly. "Oh, yes, no doubt there'll be no end of that, eh?" he said, and chuckled again. And then wanting to keep the conversation, this exchange between colleagues, going, added, "But it's nice, Sidney, you know, people wanting to keep up, and all that."

"Oh, they do that all right. Writing to each other, phoning. They've even got a newsletter."

"You don't say!"

"Yes. Yes, she had a lot of friends there, my wife. She's that sort of person. Know what I mean? Outgoing."

Dewi, who had never met Sidney's wife, nodded at this insight. "Yes, outgoing, I know. I get you. A friendly, extrovert sort of person, you might say."

"Yeah, that's it. Well, I'm the opposite. But there you are."

"Well…!" Dewi said, dismissing the difference.

"We can't all be the same, can we."

"Indeed not, Sidney. And it would be a poor world if we were. And they say opposites attract, you know. So that might be the key to your matrimonial harmony right there," Dewi said, offering it to him, leaning back expansively and quoting a phrase he'd read once in a magazine, flushed with this new rapport between them and sensing that Sidney also wanted to talk.

But Sidney just grunted by way of reply, and glanced round the office as if looking for something to complain about.

"Don't spend all morning on those letters," he said then, as if finding it.

And as if, Dewi thought, they were of no importance, and as if he'd been working on them in the firm's time and not his own, and coming in early to do so. Before remembering that he wasn't actually writing letters on anybody's time – which was just as well, because had he been he'd have chucked the lot in the nearest litter bin after that, the way he felt.

Behind that attentive, accommodating expression, his usual office face, Dewi was also back.

"I want to see some figures for the Shrewsbury run, now their boat's sprung a leak," Sidney said, quoting Mervyn without the humour, resenting what that leak had cost him. "We've had a week at it now, we should have some idea."

Not that he expected it to last, no matter how much he'd got back, that's what his tone said. Not without Lennie's statement to sink the boat company once and for all. He was beginning to wonder if Lennie actually was in Worcester – or anywhere else. He was beginning to wonder if this big shot American hadn't decided to make sure Lennie wouldn't be *able* to testify – permanently.

Dewi glared as if struck at the door Sidney had closed behind him, firmly, as if emphasising on what side of it he,

Dewi, belonged. And to think he'd been about to offer him tea, Earl Grey from his briefcase, with a few Grosvenor Select biscuits on a side plate.

He had decided when talking to him, colleague to colleague, not to bother Sidney with the death threat. He considered he had enough on his plate, what with his bald patch and a home life that should be a refuge at the end of the business day, but which, reading between the lines, he suspected was not all that it should be. He had been willing to listen, to lend a shoulder to his burdens, and to offer as an older man what advice he could. And had had it flung back in his face.

Well, two can play at that game, he told himself, and Sidney. As far as he was concerned he deserved all he had coming to him, which included his recorded delivery. See how he likes that. He'd take it into him now, with the rest of the post, knocking first, of course, he knew his place. Yes, sir, no, sir, three blasted bloody bags full, sir! he snarled in the direction of Sidney's office, and was about to stuff the letter back into its envelope when he realised that the handwriting he was looking at on it was his own.

And on a morning busy, it seemed to him, with letters, he was unsure for a moment whether he was writing to a customer or to Sidney again.

Then he remembered. He had put the letter face down on his desk to hide its contents, and after saying he had come in early to write to cash customers, had then unthinkingly scribbled a couple of lines on it to prove it.

A letter that not only a cash customer wouldn't get, neither would Sidney. The scrawled words were meaningless, but at the bottom of them, as if a real letter, to a real customer, he had signed his name.

They were waiting for Lennie in Batch Magna as well, on its river where Tom kept the fires of the PS *Batch Castle* alight, if only because he couldn't bear the thought of them going out for good, not now, not yet. And in Batch Hall, where they got on with things because things had to be got on with, and tried not to listen too hard for the telephone.

Mervyn was also waiting for Lennie, but rather less anxiously. He knew Lennie. Lennie wasn't the problem, Sidney was. It was Sidney, Sidney who was standing in the light whenever he looked into the future.

As a department head Mervyn was attending the weekly meeting in the town hall's Council Chamber. Councillor Holley, of Sports and Recreation, was on his feet, addressing the mayor, sitting in his robes and chain, the mayoral mace in front of him, and through him the entire chamber.

The councillor was putting the case for a police constable to patrol Julian Culpepper Park in the evenings following an outbreak of vandalism to the play area and park benches. Normally, damage to council property would have had Mervyn's disapproving attention. Normally, almost anything said in this place would have his attention, the deliberations on anything from drains to burials dressed in stained glass and oak-panels, under the oils in gilt frames of past mayors, their gaze stern with civic duty, and the borough coat of arms with a mural crown and a motto proclaiming justice and virtue, a weekly rite to which, whether he was to speak or not, he paid willing and full observance.

But today his mind was elsewhere. He was going over again his new plans for Sidney's contribution to the bigger picture.

He intended this time for the encounter to be a much closer one, the personal touch, as he thought of it. He felt it was more fitting somehow, something their relationship, if only one of business, called for. This time the weapon would be the more reliable one of a knife. A workman-like kitchen knife called a Chef's Friend, eight inches of polished Sheffield steel with a good grip and weight to it, judiciously chosen from a wide selection of them in a caterers' suppliers in Birmingham.

One good skewering with it and it would all be over, leaving little blood and sending Sidney home to his reward as quickly and painlessly as the situation allowed. He had, after all nothing against him, apart from the fact that he was English. It was simply a business move, an extreme takeover bid, as it were.

He was going to do it in Sidney's office, early on Sunday morning, when there was hardly anyone around. He had dangled the bait of money when he'd phoned to arrange it, stressing the need for the utmost secrecy while hinting at the amount involved. Sidney, as he knew he would be, had been as a moth to a light.

Sidney hadn't mentioned the death threat, nor sounded any different from usual, suggesting that the letter hadn't yet arrived. Which didn't surprise him. The Royal Mail's vaunted promise of next day delivery for recorded mail frequently meant a few days after that, and even the following week or beyond.

But it would arrive. This week or next, it didn't matter. It wasn't meant for Sidney, but the police. An invitation to add two and two together, the arithmetic of an open and shut case.

Chapter Twenty

Paula found Lennie at home as the three bears had found Goldilocks, starting in the kitchen where, instead of used porridge bowls, there was the lavish debris of a fry-up.

He'd kicked off his bovver boots in the sitting room, where he'd unearthed her new hiding place for her cigarettes and had then watched television, judging by the amount of ash that had missed the ashtray balanced on the arm of a chair.

He was upstairs, on his bed in his underpants and a T-shirt with 'We Are The Flowers In Your Dustbin' across the chest.

She picked up the rest of his clothes from the floor and downstairs washed up his plate and the other things he'd used, complaining about it to herself while doing it, just like any other mother, relief turning her briefly, as if showing her the error of her ways, into a mother just like any other. She had started to worry that the American had finished the job.

Lennie was still asleep when Victor came in later, Paula, smoking what he'd left her of her cigarettes, taking her eyes away from the television long enough to tell him that his brother was in bed.

Victor immediately shot off out again, down to the phone box on the main road to call Mervyn, and when he got back went straight upstairs.

Lennie was still asleep, on his back, blowing as if taking a breather from doing something strenuous. Victor took advantage and punched his meaty shoulder, and then did it again, returning just two of the blows he was owed over the years, knowing Lennie would barely feel it even if awake.

"Lennie!" he bawled then in his ear.

Lennie stirred and looked blearily at him.

"Had a good time in Worcester, did ya?" Victor leered.

"What do you bleedin' well want?"

He told him about Mervyn. "All we've got to do is tell a few porkies. We can do it tomorrow. I'll tell you what to say then," he said, knowing that if he told him now he'd only have to do it again tomorrow. "We make a statement, sign it, and then—"

"What statement?"

"Witness statements, Lennie, at the cop shop—"

Lennie looked suddenly awake. "The cop shop?"

"Yeah, but you'll be going as what Mr P called the aggrieved party this time, Lennie."

His brother looked unimpressed. "What's the wages? How much is he paying?"

"You ain't been listening, have you. I *told* you," his brother said, and then told him again. "If we do as they say, in the future there'll be loads of wages."

"I dunno," Lennie said, making a face.

Victor knew that face. It meant he did know. It meant he wasn't going to do it.

Lennie wasn't interested in that sort of future. It was the future that the teachers and probation officers and the local bench went on about while he pretended to listen. The future to Lennie was the next giro cheque or Saturday and Kingham Athletic playing at home. To Victor it was now the promised land.

"Come on, Lennie. We're talking about the big time here," he said, grinning at him, urging him to see what he saw. Then he remembered something Mervyn, who knew all he needed to know about Lennie, had said when he'd phoned him.

"And don't forget the compensation, mate, will you."

Lennie blinked, taking it in. "Eh?"

"That will come to a good few quid."

"What are you rabbiting about?"

"Money, Lennie. Bread. Compensation due to you as the aggrieved party in the matter. Comes out of the boat company's insurance. Mr P even gave me the name of a solicitor to pass on to you. Says to mention his name."

"How much?" Lennie asked, sounding like an aggrieved party, an aggrieved party who doubted that money could compensate for his ordeal, but who was open to offers.

"I dunno. Could be thousands."

"Thousands…?"

"Yeah. Well, you read about it all the time in the papers, don't you. They're always paying out. Insurance money, see, Lennie."

"Yeah, right. Right. OK, Vic," Lennie said, happy for once to give his due as the brains of the outfit. "When do we see him then, this solicitor geezer?"

"Tomorrow – after the cop shop."

"Why have I gotta do that? What have I gotta go to the bleeding nick for?" Lennie snarled.

"I've told you – to make a *statement*. You've got to make a statement as the aggrieved party before you can claim compensation. It's official then, once the Old Bill gets it down on paper. First thing the solicitor will ask about. He'll have to see a copy of the statement before he can act on your behalf, as your legal representative, screwing as much as he can out of them," he said, more or less quoting Mervyn.

Lennie snarled again, at the police and solicitors and forms and signing things standing between him and a world with thousands of pounds of spending money in it.

"All right, all-bleeding-right! I'll do it, I'll do it. OK? Now let me get some bleedin' kip, will you. That's what I've come back for."

On the Saturday after that, Inspector Cholmondley-Jones drove over to Batch Hall. She had already told them that the principal witness was on a visit in Worcester and they had been unable to locate him, and she now had an update.

The sort, she considered, that ought to be delivered in person.

But when she reached the Hall there was no one there to deliver it to. The kitchen, which almost always had somebody in it, bare, silent even of the dogs. She tried upstairs as well as down, and then went through the drawing room to the terrace and shouted *cooee* at the grounds, before coming back through the house and standing with her hands on her uniformed hips in the hall.

"Honestly, they really *are* the giddy limit! Anybody could just walk in and take what they want," she told herself, speaking as a police officer, but with the fond exasperation of a friend, and that faint, vague concern that was never absent for long when it came to the ways of the Hall.

She left a note on the kitchen table and drove back through the village for the road out of the valley.

She was passing Upper Ham, when through the open window of the car she caught what sounded like an outbreak of public disorder.

She reversed for the turn-off, glad of the two-way car radio in case she was driving into trouble.

The din was coming from the PS *Batch Castle,* and it wasn't shouting, she realised as she went past the ticket office, empty now this past week and more of Priny, but singing – of a sort.

It was the Commander, sitting on a deck bench in full master's uniform, with Phineas beside him making trumpeting noises.

"*Take my drum to England, and hang it by the shore,*" the Commander roared, as if to a ship's crew in a storm, his good eye fierce, "a*nd strike it when your powder's running low. If the Dons sight Devon, I'll quit the port of Heaven and drum them up the Channel as we drummed them long ago!*"

Phineas lifted a pint glass with the remains of Sheepsnout in it. "And they'll never drink old England dry!" he shouted, as if about to fight, or cry.

There was more song in the stern, or soon to be, Jasmine and the young man she knew to be Ffion's new boyfriend tuning their guitars together. Half the village, it seemed, was on deck, children and dogs everywhere, two of the Owens' trestle tables on the fore-deck loaded with bottles and glasses, and the smell of frying onions from the galley on the air.

And the Inspector, taking it in from the top of the gangway, wondered how they knew.

She saw Clem then, leaving the deck saloon which had been turned into a sort of nursery for the occasion.

"Clem!" she called, going to her.

Clem smiled and touched her arm. "I know, Pet. He's back, isn't he. Our star witness."

"Yes – yes, he is. But how did you know…?"

"Well, not *know*, exactly. But unless someone had finished what Humph is alleged to have started, we knew he would be any day now. And then… That's what this is about," she said, indicating the rowdy gathering. "What my Irish cousins would call a wake."

The Inspector realised then. The news, she saw, was all hers. "Clem – Clem," she said, grinning at her friend, happily sharing it with her. "Clem, Humph is in the clear. There won't be any charges against him, of any sort. The principal witness, the one who went overboard, turned up at the station earlier and made a signed statement testifying that it was an accident, and that *nothing* was said. Humph is in the *clear*, Clem," she said again, felt she had to say again, as Clem didn't appear to have taken it in.

"And that's it…?" Clem said then, in a small, cautious voice.

"Well, the only other witnesses to come forward following our appeal simply said that they saw a fight. So, yes, that's it," the Inspector said with a laugh. "The secondary witness either misheard or lied – and we'll be talking to him about that. But as far as Humph's concerned, it's over."

"It's over," Clem told herself, and all she had been holding in since that day in the Hall's kitchen threatened to spill over, her eyes sparking with it.

She sniffed, made a sound like a laugh, and hugged the inspector. Then stood back, sniffed again, and wiped at her nose.

"Thank you," she said solemnly.

Humphrey was in the galley, saying goodbye as it were, in his Food Dude apron and Master Chef's hat, frying onions for the last time in that place to go with the Conies and Famous Stars and Stripes Extra-Special Relish, given away with the crisps and pork scratchings, and the rest of the stock they would no longer need.

He thought it had come then, that which had stalked his days and followed him to bed each night, when Clem walked in with the police, even one in the familiar and friendly form of Petunia Cholmondley-Jones.

"Humphrey, Petunia has something to tell you," Clem said, feeling the occasion called for their full names, while Humphrey waited lugubriously, as if for the handcuffs.

He nodded ponderously, head lowered to her words, Master Chef's hat wobbling, as the Inspector told him what she had told Clem. And when she had finished held out his arms to her, an odd courtly gesture as if inviting her to dance, to trip a measure, and gathering her, carefully, to him, closed his eyes as if resting from it at last.

The Inspector was sort of passed around after that. Even Phineas, who, after what he thought of as the misunderstanding between them, usually treated her with a sort of careful physical consideration, like someone he had once accidentally run over, was moved to hug her.

And straightening her uniform jacket and re-pinning her hat, she brushed away her own tears, and clutching a glass of Annie's home-made strawberry wine, said again that it was really nothing to do with her.

It was Lennie's doing. It was Lennie getting in the way of Mervyn's bigger picture and his brother's executive lifestyle, and his mother's hopes of getting the phone bill paid. It was Lennie, and he wasn't shifting.

"I'm not saying that! It's not right," he'd said indignantly the next morning when Victor told him what he had to put in his statement, looking as if he'd surprised himself by it as well as his brother. "The geezer didn't say *nothing*. It was an accident. And I've have drowned if it wasn't for him. It's not right. It's not right," he said again, as if liking the sound of it.

Mervyn came round and offered him money, upping the amount when he thought Lennie was holding out for more. He tried threatening him then with Mr Big, warning him what he'd do when he heard, and his mother tried tears, and talked about the sacrifices she'd had to make. But Lennie just shook his head at it all, as if he'd asked a question and kept getting the wrong answers.

"No. It's not right."

"What are you bleeding well talking about!" Victor screamed in frustration, meaning what has that got to do with it?

Lennie's expression suggested both a struggle to tell him and a desire to punch him. He knew what other people meant by right and wrong, he'd had to listen to it enough times. But that was their world. In his, right and wrong never came into it, until now.

"It's just not *right*," he got out then. "OK…?" he added on a quieter, loaded note, one which shut his brother up immediately. That sort of enquiry from Lennie, said like that, usually ended in what the courts termed an offence against the person.

And that wasn't all. The next day, Saturday, Lennie, propelled there by this new-found moral conviction, and a sense of something he identified from television and films as duty, presented himself at Kingham police station.

Chapter Twenty-One

The following morning Mervyn left home to murder Sidney as if for work, carrying his briefcase containing the Chef's Friend and an old shirt to wrap it in afterwards, on his way to make a start on the bigger picture.

Afterwards, it would be weighed down and added to the typewriter and Lee Enfield in the Cluny. And then back for a light breakfast with the Sunday papers, and change for chapel. He tried not to miss an attendance there, it could be as useful as the Rotary or golf club, and today there must be no departure from routine.

But it was an outing he wasn't looking forward to, not today, visiting a past that for the rest of the week he was free of. It was in chapel that his sins found him still, dragging him back as if by the ear, no matter how far he thought he'd come. It was there that his conscience spoke again, not in words of fire but with that uncomfortable, irksome feeling he remembered from his first starched Sunday collar.

That God of the Valleys was old now, enfeebled by a world that had moved on, like some relative he visited regularly still for his own reasons, paying lip service to a past that for the rest of the week he was able to feel he had outgrown.

He parked round the corner from Sidney's firm, and walked slowly past the building. The cobbled yard looked empty of cars apart from Sidney's, its large wooden gates, in need, he noted for future reference, of a new paint job, opened fully, inviting him in.

Chapter Twenty-Two

The door of Sidney's office was also open, waiting for him. It was Mervyn's first time there, and when he entered, his mind on full beam, he saw in one sweep both where he would do it, and that Sidney did not have the air of a man threatened with ending up being fly-tipped off the M1. Her Majesty's recorded mail had evidently once more lived up to its reputation.

In fact Sidney, Mervyn was pleased to note, was looking, for Sidney, quite cheerful. And he intended that for the little time he had left he should stay that way. He didn't know about Lennie's return and Mervyn wasn't going to tell him. Not only would he not leave this world on a note of disappointment, he would do so with expectations. The last favour Mervyn would be able to do for him.

Sidney was sitting at a desk that looked too grand for the office and too large for its owner, as if his feet didn't quite touch. "Morning, Mervyn," he said from behind it, his expression suggesting that he had got to it first, bagged it before Mervyn or anyone else could.

"Good morning to you, Sidney," Mervyn said, smiling at him, and meaning it. A smile that, up to a point, wished him well. A smile which, had Sidney been able to read it, would have told him that there was nothing personal in what he had come to do, that there was even a sense of regret that he had to do it.

"Nice day," he added, on a sudden, awkward social note, words that went with the smile.

"Yeah," Sidney agreed.

"Well, now," Mervyn said then, clapping his hands and rubbing them briskly together. "Well, now, boy – so this is where it all happens, eh? The centre of operations. The executive bridge from where the ship of commerce is steered."

"This is it."

"And very nice, too, it is."

"Eh – eh, and you say that, Mervyn, about steering from the bridge. I'm sitting here on what they call a captain's chair," Sidney said.

Mervyn chuckled with him. "And I *like* the desk," he said, pulling his head back to take all of it in.

Sidney patted it. "Nineteenth-century antique. Well, reproduction, of course. All the genuine stuff's gone to America or to the Arabs. It's what's called a partners' desk. It's from a time when two bankers, senior officials, obviously, would work together, facing each other. That's why it's big like this, and got drawers in the front as well as the back. I bought it with the chair from the same place in Shrewsbury. It's antique red walnut with gilt tooled burgundy leather top. Cost me a few bob, I can tell you."

"Well, it certainly leaves no doubt who's in charge. Very impressive. And a nice roomy office, as well. What's downstairs, the two doors I passed coming up?"

"The control room and the drivers' room. And on this floor there's this office and a general office across the way there. And two toilets," Sidney added delicately. "One for each floor."

"Well appointed, I'd describe your set-up here, Sidney, and that's a fact. Well appointed. And is there only you in the building?"

"What, at the moment, d'you mean?"

"No, I meant your business."

"Ah, right. Yes, just us."

Mervyn nodded approvingly. "A good solid presence. Suggests a history in the town, suggests trustworthiness and stability."

"Yes, I was lucky there."

"Luck you helped along, Sidney. Gave fate a bit of a nudge, like. Unlike some people who sit around waiting for it to ring the doorbell. That was you, Sidney, giving yourself a leg-up with your future."

"Yeah, well, I suppose there's something in that," Sidney muttered vaguely.

"*Def*initely there is!" Mervyn said with the passionate conviction of a man about to gamble all on giving his own future a leg-up.

Careful not to touch it, he admired a globe drinks cabinet elegantly bearing the weight of the world on curved legs, its wood veneer printed with an antique map, and then peered at a complicated-looking wall chart.

"The ups and downs of business life, eh, Sidney?"

"More downs than ups at the moment," Sidney said automatically, his cheerfulness undiminished.

Sidney, Mervyn knew, was waiting for the one who had arranged the meeting to make the first move. Sidney had learned well.

"And a good view of the town, by the look of it," Mervyn said then, as if just noticing it, drifting across to the sash window directly behind Sidney's desk, the thing he'd put together when he had entered.

"Good view of the roofs, more like."

Mervyn opened his briefcase. "And of the yard, Sidney. And of the yard, so you can keep an eye on things. See who's up to what, and all that, eh?" he said, his voice riding a brief, high unsteadiness as he turned with eight inches of polished Sheffield steel in his hand, ready to make a start on his future. And then he froze, seeing only the top of Sidney's head, the rest of him hidden by the high back of the captains' chair.

Sidney had a bald patch on the crown the size of a tennis ball. He had not noticed that before.

He hesitated, and then hooking his left arm as if around a throat, stabbed savagely at nothing a couple of times, dry runs for a change of plan, for doing it from the front.

Then Sidney moved his head in his direction and the Chef's Friend disappeared behind his back.

"How long will this take, Mervyn?"

Mervyn was thrown for a moment, his thoughts scattered, before realising that he meant the meeting.

He hesitated again. "Well – well, it's a bit complicated see, Sidney."

"Yeah, I thought it might be," Sidney said, and chuckled. Complicated was good. Simple might mean there was just a few quid in it. Complicated promised much more. It was complicated that had allowed him to change his life in the first place.

Sidney stood. He was wearing jeans, but with a blue-striped business shirt, as if in part concession to the meeting, or to remind himself, and others, who he was the rest of the week. "In that case, how about doing it over a cuppa? I didn't have time before I left. And I suspect I'll need the old grey cells working fully for this one."

"A cuppa?"

"Tea." Sidney laughed at his expression. "It's all right, Mervyn, I won't poison you. Come on, you can give me a hand. We have to go across the way for it."

Mervyn followed him, followed Sidney's back.

He marked the target with an eye, the backdoor to Sidney's heart, and crept nearer, as silent in his weekend chukka boots as a shadow on a wall, the knife lifted, his left arm a hook, ready for Sidney's throat.

And then Sidney, about to open the office door, glanced round at him, and Mervyn found a weakness in himself, a weakness that afterwards he would try to call something else. He could not do it to his face, could not kill Sidney while Sidney was looking at him, the other man's eyes like a bright light shone suddenly on something he'd been about to do in the dark.

He hid the knife again, as if shamefully, as if even from himself.

"I might even run to a few Grosvenor Select biscuits," Sidney said roguishly.

"Sounds good to me, boy. Lead on!" Mervyn said, trying for a hearty note.

He had moved in again, following Sidney across the landing to the other office, was almost there, when something in him jumped at the sound of a door opening and closing below.

He hadn't expected that, hadn't expected anyone to be at work this early on a Sunday. He listened for more activity, even footsteps on their way up, the strain showing in the public face he was unaware of, smiling his councillor's grin at nothing as Sidney got the first few keys wrong on a ring bristling with them.

"I don't normally unlock this in the morning," he explained, opening the door.

Mervyn followed him in and closed it, quietly, with a delicate click, after them. It had to be done now. Before his chances increased of leaving the police a photofit on the way out, or, worse, disastrously worse, bumping into somebody he knew.

He moved swiftly, in a few long strides on the balls of his feet, grimacing with intent, a cartoon cat given another chance at the mouse, and then had to pull up abruptly, almost shunting into him when Sidney came to a halt, turning to him.

"That's Shirley's desk, my secretary," he said, pointing to a desk on his left, and then the one opposite. "And that's Dewi's, Dewi Brice, my bookkeeper and office manager."

"Ah," was all Mervyn could find to say.

"Between you and me, I keep Dewi on more for local knowledge and contacts than anything else," Sidney said, a businessman showing a visitor around, Mervyn walking with him, hand behind his back. "Or though, I have to say," he went on grudgingly, "and I know about figures, he's a good bookkeeper. But he's liable to be forgetful. His work needs constant checking. Know what I mean?"

Mervyn said that he did. And while Sidney gave him the latest instance of Dewi's forgetfulness, mentally rehearsed taking a quick step back, grabbing him around the neck and then doing it.

Then Sidney stopped again, at another door, between the desks and a bank of green metal filing cabinets. He moved to open it and Mervyn moved with him, making up for lost time as Sidney, stepping back with the door, trod on his foot.

"*Oh!* – sorry, Mervyn."

Mervyn hid the knife he'd almost dropped with one swift movement and chuckled, as if Sidney had almost caught him out that time.

"No, it's I who should apologise to you, Sidney, for not looking where I was going," he said, and found that he meant it, feeling an odd sort of intimacy in another failed attempt, as if they were in it together, two colleagues sharing the difficulties of getting an unpleasant job done.

"It's this door. Not a lot of room in here for it to open inwards, as you can see."

"Yes, indeed I can, Sidney," Mervyn said, looking around at it.

"Used to be a small storeroom. Not much more than a cupboard really. We just use it to make drinks, and that, but Wilf Ellis, the bloke who had the business before me, used to cook his meals in here, on a Baby Belling. He had extra wiring done and the sink put in."

"Very handy," Mervyn agreed.

"Saved me a few bob." Sidney lifted the electric kettle on a worktop and finding water in it switched it on. "The office itself, believe it or not, used to be a French polisher's shop. When the weather's hot you can still smell the polish," he went on chattily, opening the cupboard over the sink for the tea caddy. "There were four businesses in the building then. My office was a tailor's workroom, repairs and cutting, and that, and downstairs there used to be the office and press of the *Bugle,* before they moved to Drovers Lane. And opposite that, what's now the control room, was the office of a second-hand car dealer. He kept his jalopies in the yard."

"And now it's all yours, Sidney!" Mervyn said, grinning as if including himself in the congratulations.

"Well, not *mine*, exactly. But yes, it's true that the Kingham Prestige Car Service is now the only company occupying the premises. The used car bloke was the last of the old tenants to leave, so my cleaner tells me. She used to do for him as well. Right Jack the lad, he was, by all accounts."

Sidney told him a couple of things the used car dealer got to while waiting for the kettle to boil. He put out a couple of mugs and side plates from the sink's drainer, and Mervyn realised that it had to be done there, in that room. He couldn't see a tray to carry things, so with only one hand free, and tea and biscuits to take back to Sidney's office, it had to be there.

Mervyn watched him make the tea, the weight of the Chef's Friend behind his back quite a familiar one now, like something he often carried about with him.

"The tea's Earl Grey, but there's only one cup and saucer, the bone china set I use. So we'll have to use mugs, I'm afraid," he said, as if apologising to the elegance of his Royal Albert teapot and its contents rather than Mervyn.

"Very democratic of you, Sidney," Mervyn said, giving him some of his attention, the rest of it on the small fridge against the end wall Sidney would have to stoop to for milk, presenting his back.

Sidney got his Fortnum & Mason biscuit barrel out of the cupboard, shook it with a frown, and opening it found it empty.

"That's odd. I thought there was some left."

"Staff got there before you, Sidney?"

"They've got their own. Not the same quality of course. Still, as we're drinking out of mugs."

"I don't think I'll bother with biscuits, you know. The old tum's playing up a bit this morning. Just the tea will do me."

"Yeah, and me, come to think of it," Sidney said, shoving Shirley's Roses chocolates tin back into the cupboard. "Sugar? We've no lemon, I'm afraid."

"Just the one, please, Sidney. Have to watch the old weight these days."

Sidney poured the tea through a metal strainer. "I normally insist on the infusion standing for three minutes, as per the recommendation of connoisseurs of the brew," he went on, his elocution lessons taking a firmer grip. "But I have to admit that I am rather anxious to get back, to hear what this is all about."

"Well, that's what I'm here for. Got all the info in my briefcase. The road map to both our futures. I tell you, boy, play our cards right with this one and we can both retire. The pension pot, I call it."

Sidney paused, his eyes widening, taking in the size of the promise. "What – that good…?"

"That good. What d'you think all the secrecy's about? Sidney, it is *big*. It will make us both wealthy men. Very wealthy. Very, *very* wealthy," he added, doubling up. When it came to the few seconds Sidney had left in this world the sky was the limit.

"'Ere cop for that," Sidney said, the old Sidney in his enthusiasm getting there before the new and elocution lessons.

Mervyn, hoping Sidney wouldn't notice he was doing so with his left hand, took the mug, and then frowned. "What about milk, Sidney?" he said, as Sidney went past, already on his way out, and saw that he no longer needed the fridge.

Sidney stopped abruptly, the mention of milk bringing him up short. Mervyn, about to close on him again, stopping with him, the Chef's Friend disappearing with practiced ease, his face wiped clean, innocence of intent.

"Mervyn – it's *Earl Grey*. The finest Earl Grey obtainable. A product of over seven years of botanical trials in the uncompromising pursuit of excellence. Cultivated in a walled garden in an enclosed order in Kent for a select few outlets," he said, as if reading it off the box. "Each leaf handpicked and delicately scented by monks in their flavouring room with oil extracted from the rind of the bergamot orange. One does *not* put milk in it!" he added, a man burdened with the ways of the untutored Welsh, and was almost out of the room before Mervyn realised that fate was waiting with another chance.

He moved swiftly, intending to be behind him when Sidney stopped to close the door after them, the door that Sidney then walked straight out of, leaving it open.

"I'm a bit too young to retire, I know," Sidney said, after waiting for him to catch up. "But I have to say that one could be tempted."

"Somewhere like sunny South Devon, Sidney, perhaps," Mervyn suggested, drawing on a recent TV ad. "One of England's most scenic regions, with beautiful countryside and miles of stunning unspoilt beaches. A golfing paradise replete with top-notch coastal courses, all with breathtaking views and benefiting from a temperate climate," he said, a salesman selling him a future like a holiday, something to look forward to before he went, before he reached the next door. The door that he had closed behind them and which Sidney would stop to open. A chopping board for the Chef's Friend and the way home for Sidney, to no more run and be weary, his tears and strivings behind him.

Because this time, no matter what happened, this time it would end there. End for Sidney and begin for him.

"Or even *abroad* somewhere, Sidney."

"Abroad?" Sidney looked startled.

"*Yes*. A life of ease and plenty in the sun. Why not? Why *not*, boy?" Mervyn demanded, as if indignant for them both, for both their futures. As if they were somehow in it together again. He had never felt more fraternal.

"I wouldn't mind getting away from all this bloody rain sometimes, I can tell you."

"Oh, I'm with you there, Sidney," Mervyn indulged him unpatriotically, knowing which side of the border Sidney considered was responsible for most of it. "And, well, you could afford it. Go anywhere, you could. The Caribbean, now. Barbados," he recommended. "That's the place, I'm told. A favourite with the millionaire class. Golf and country clubs with the word royal before their names, white sands and rum punches, in a hammock, I wouldn't be surprised, while being fanned with a palm frond, and the sky and sea the bluest money can buy. Think of that, boy. *Think of that, Sidney…*" he urged softly, a last kindness.

"Yeah, well, wherever it is, it'd have to be someplace where there's no foreigners," Sidney said, about to open the office door, Mervyn quick-stepping behind him in a brief dance, the blade of the Chef's Friend a sudden flight of bright menace.

"Ah! *There* it is. I've been looking for that," Sidney said, darting off to the left as the door was opened from the other side knocking Mervyn's tea from his hand, the end of the Chef's Friend, travelling with the force of uncorked frustration through the space Sidney had just left, embedding itself with a thud in the solid pine of the door.

The pale moon face of Reg, one of the drivers, a face open to the world and whatever it had to tell him, peered cautiously round it at them from under the shiny peak of the chauffeur's hat Sidney insisted his drivers wear.

"Oh, it's you, Mr Acton," he said on a brief laugh of relief. "I heard somebody up here, and it being Sunday, like…" He looked at Mervyn, and then down at the pool of liquid on the linoleum. "Sorry about that. Still, at least the mug's not broken," he added, cheerily pointing out the bright side.

Sidney, holding the copy of Kelly's business directory, left on top of the bookcase that side of the door, remembered the need for secrecy.

"This is – er – this is Mr Jones, Reg. He's here on business."

Mervyn nodded absently at him round the door, a man with other things on his mind.

The driver looked at him, and then, amused, pulled back as if for a better look. "That's not Mr Jones. That's Councillor Probert," he said, and looked from one to the other of the men as if waiting to be let in on the joke.

"Yeah, well…" Sidney said vaguely, and left the rest to Mervyn.

"It's something we do at the town hall," Mervyn said dismissively, making it clear to Reg that town hall business was none of his business. Behind the door he had pulled to him for cover he was having trouble freeing the blade.

"It's something they do at the town hall," Sidney told Reg, as if he'd needed Mervyn's OK to do so. "But thanks anyway, Reg, for checking," he added, by way of saying goodbye to him.

But Reg wasn't going anywhere. Intrigued by this insight into local government, he was regarding what he could see of Mervyn with interest.

"Why's that then?" he asked.

"Why's *what* then?" Mervyn frowned round at him as if surprised to find him still there.

"Why do you do that? Use two names, like?"

"As I've said, it's the town hall business," he snapped. "Now if you don't mind!"

"Yeah, we've got things to discuss, Reg," Sidney said, as if explaining Mervyn's manner, and adding a smile to go with it. Reg, who went back to the previous owner, was an asset to the firm.

But Reg did mind. He moved from one foot to another, obstinately shifting his large frame. "Yeah, but why? That's what I'd like to know. Why?"

Reg paid his rates on time each month in that same town hall and voted in council elections. As far as he was concerned town hall business *was* his business. Especially if he thought there was something dodgy about it.

Mervyn knew it was no good. He knew Reg wasn't going to go away. He'd known many Regs over his years of public service. One thought, one question, would follow another, ploddingly, implacably, until he had exhausted his curiosity. With someone like Reg it could take half the morning.

He hid what he felt for a brief moment behind the door, before composing himself and grinning round it at him as if greeting a constituent on the street, the public face of Councillor Probert, hastily put together on this occasion and not quite right somehow, like someone who had dressed in a hurry.

"Yes," he said, and chuckled, playing for time while worrying at the blade. "Yes, good question, my friend. Good question. And, well, quite frankly, I can see why you felt obliged to ask it. As indeed I would myself. But I can – er – I can assure you that there's nothing untoward about it. Nothing untoward about it at all. It's all perfectly in order, all above board. It's just that in the town hall, you see, in my official capacity there as head of Planning and Strategic Development, I am, as you rightly pointed out, Councillor Probert. While outside of it—"

"When he's off duty, like," Sidney put in, catching up.

"When I'm off duty, I'm plain Mr *Jones*." Mervyn grunted the last word, wrenching at the same time at the knife.

"I see," Reg said slowly. "So, isn't that your real name then, Probert…?"

"Yes. Yes, it is," Mervyn said with a show of frankness, and then couldn't think of anything to be frank about.

"I see," Neville said again, satisfied with it as far as it went, and waiting for the rest.

"But, well, it's – er – it's not as simple as that. It's – er – it's complicated. It's…" Mervyn faltered and stopped, as if running out of breath, unable to think beyond the nightmare nakedness of an eight-inch kitchen knife sticking out of the door, a nakedness about to be exposed any moment now.

He gave a sudden, desperate tug at the Chef's Friend and felt his tendonitis flare up, the sudden weakness of his golfer's wrist. "It's – er – it's so I don't get bothered all the time. That's what it boils down to. Basically," he said, was all he could think of to say.

"I see," Neville said, not sounding as if he did.

"When he's off duty, Reg, as I said. Such as now," Sidney added.

"No peace for the wicked, eh?" Mervyn added, and laughed distractedly, sweat leaking from his Brylcreemed hair.

Reg, in the presence of his boss and a town hall worthy, nodded. "I get you," he said, decided to say, still not doing so but flattered that they should think he would.

"Right, well, where does Agnes keep her things?" he said then, moving briskly on to something he did understand, and referring to the cleaner. "I'll get this mopped up."

Sidney, his hands full, jerked his head towards the rear of the office. "Up on the left there, Reg, where we make the tea. The door's open."

Reg, excusing himself to Mervyn with a smile, pushed a little at the office door to get in.

Mervyn pushed back. "No! No, no, that's all right, I'll do it," he said on a sudden high note, a brief song of panic.

"No, no. I did it, so I'll clean it up. That's only fair," Reg said ponderously.

"Let Reg do it, Mervyn, then we can get on," Sidney said, frowning at him.

Reg's large hand pushed again at the door and Mervyn felt his own hand on it weakening, giving in, surrendering from the ruins where his takeover bid had ended up, the bigger picture now one that promised to end in ignominy and a crown court dock.

"You all right, Mervyn?" Sidney said.

"Yes, fine," Mervyn said, as if he hadn't noticed Reg was trying to get in. "Just finding it a bit warm in here, that's all," he said shakily, wiping at his brow to prove it, and looking wildly about as if for escape.

"Tea!" he said then, his gaze meeting Sidney's mug and clutching at a straw. "That's it. That's what it is. Tea. I didn't have my tea. I'm in need of tea. It does that to me sometimes – and not only that, not only that, Sidney," he went on, rallying, finding his tongue again, "I was looking forward to my first taste of *proper* tea. Your Earl Grey. From a monastery garden," he said, as if about to start singing it. "So I'll mop this up and get myself another one from the pot while I'm at it. See…?" he added, looking at him as if in appeal.

"Yeah, all right, Mervyn," Sidney said, as if humouring him, amused by the passion the Welsh could bring sometimes to the smallest of things.

"Are you sure, Councillor – er – Mr Jones?" Reg said with a small frown, as if suggesting that it was something that he, as an official employee of the firm, had more right to do.

Mervyn, tightening his grip on the doorknob, his grin like a snarl, said that yes, he was sure, thank you very much.

"Right. Right, well, in that case I'll get on, then," Reg said, as if rebuffed.

"Yeah, thanks, Reg." Sidney said.

"The church jobs should start coming in soon," Reg said on his way to the stairs, as if to let them know that his labour was wanted somewhere if not there.

"I'll see you in there, then, Mervyn," Sidney said.

"All right, Sidney," Mervyn said, coming up with another grin. "Won't be a tick."

He waited until Sidney had crossed to his office, and Reg was on the stairs, and once again that morning quietly closed

201

the door of the office. His face set with the determination of a last chance, he put both hands on the handle, and ignoring the shooting pain in his wrist, worked the blade this way and that, until it came out, suddenly, leaving him almost giddy with relief.

Holding it in front of him this time in case the door opened again behind him, he scurried for the safety of the cubby hole, and wiping the handle with a tea cloth hid it behind some of the cleaner's things in the cupboard under the sink. The mop was sitting with its bucket in a corner.

There was nothing he could do about the cut in the door. The knife had gone in cleanly and had come out more or less the same way, so it could, he supposed, be taken for a crack in a door that was probably as old as the building, and, like the rest of it, in need of repainting.

He made up for it with the spilt tea, mopping it up carefully, as if removing evidence. He took a breather afterwards, needing it, leaning on the mop as if he'd just finished a day's work with it, and when he looked at his watch was surprised to see how short a time he'd been in the building.

He returned the mop and bucket and rejoined Sidney in his office, shaking his head on his way to his briefcase under the window.

"We'll have to forget about it for now, Sidney. Now your driver's seen us together."

"Who – Reg! Nah, I don't think we need—"

"No, no, Sidney. Trust me. This is *far* too sensitive. It's a pity, but there it is. We'll just have to leave it for a while.

It'll still be there," he told him, leaving the promise of it with him like a present. "I'll be in touch."

Sidney watched him leave from behind his desk.

"You didn't even get your tea," he said plaintively, as if adding another disappointment to the morning.

Mervyn paused long enough to tell him that he hadn't felt like it, that his stomach had taken a turn for the worse.

He wasn't sure what was wrong with him, except that it wasn't his stomach. All he knew was that he wanted to go home, maybe back to bed even, the way he felt, like a man who had drunk too deep of something and was now paying for it with a hangover.

Chapter Twenty-Three

On the following Tuesday the letter they'd been waiting for arrived at Batch Hall by first post. Clem got to it first.

They had phoned Odgar Llewellyn-Jenkins's office soon after it opened yesterday, and were told in incredulous, even outraged, tones that any decision made by the council would be conveyed to them in due time and through the proper channels. And here it was.

Clem opened it, and slumped with relief. She handed it to Humphrey.

It informed them that after consultation with the police it was decided that their passenger licence should be restored. But then, in the next paragraph, as if begrudging the decision, it went on to stress the council's obligations and powers under the Public Health Act, and that any further occurrence of public disorder would almost certainly result in a permanent loss of that passenger licence.

"Well, we'll just have to make sure that there isn't another one," Clem said vaguely.

"Yeah, we'll just have to watch it, that's all," Humph agreed, and stared off into the near distance for a moment, frowning at whatever he saw there, before grinning again, looking at her and grinning.

"I know," she said, grinning back at him. "I know."

They'd known since Saturday and the Inspector's visit – known that it would be all right, in-between knowing, just *knowing,* that it wouldn't be. And now here it was, in black and white.

And tied up at the landing stage the PS *Batch Castle* waited, ready to ply the river again, or to say goodbye to it on a last, crew-only trip, returned, however briefly, to where she now most belonged, more part of it than of the land. Sion and Tom had seen to that. They had gone ahead anyway, as soon as they could on Saturday, lighting her fire again, putting the heart back into her, her steam escaping now like living breath into the crisp river air. And then the phone went in the ticket office.

Tom, white engineer's overalls freshly laundered, the cap with the gold CSC ribbon rescued again from the past, in the great good humour of the occasion pretended to pipe the Commander aboard as he came up the gangway, Stringbag at his heels. The Commander playing his part, returning the salute and then inspecting the ship's company lined up at attention on deck, adjusting Tom's cap and telling Sion, fireman's shovel at the shoulder arms position, to get his hair cut.

It was a trip that meant as much to them, perhaps more, than the inaugural one. And although there was no band this time to play them out to midstream, two representatives of the local press were there. Clem had seen to that yesterday morning, intending either to air today an injustice or to advertise that the CSC was back in business.

And having got the latter in, including sailing times and prices, she turned into the little woman for the photographers, holding Hawis by the hand and with Ralph Franklin T Strange on one hip, standing next to her husband, gazing at him as he spoke.

"Still, worse things happen at sea," Humphrey said, after talking about the threat of a charge of attempted manslaughter, even murder, treating it almost as if it were just another business problem.

And then, having got that over with, he lifted a finger and grinned, slowly. "Or – or, on the river," he said ponderously, and chuckled, his body heaving with his own wit, before remembering that Clem, with public sympathy and ticket sales in mind, had warned him not to joke about it.

"But it's not something to joke about here," he added sternly, looking at the two reporters as if one of them was responsible.

"And I wanna say something else," Humphrey said then, on a different note, a note that suggested that if what had gone before had embarrassed him in some way, because it had been all about him, this would not at all.

Clem, as much in the dark as the reporters, shifted Ralph onto the other hip and waited. "I wanna say this to the guy they said I'd tried to drown," he went on, gruffly, the reporters, with a dramatic detail that had the front page written on it, busily turning it into shorthand. "The guy who knew what the truth was and who made sure it got heard.

I'm not allowed to know who he is, his name and that, but I wanna say this to him. I wanna say thank you. And I wanna tell him that every time the PS *Batch Castle* sails from here, there'll be a free ticket waiting for him at the office. Because without him... well, that's all I wanna say. OK?"

Humphrey was wearing his favourite Hawaiian shirt for the occasion. On it, an island festival, a street party, was in full swing in an explosion of gaiety and colour, carrying it around on his generous frame as if he were hosting it, standing at the top of the gangway, greeting the few passengers they had, welcoming them to another sort of party, one with the sun shining and the fun of a paddle on the Cluny waiting.

While in the offices of the Kingham Prestige Car Service Dewi was in the cubbyhole, standing, frowning in front of the sink. Shirley had spilt Tipp-Ex on her desk and asked him to bring her a damp dishcloth while she did what she could with tissues.

The cloth wasn't on or in the sink, on the drainer, or the worktop one side of the sink.

He put his head round the door. "I can't find it, Shirley," he said plaintively.

Shirley sighed to herself. "Look under the sink, Mr Brice. Agnes probably used it again. But there should be another one there."

And Dewi, searching the cupboard under the sink, found the Chef's Friend.

Agnes must use it for something. To scrape at things. Or to unblock a sink or drain. Or on the vacuum cleaner she's always nagging Sidney about, he told himself, reassured himself, staring at it in his hand, not wanting to consider who else might have put it there. Who might have hidden it there – until, until…

"Where's that come from?" Shirley said, a woman who knew the contents of the cubbyhole down to the last teaspoon, suddenly appearing and waking him from a dream of murdering Sidney, stalking the Englishman round his office with the long, bright blade, Sidney flapping his arms and squawking like a chicken.

Dewi turned his smile on her with a sort of wonder. She had last been seen chatting inconsequentially while putting on her coat to go home at the end of the day, while he waited impatiently for his visit to the cubbyhole, and the last word with Sidney.

"What?" he said.

"The knife," she said, smiling because he was.

"It's Agnes's," he said, as if denying it had anything to do with him. "It's Agnes's knife. She uses it in her job. To scrape recalcitrant grease or dirt off things. And to get into the corners, you know? Or to unblock the odd sink or drain. Or on that old vac. She finds it just the thing with that wide part on the end, when it gets bunged up, like, with fluff and bits of this and that," he explained, happy to do so. He was fond of Shirley. "She keeps it under there. With her other things. A tool of her trade, you might say," he said, putting it back.

"And is there a dishcloth there as well?" Shirley reminded him. "Only the Tipp-Ex is setting."

"Oh, sorry, Shirley," he said. "I forgot."

"No worries, Mr B. I'll get it," she said, her tone suggesting that she should have done so in the first place.

He watched her wet it under the tap. "It's age, you see, Shirley. You tend to sort of drift off a bit sometimes, you know?"

"Oh, I wouldn't worry about that, Mr B. I'm always doing it," she said, heels tapping busily on her way out, followed by Dewi, casting a last lingering look at the cupboard under the sink.

And in the executive Culpepper Dining Room, on an upper floor of the town hall, Mervyn was listening, or appeared to be, with an expression of fixed avid attention to the head of Commercial and Environmental Health relating a recent professional visit to a fish and chip shop, while stirring his coffee over and over and wondering where he could get hold of a bomb.

Chapter Twenty-Four

Lennie was back in Batch Magna, by bus and this time on his own.

He'd headed straight for the boat. Finding at the ticket office that Humphrey wasn't on that day, he followed the directions that Priny, who had no idea who he was, had given him for the Hall.

An alien, menacing figure in the village, this large skinhead, a figure out of news reports of football match skirmishes, punch-ups at the seaside and blood on the Saturday night cobbles of local towns, a crusader, in his Cross of St George T-shirt, looking for Welsh dragons to slay, braces holding his jeans clear of Dr Marten boots, his hair cropped for combat.

Along Upper Ham to the turn-off at the other end, up to the crossroads, marching on to the Hall like a one-man army.

Although last seen at any length head down, subdued and shivering in a blanket, Humphrey recognised him immediately. He'd watched him stride through the gates like that before, a few times since in his imagination, grim with intent, on his way up to the Hall for a re-match.

But bigger and more menacing looking now than he remembered or imagined.

When Humphrey acted from his heart, fired into action by love or indignation, his was a weight to be reckoned with. But on the odd times when starting, as it were, from cold, when he had stopped to think about it first, stopped to wonder what his childhood hero John Wayne would have done, John Wayne was no longer there to tell him. And John Wayne was no longer there now.

Humphrey had been working with his young helper George on renovating the lodge, a cottage that in the estate's palmier days had once housed a gatekeeper. He had just dumped the latest delivery of wet plaster from the sitting-room ceiling in what one day would again be a front garden, when he'd spotted Lennie.

And almost at the same time Lennie spotted him, and while Humphrey gawked on at him over the lodge's hedge, Lennie veered off and marched determinedly in his direction. Lennie was busy discovering Lennie still.

And Humphrey, who, without John Wayne to guide him, had been wondering whether to hit him with his shovel as the skinhead pushed open the garden gate and headed for him across the trodden lawn, found himself being invited to shake hands, Lennie thrusting his own, large-boned heavy-duty hand at him, the fingers like spanners.

"Put it there, mate," he said.

Humphrey did so, looking as if he had still to catch up, their two great paws meeting and moving up and down in a solemn, hefty dance, as Lennie recited the short speech he'd been rehearsing since leaving home, thanking Humphrey for saving his life.

"You risked your life, mate, to save mine," he said at the end of it, as if it carried a question mark, as if he still didn't understand why and it was part of the reason he was there, for Humphrey to explain it to him.

"Yeah, well, you know…" was all Humphrey said, and shrugged.

Hearing their voices Humphrey's helper George wandered out then to see who the visitor was, and Humphrey, embarrassed and glad of the diversion, pointed at him and said, "That's George."

"Right," Lennie said, and nodded briefly at George.

George was impressed. It was the closest he'd been to a skinhead, and one at that who was as big as Humph.

"George, this is – er…"

"Lennie," Lennie said.

"And I'm Humph, Lennie. George. Georgie," Humphrey said, pointing at Lennie, "this is the guy who saved—"

"Yeah, and you saved my life, mate. That's why I'm here today. That's why I'm here today. To thank your dad," he told George sternly, as if instructing him on the proper way to act if ever someone saved his life.

George's pale serious face broke in a slow grin. "That's not my dad. My dad's dead," he said, not without pride. He may not have a T-shirt like that and Dr Marten boots but he had a dad who was dead.

"So's mine," Lennie said, looking for that moment much younger than his nineteen years.

"And mine," Humphrey put in.

The three of them shared a silence, and then Lennie felt obliged to add, "Well, I don't know if he's dead exactly. He's just sort of... you know." He shrugged. He had no idea where, or even who, his dad was, and in his world wouldn't have needed to say so.

"Missing," George said, as if getting it then. "He's missing believed dead." He'd read about something like that in the new war serial in the comic stuffed in his pocket.

"Yeah. Yeah, that's right. Missing believed dead. Yeah," Lennie said, taken with it. And then looking at the lodge said, "Doing it up then, are you, your gaff?"

While Humphrey was trying to remember what a gaff was, George said, "That's not his gaff. That's his gaff up there, up the drive there," he said, pointing to where the screens of rhododendrons and the ancient beeches led. "Batch Hall. Big place it is," he said, boasting on Humphrey's behalf. "His real name's Sir Humphrey. He's what—"

"Humph," Humphrey said.

"He's what they call a baronet," George said proprietarily, and Humphrey gave a short, vague laugh, something he was used to doing, laughing at the idea before somebody else did. He still considered it lousy casting, still couldn't entirely shake off the thought that somewhere along the way a mistake had been made.

"What, that's American, is it?" Lennie asked, without much interest.

"No. No, it's not. It's British," Humphrey said, as if shifting the blame. "It's something I inherited, that came down through my family from here. It's a sorta ancient Britain title kinda thing."

"I get ya," Lennie said, meaning he hadn't the remotest idea what he was talking about, and not the slightest interest in finding out. "So what's this place then?" he asked, nodding at the lodge.

Humphrey told him something of the lodge's past, the ornate Hall gates, under the lion and otter rampant surmounting its pillars, that had now long stayed open, rusted on their hinges, once run back by the gateman for carriages and the first motorcar of the valley.

"I get ya," Lennie said. "Right, well, I'll be off then."

"Where d'you live, Lennie?" George asked.

"Kingham. See ya."

"Hey, Lennie. Did you read about the ticket?" Humphrey remembered to ask.

He said that it had been reported in two local newspapers, and when Lennie still looked blank, told him that he had a permanent free ticket for the *Batch Castle*. "Because without you, without what you did, there wouldn't be any sailing, and I'd be on bread and water. So, that's just to sorta say thank you. From all of us. Any time the *Castle* sails, Lennie," Humphrey went on, emphasising it by waving his shovel at him, "there's a place aboard for you."

"Yeah, well, it's good of you. You and – er – and everybody. I appreciate it. Thank you," Lennie said in an embarrassed, formal sort of way, as if acknowledging a public award. "Well," he added, now that was over, "I'll be off then."

"Yeah, we've got to get on as well. We've got a ceiling to put up," George said, a workman in workman's trousers, the state of which his mother would have words about later, his face the smaller size of the same face he'd have at forty or even older, under a shock of black hair that seemed to have got there before him.

"And then watch it come down," Humphrey said. He made a face. "Plastering."

Lennie nodded at the heap of plaster on the lawn. "Is that where that's from?"

"Yeah. That's the new sitting room ceiling, or a good bit of it. I put the plaster up and a few minutes later down it comes again."

"It stayed up a bit longer though this time, Humph." George put in loyally. "Nearly five minutes," he told Lennie.

"Yeah, thanks, Georgie," Humphrey said. "The trouble is the book on plastering from the How To series in the library is out, been out for ages."

Lennie laughed. "Then get a plasterer, a professional to do it."

"We did, for the upstairs. Then we ran out of money."

Lennie looked at him. "Ran out of money? I thought you was rich." Lennie sounded indignant. "With the big place up there, whatsit Hall. And that boat. And this ancient title thing. And you being an American," he said, as if accusingly, as if Humphrey had let it all down, including America.

"Yeah, well," Humphrey said defensively. "Things are not always what they seem."

"They just about keep their heads above water," George said, quoting an adult remark and looking adult about it.

"It's not their fault there're broke, Lennie!" he added in a small explosion of temper.

"I'm not saying it is," Lennie said, looking uncomfortable, more at home being blamed than blaming. "Anyway, I've gotta be off. Thanks for the ticket."

"You earned it," Humphrey said.

"Bye, Lennie," George said.

"Yeah, bye, George," Lennie said, and dropped a shoulder as if about to throw a punch, putting a swagger into it for George's benefit. "See ya," he said, waving an abrupt hand as he went.

He got as far as the gate, and glared at it as if about to kick it.

He knew this was going to happen. He just bleeding well *knew* it.

He stomped back across the lawn, the old Lennie burdened with the new.

They stared at him, and then at the new heap of plaster he pointed a large finger at.

"Well, that don't look right, for a start! You putting enough water with it?" he demanded.

Humphrey looked from the plaster to Lennie and said, "Well, I guess so. I don't know, I—"

"Fifty–fifty's about the mix for plaster."

"Something like that, yeah," Humphrey said vaguely.

"And is it clean, the water you're using? Where you getting it from?"

"From the water butt there. We haven't got the water on yet."

"And you putting it in first or last?"

"Well, last. Like mortar. I—"

"First mistake, mate. It's always plaster to water. You've gotta get the mix right first. Plastering starts with the mix, not the trowel."

"Well, like I said, the plastering book's out. Somebody keeps renewing it."

"Do you know about plastering then, Lennie?" George said.

"Probably got the same problem I've got," Humphrey went on, more to himself, talking about the book borrower. "Probably still watching his plaster come down."

"Yeah," Lennie said to George, sounding reluctant. "Yeah, I did a course on it, when I was in – when I was at this place I went to. To do the course."

"What, like Humph did at night school for bricklaying, do you mean?"

"Yeah, something like that. In there then, is it?" he said, indicating the open front door of the lodge, and heading for it without waiting for an answer. "You've got the right trowel, I hope. And a good paddle."

"A paddle?" Humphrey said, staring after him. The only paddles he knew about were on the river.

"A paddle. For mixing the plaster."

"No, we used a stick – but—"

"Are going to do it, Lennie? You going put the plaster up?" George asked, trotting along with him.

"Might as well while I'm here," Lennie said offhandedly.

Humphrey caught up with them. "But, Lennie – Lennie, we can't afford to pay you, fellow. That's why—"

"I haven't asked you to have I. Well, you got the plasterboard up all right. You've even got the joins taped,"

Lennie said, after stepping into the room off the hallway of the lodge.

"I saw it done upstairs. And I thought the plastering looked easy enough."

Lennie laughed, one up and without having to punch anybody. "It's a skilled job, mate. More to it than meets the eye."

"You can say that again," Humphrey said with feeling.

"Yeah, well, even builders get it wrong," Lennie said then, on his own ground and prepared to be generous. "Right!" he said then, taking off his bomber jacket. "We need everything clean, tools, buckets, that spot, the hawk, everything."

"I'll do it. I'll get the water, Lennie. I'll clean them," George said.

"Dirty water makes the plaster go off quicker," Lennie told Humphrey. "Which is probably one of the reasons you kept losing it. Plaster goes off quick enough as it is. It's a time game, plastering. Once the stuff's in the mixing bucket the clock's ticking."

Working on the two scaffold planks supported between step ladders he scraped off what plaster of Humphrey's had stayed put, while George was happily busy with the tools and water.

"See that?" Lennie said then, after knocking up a fresh batch in the bucket, and pointing at the stick he'd used, standing upright on its own in it. "*That*, mate, is a proper mix of plaster."

With George splashing water about and Humphrey labouring for him, mixing under Lennie's watchful eye and feeding him more plaster, piled like ice-cream on the wooden hawk, there was no more nonsense from the ceiling. This was a tradesman at work on it. What he put up there stayed up there.

And when he'd finished laying that coat he started immediately on the second, the skim coat, and when that was on, the ceiling was finished, made new again, the colour and shiny smoothness of sand left flattened by a tide.

"It's bloody great, Lennie," George said, using language with the men that would have earned him a clipped ear from his mother.

"Yeah, great, Lennie. Great job," Humphrey echoed cautiously, eyeing it up as if waiting for it to come down again.

Lennie laughed. "It ain't going nowhere, Humph," he said matily, sitting on the planks and getting his tobacco out. "You can put paint on it in a few days. When it's gone a nice pale pink," he said, glancing up at it, proud as a parent.

And Humphrey saw not a ceiling that could fall any minute, but one with paint on it. A ceiling here to stay.

He spread his hands. "What can I say? Thanks, Lennie. Look, buddy, I tell you what, it's lunchtime. We can't pay you but we can feed you. And you can clean up there if you like. It's Conies and chips today. Double helpings for the workers of course."

"Chips – yeah," Lennie said, as if realising he was hungry, starving even. "Yeah, I'm on for that. What's Conies?" he asked then, on their way out.

A while later he had found out. And was now sitting back with a mug of coffee in the Hall's kitchen, sharing his rolling tobacco with Clem because she'd run out. His bomber jacket was on the back of his chair, and he'd even slipped off his braces, leaving them hanging from his waist, a soldier among friends.

He couldn't eat any more, he'd told Annie and Shelly, putting up a hand as if in surrender after finishing a second helping, leaving only a few chips on the plate. "It was…" he said, and then tried again. "It was – it was *delicious*."

It was the first time he'd said that about food. Food was just food, even chips. But then it was the first time he'd eaten at the Hall, the first time he'd tasted jumbo-sized hotdogs running with Shelly's Stars and Stripes Extra-Special Relish, on thick, fried succulent nests of caramelised onions, mushrooms and tomatoes, with basil and garlic, his plate piled with the chips Annie made, plump country cousins to the anaemic Kingham fish and chip shop variety, double dipped as if in sunshine instead of beef dripping, golden and bursting with taste.

He'd even offered to do the washing-up afterwards, out of sheer gratitude, until told to sit down.

He was told to do that when he walked in with Humphrey and George, sit down and make yourself at home, as if they had somebody like him dropping in every day.

And he had found himself doing just that, after losing his uncertainty about how to behave there, covering it with bluster and a couple of silly jokes. He had never been in a house like it, except to rob it, and the last time someone with Clem's accent had addressed him it had been from the bench of a local magistrates' court. But this was Batch Hall with a welcome of its own, and an oddness that went beyond the two slot machines he'd played in its kitchen.

But this was Batch Hall, its arms open wider than most, and so Lennie sat with his bomber jacket off and his braces slipped, sharing a roll-up with Lady Clem.

And a short while after that Ffion Own dropped in, and Lennie looked at her as if she might be the pudding.

When she was told who he was, and the conversation had moved on, she mentioned that, as she had to work on that coming Saturday, she and Tim had arranged to take a trip on the *Castle* on the following Saturday. And he decided there and then that that Saturday would be the day he'd take his first free trip. That she had also mentioned a male who, by the sound of it, was her boyfriend bothered him not at all.

In some things, the old Lennie had yet to catch up with the new.

Humphrey gave Lennie a tour of the Hall before he left, and it was a measure of how he had come to regard the family that not for a moment, then or afterwards, did he consider returning to rob the place.

Chapter Twenty-Five

After giving it a good deal of thought Mervyn had given up the idea of blowing up Sidney, defeated by the logistics involved.

And if the logistics of it didn't defeat him, then there was a good chance the Royal Mail would. He'd phoned Sidney twice that week, first to tell him about Lennie and then to arrange a second meeting. Sidney had been aggrieved of course about Lennie, in his lugubrious way, as if he hadn't really expected anything else, but it was clear to anyone who knew him that he had not received a death threat.

So even if he had managed to make a bomb, he would still have to post it, still have to deliver it into the hands of the Royal Mail, and risk it doing the rounds with his letter of the sorting offices of Great Britain.

After that, he'd thought of arranging a meeting in the secrecy of an early morning beach at Aberystwyth, and there producing a hipflask to warm them up, a hipflask with a quick-acting Mickey Finn in it, politely offering it first to Sidney, and then drowning him after it had acted. Before realising that even if he knew what a Mickey Finn was, he had no idea where to get one, quick acting or otherwise.

He'd discounted a few other schemes as impracticable or incriminating, before coming up with a plan that was so perfect, so complete in itself, that is seemed to have fate written on it.

He was using the garage of his own home on a private estate this time for the venue. He had hauled a hydraulic trolley jack with a three ton lifting capacity up a pair of stepladders and manoeuvred it into position, balancing it between a shelf above the garage side door and the top of the door when partly open, waiting for the eager hand of Sidney.

They were meeting again early on a Sunday. He'd given Sidney his address and suggested for secrecy's sake he park in the car park of a nearby pub and walk round. And then, when he arrived, he'd say he was going to show just how much money he was talking about.

"It's in the garage," he'd say, leading him to the side door. "Your share as well. And it's just the start, Sidney, the first installment on our futures," he'd say, and then pretend he'd heard the phone ringing in the house. "I'd better get that. Could be the hospital. I've got an auntie who's not too good. Heart, you know. But you go ahead, boy. Feast your eyes. Oh, and Sidney," he'd say, Sidney already on his way, "the old door's a bit heavy and it's sticking. Just give it a good *shove,* boy."

Sidney wouldn't, he reassured his conscience, preparing it for chapel later that morning, feel a thing, before leaving this vale and its riches for a greater treasure, one which a thief cannot steal nor moth or rust destroy.

Afterwards, he'd drive Sidney's car to the Claypit estate, which largely never stirred on a Sunday much before the pubs opened, and leave it there with the keys in. Where it would end up after that would be anybody's guess.

And then collect the late Sidney, driving him in the back to Batch Valley and Cutterbach Wood. And after depositing him there he'd phone the police, purporting to be a villager, too frightened to give his name, but telling them that the American squire – a man already not unknown to them – had murdered someone who'd got in his way, and suggesting that they search the wood, part of his estate, his personal fiefdom.

"Two birds with one car jack," he told himself gleefully, as a future director of the Kingham Prestige Car Service.

He'd finished his labours earlier than he had thought, and decided he had time to grab back an hour's sleep before Sidney was due. He was thinking about his future, going over the bigger picture again, telling it himself like a bedtime story on his way up the stairs, when the phone went below in the hall.

He stood still, thrown for a moment, confusing it with the call from the hospital, the call he wasn't supposed to get until Sidney had arrived.

The call, he reminded himself with a chuckle, going back down to answer it, that wasn't a real phone call at all, but a pretend one.

"Hello…?" he said cautiously.

It was Avenable Blevins, a girlfriend, a woman who could usually be relied on to stay in bed on a Sunday.

"Bore da, cariad. So you can't sleep either, is it, lovey? It's this weather. Hot, isn't it. I'm naked here, me. Not a stitch on. Naked and hot, I am," she said, breathing it at him down the phone. "And I was thinking, I'm only down the road, so why don't I just throw a coat on and come as I am? Be there 'fore you know it," she promised on a throaty note, and without waiting to hear his views on it, blew him a kiss like an afterthought and rang off.

Avenable, a businesswoman, hadn't got where she was waiting for an answer to something which wasn't really a question at all, but a compromise between that and a statement of intent, and the only concession whoever it was addressed to was likely to get.

She left Mervyn staring at the phone. He couldn't ring her back to put her off without arousing her suspicion which, with Avenable, would be the same as inviting her over. And he couldn't risk taking a firmer line and offending her. Avenable was not only a woman of uncertain temper, she was also someone else who knew too much. People who bought property from Blevins's estate agents never had problems with planning permission.

After going round in circles, searching for ways to get out of doing so, he reluctantly decided that he had no choice but to put his future on hold again. He picked up the phone, and then put it down, realising that he couldn't ring Sidney either, to put him off, because he didn't have his home number.

"The bloody woman's insatiable! And on a Sunday!" he cried, on his way out to the garage.

He'd readied the stepladders again, this time to get the trolley jack down, muttering to himself about the effort it took to get it up there, when he froze, hearing someone walking past on their way to the front door.

He hadn't heard a car pull up, but it must be Avenable, Avenable with her foot down. She'd walk straight in, and when she couldn't find him downstairs, or upstairs in bed, ready and waiting, she'd try the back garden before leaving, flouncing out past the open door of the garage, noticing then that it was open.

He blew a couple of times, as if from exertion, pressure escaping from him like steam. He had to get the jack down before she…

"Before she…" he said to himself absently a few moments later, his eyes elsewhere and full of it, seeing her pushing at the door in that aggressively nosy way of hers, as if she had a warrant – *having* to push at it, because the jack was still perched on top of it. And seeing fate, like a game of Monopoly that was on his side, adding Blevins's estate agents and the employment bureau above it to the Kingham Prestige Car Service.

There was room in the back of his car for two, and he easily had time to tidy her away there, and to haul the jack back up for Sidney's turn. Then two cars delivered to the light-fingered boyos on the estate, and a trip for them both afterwards to Cutterbach Wood, their day done, leaving their knowledge of this world, and him in particular, behind them.

And a new embellishment when he phoned the police, a headline for the *News of the World* – a love triangle involving two prominent members of the Kingham business community, and multi-millionaire tycoon and playboy Sir Humphrey Strange of Batch Magna, known elsewhere as the Burger King, a man who had already got away with attempted murder, after frightening his intended victim into saying it was an accident. The American, as the two lovers had fatally discovered, was not a man to be crossed. Chapel-going Avenable Blevins when found would be naked, and taxi firm proprietor and Rotarian Sidney Acton without his trousers, because, the police would be led to believe, that was as far as he got before the avenging aristocrat found them, armed with his usual weapon, a baseball bat to remind him of the old days.

Mervyn looked lost to the activity going on in his head, grinning fixedly at it, his eyes avid, putting it together step by step in a mad dance.

And then he cocked a sudden ear, listening to her footsteps again on the path, and then hearing them stop.

"She's looking at the door," he whispered, as if telling someone else it, hiding behind his car, waiting for Avenable.

He expected her to call him first, in that impatient, demanding way of hers, like a wife, expected Avenable's voice, and heard with a small shock a male's.

It called again then, asking, querulously, if he was in there, as if he, Mervyn, were playing with him, hiding from him. It was Sidney. That's why he hadn't heard her car pull up, or its door slammed, as she normally did.

But if it was Sidney, then where was Avenable? he asked himself in confusion, before remembering with a much bigger shock not only where Avenable was, but where Avenable would be, any minute now.

"Sidney – stay there… *Don't touch the door!*" he screamed, almost going over the bonnet of his car in his haste as Sidney's shadow broke from the doorway, seeing him falling, bloodied, just as Avenable tripped down the path.

Sidney stayed where he was, and Mervyn collected himself before coming forward out of the gloom, smiling like a salesman. "Good morning, Sidney. Sorry about the, er…"

"What's that?" Sidney was staring up at the jack.

"That?" Mervyn showed his teeth in a chuckle. "That's a car jack, Sidney," he said, as if surprised at the question.

"Yes, well, I can see that, Mervyn. But what's it doing up there?"

Mervyn looked at it as if trying to remember.

"Hinges," he said then. "The hinges on the door. They needed – er – needed tightening, you know? It's a heavy door, as you can see, and the screws on them had come loose over time. And I wanted something to hold it steady for the old screwdriver, like. To get a good bite on the rawl plugs, you know?" he said, one male to another concerning a bit of DIY.

"Bit dangerous, isn't it?" Sidney sounded doubtful, and vaguely suspicious.

"Not dangerous at all," he said, his resentment showing at how non-dangerous it had now become. "I wasn't expecting anyone to walk in at this hour." He looked at his watch. "I mean, you're—"

"Yeah, I know, Mervyn, I'm early." Sidney gave a small embarrassed laugh. "Tell you the truth, I couldn't sleep. It's like Christmas morning, the thought of your pension pot waiting—"

"*Our* pension pot, boy."

"Our pension pot," Sidney said with a chuckle, happily agreeing. "Anyway, I thought maybe you weren't up yet. I tried the bell, and when there was no answer, I thought I'd see if you were round the back somewhere. Then I saw the door open."

"Yes, well—"

"And well, quite frankly," Sidney said, sobering, a man who desperately wanted to believe in Christmas, "I could do with a fresh injection of the readies right now. Wouldn't half solve a few problems, I can tell you."

"Yes, well, we – look, let's get out of here," Mervyn said, shepherding him out and following him, cautiously, round the partly open door.

He glanced about him out on the path, the avenue empty of people, the Sunday curtains drawn in the houses opposite, and then lowered his head to Sidney's like a conspirator.

"We have a problem, Sidney. This bloody woman."

"What bloody woman?" Sidney said, knowing that whatever it was about he wasn't going to like it.

"She's a girlfriend – well, sort of. Doris, her name is. Doris Thomas," he decided, purely out of a habit of secrecy. "She phoned just now, saying she had to talk to me. All tearful, like, you know? I haven't a clue what it's about. She didn't say. Only that she had to talk to me, and was coming over. Just like that!"

"I see." Sidney, who did have a clue what it was about, was seeing the councillor in a new light.

"Put the phone down before I could get a word in, she did. But the thing is, boy, she's buggered up our bloody meeting.

229

We've no choice but to put it back it again. As I've said, with what I've got planned secrecy is paramount. *Paramount.* She's a niwsans! A bloody *menace!*" he snarled in English.

"A bloody menace," he said again then, absently, his mind moving on, dancing again.

He had realised that there was no reason for Sidney to know that Avenable wasn't Doris. Avenable didn't play golf, wasn't a member of the local Rotary Club, and spent her business hours not on public view in her estate agents but in the back office of the employment bureau.

He saw himself telling Sidney that, the phone call aside, the woman was becoming increasingly unstable – and worse, for reasons he hadn't time at the moment time to go into, 'Doris' knew about a certain crime in the past that had both their names on it, and had started threatening to go to the police. And of course if that happened – and in his opinion it was only a matter of time – then not only would she rob them of all that money, rob them of their future, she would reduce what they had now to ashes and a prison cell.

This is a tide, Sidney, he would tell him, in both our affairs, which must be taken at the flood.

And after Sidney, driven into that corner of himself that Mervyn knew well, and ready to strike, or at least not hinder, had helped him see Doris to her rest, he in turn would put Sidney out of his misery, the swamps and shallows of his life, with, he decided, the big monkey wrench, a tool he had not until now found a use for.

"Mervyn… Mervyn," Sidney said again. "She's here."

Mervyn came back from another trip to Cutterbach Wood, and frowned.

"Who?"

"Your girlfriend, Doris. She's arrived."

"She can't have," he said, as if telling himself that.

"Well, somebody's just pulled up."

A car door was slammed and Mervyn's gaze for a moment was fearful as he looked towards the gate, waiting for someone he knew didn't exist to walk through it, before telling himself that it must of course be Avenable.

Avenable who, for Sidney, would now and forever be Doris. He was about to start the relationship, to mention her by that name, to comment on the sort of woman she was, slamming car doors on a Sunday, when she appeared at the gate and Sidney said, "No, it's not your Doris. I know her. It's the estate agent woman, Blevins. She was in the *News* recently, in the business section."

"Yes," Mervyn agreed, as if he'd seen the same article, before realising that when he'd seen Avenable in a newspaper, in several newspapers, she had been with Sidney, side by side, together again above a dark tale of Cutterbach Wood.

Avenable bounded down the path in flip-flops and a pink polka dot raincoat, putting Mervyn in mind as she always did of some large flightless bird, the way she seemed to run at things, as if for take-off, or attack.

"Bloody hell!" Sidney muttered, and Mervyn laughed briefly and without humour, and waved a vague hand in her direction, a gesture that spoke of what he had to put up with, and of a tide that had once more left him behind.

Avenable, as she had suggested she should, had come as she was, the thin transparent plastic over her nakedness holding in its high street ordinariness the mystery and promise of a veil, an exoticness she seemed to respond to, as if about to start dancing.

"She hasn't been well," Mervyn said.

Far from being in any way abashed by Sidney's presence, she regarded him as she drew near with shameless interest. The more the merrier, as far as Avenable was concerned, when it came to the bedroom.

"Hello, Aven," Mervyn said, as if he'd had this problem before.

"Hello, lovey," she said, pouting at him, and then lowered her eyes at Sidney.

"This is Ted Smith, a neighbour. He – er – he just nipped round to borrow a screwdriver," Mervyn improvised. "Unfortunately, I hadn't got the size he wanted."

"*Mmm*," Avenable murmured suggestively at Sidney.

"Anyway, Mervyn, thanks – er – thanks for looking," Sidney said.

"Oh, you off then, Ted?" she said, the lilt in her voice carrying both an invitation to stay and a suggestion of what he'd be missing if he didn't.

"Yes, I – er – I'd better get on. Nice to meet you – er—" he said, edging round her, while looking elsewhere.

"Bye, Ted," Mervyn said. "Come on, Doris, let's get you inside," he said, anxiously eyeing the street, Avenable as obviously naked from the rear as she was from the front.

Avenable stayed where she was, her eyes turned to stones, the other Avenable, the one who had elbowed her way to a prime position on the high street.

"And who, may one ask, is Dor-is?"

You'll find that out any minute now, love, Sidney thought on his way up the path. And then the fur will fly. One girlfriend on her way pregnant, and another turning up naked to save time. No wonder Mervyn's been looking under a bit of a strain lately.

"Doris is my cleaner, Aven," Mervyn said almost immediately. "She's been on my mind lately, that's what it is. She's getting on a bit, see, and is in hospital after a fall at home. And not doing too well, apparently. Very poorly, she is. Touch and go, they more or less said when I rang up yesterday. But it's silly you are, to be jealous, Aven! You should know there's only you, dearest."

He flashed a grin of polished teeth at her, and glancing furtively over his shoulder at the avenue took her arm. "Avenable, Myfanwy, ngoleuni fy mywyd, pert bach, sweet plum," he said, cooing endearments at her as if soothing a horse, as he led her, sulky with suspicion still but willing to be led, round to the front door. "I am not a bard, cariad. I cannot speak of love as they do. The words I have for you must stay in my heart. But since your phone call earlier, annwyl, music has been in the air, the music of the harp, playing only your name over and over, isn't it," he said, opening the door and ushering her in with another hurried glance back at the street.

After setting the alarm for his future, rising optimistically early for a morning that had promised much, but which had left him with the same old past, and after bed with Avenable that she had turned as usual into something more akin to a contact sport, one she was determined as usual to win, Mervyn slept.

And woke to Avenable vigorously shaking his shoulder. He groaned, expecting another bout, but when he opened his eyes she was standing over him, buttoning up her polka dot raincoat.

"Gotta go, lovey. I'm going with friends to one of them car boot sales at the football club. Come with us if you like."

"A car boot sale? No, thank you, Avenable. It's Sunday. On Sunday I attend chapel," he said, meaning unlike some people he could name, and intended to let her know what he thought of something called a car boot sale.

But Avenable, finding a second flip-flop where it had landed after she'd kicked it off, her mind already on bargains, simply blew him a vague kiss off her palm.

"Talk later," she said, and fluffing up her hair left.

"Not if I can help it," he muttered, and settled down to get an extra hour in.

And then his head came up off the pillow. The trolley jack! The trolley jack was still sitting on top of the garage door. The door she couldn't help but see was open now, on her way out, an invitation she wouldn't be able to resist. And a sticking door she'd give short shrift to.

He leapt out of bed, shouting her name to himself in a hoarse whisper, and almost fell down the stairs in his panic.

She wasn't on the path, and with a laurel bush in the way he couldn't see the garage door.

"Avenable!" he shouted, a wail of despair as he ran down the path, seeing another sort of future, seeing her crumpled body and Sidney testifying that the deceased was alive when last he saw her.

"Avenable!" he shouted again, getting to the garage as Avenable, who'd just gone through it, peered back over the gate with a quizzical half smile, a woman in a hurry but showing interest in the possibilities.

Mervyn stared at her, dumb with relief, and then saw that they had an audience. He clasped at his front with both hands, grinning feebly, as if a curtain had gone up unexpectedly on his nakedness.

It was an elderly man, out walking his dog, a stranger to him but a face he knew well. It was what he mockingly called a chapel face, a face that had followed him from childhood, and the look on it now stripped him of the years since.

Mervyn's grin came and went as he teetered between attempting an explanation and making a joke of it, staring into that uncompromising face on which the old man's thoughts were written as if on stone, the grey stone of the Valleys when rain fell on a Sunday.

Then his nerve broke and he bolted for the nearest cover, the side door of the garage.

He knew what he had done as he was doing it, and threw himself backwards, saving his head but breaking a foot, as the trolley jack finally did what he'd been waiting for it to do since putting it up there.

Chapter Twenty-Six

Gareth, Ffion Owen's ex-boyfriend, had just made a Saturday morning home visit a few miles distant from the practice he was now working at in St Moefyn, on the Welsh side of the border.

It was at a large house of mellow red brick and wisteria on the edge of a village, sitting with Georgian elegance in a few acres of grounds, with a stables and a paddock, he had no doubt, having imagined it, or something like it, often enough. It was the first time he'd been there, and when he was invited in it was like being introduced to his future.

This was where he wanted to be, this was what the lights burning late over books on equine health, and his courtship of Poppy Cadwallender, was all about. This was what he hungered for.

This, or something that looked like it. For this was old money, passed on with the polished patina on furniture and the good carpets worn by the same years, the same family, an elegant sprinkling of notes from a Chippendale long-case in a hall smelling of beeswax following him as he went up the stairs.

His patient was on the floor of the smaller of the house's four bathrooms on a bed of newspapers, a field-bred English Springer Spaniel, who had produced a short while before the last of a litter. There were eight of them, liver-and-white bundles birth stained and with pieces of back copies of the *Telegraph* and *Shooting Times* sticking to them, making small keening sounds, the muffled howling of wolves lost in their deaf and blind wildernesses, until silenced by the milk and the warmth of their mother, and each other.

Gareth was there simply to check parent and offspring over, and he took his time doing so, and lingered over the coffee he was offered afterwards, feeling at home there after bringing Poppy and her family into the conversation, in the company of friends rather than clients, his accent leaving Cardiff, his past, further behind, on a visit to his future.

He had seen beforehand that the house was a mere five miles or so from Kingham, and he intended a quick shop in the town afterwards. Poppy's parents were throwing a party that evening and he wanted to buy a new shirt and tie for it. He knew the sort of thing he wanted and knew he wouldn't be able to get it in St Moefyn.

Both Poppy and her mother had indicated that Mr Cadwallender was coming round to him, coming to see what they saw in him. Which, while of course pleasing Gareth, the door opening further, did not greatly surprise him. What his wife and daughter saw in Gareth was what Mr Cadwallender was coming to see, Gareth's version of

Mr Cadwallender. Gareth had taken Mr Cadwallender's views on life, which largely meant his likes and dislikes, and made them his own by changing the words, or simply by suggestion, by taking a particular dislike of his and lauding the opposite of it.

And Mr Cadwallender, with two daughters but no son to pass on who he was to, was slowly coming round, slowly turning his face towards Gareth.

His shopping in Kingham, in Merry's Gentlemen's Outfitters in the high street ('We Dress the County'), didn't take long. He knew exactly what he wanted. It was the sort of shirt and tie favoured by Mr Cadwallender. There were days when Gareth hardly had to pretend at all.

He'd parked in a side road and was waiting to rejoin the high street, when a car he recognised slowed in the Saturday morning traffic as it went past. It was a yellow French Deux Chevaux, a typical hippie car, painted with flowers, and with a hippie at the wheel, the hippie from the boat, with Ffion Owen next to him.

He moved quickly, and without thinking, as if he'd just noticed the traffic lights had changed to green, forcing a gap in the traffic to follow them.

He had no idea what he intended doing, but whatever it was he felt he had a right to do it. He didn't look further than that, beyond the heat of indignation, the sense of having been wronged. An indignation fuelled now by what he saw as his new station in life, that she should prefer a jobless hippie to him.

He tailed them past the turning for his old practice, the memory of it, of Ffion behind the reception counter that day, a sore touched, and then past the general hospital, where a bust of composer Julian Culpepper gazed with pinched aloofness over the heads of the ailing in the casualty waiting room.

And when they took the turning off for Batch Magna he followed them without giving it a thought.

To Gareth all hippies, almost by definition, were jobless. But in Tim he was wrong. Tim had a job. He was a junior reporter on the *Church Myddle Chronicle*, sister paper to the bigger of the two the *Kingham News*. And according to him now, talking to Ffion, likely to stay a junior reporter.

"Nothing ever happens there. It's why I've got the day off. On a Saturday. In summer, and not even a wedding to wax lyrical about."

"Well, don't look at me," she said, "I'm too young."

"All right, well, how about a murder then? How about murdering someone for me in Church Myddle? That would really do it. Get me on to the *News*, that would."

"I don't know anyone in Church Myddle. Well, apart from Mrs Shearman, who used to keep her horse at the hunt's stables."

"She'll do."

"But I like Mrs Shearman. She was nice. And she always used to give us little presents and a card each at Christmas."

"I thought you said you loved me."

"Where did you get that idea from?"

"From you. Last night."

"Last night was last night," Ffion said, a woman of the world after taking her pleasure and coolly moving on.

Tim smiled at her, and then looked again, a couple of times, unsure.

"And keep your eyes on the road," she said, unable to keep it up, "or you'll have us off it."

Gareth remembered the labyrinth of lanes in Batch Valley from the last time he was there, the hedgerows under high banks turning the place into a maze, and thought he'd lost them, before picking the yellow car up again on the road leading to the humpbacked bridge and Batch Magna.

By the time he'd reached the High Street they were about to turn off it. He had expected them to do so just before the village pub, which led, Ffion had said that day, to the Owens' boat, but they took the turning on the other side of the pub. And he also knew where that led.

He went down after them into Upper Ham.

They had parked at the end of a line of cars up as far as the *Belle*, and were walking back to the entrance to the *Batch Castle*, hand in hand, when he drove past them unnoticed. He parked behind the ancient-looking Deux Chevaux, taking in as he went past the hand-painted flowers and the window stickers, Do Not Hate – Meditate, Love and Peace, and Let Your Soul Shine, with an expression that had satisfaction as well as scorn in it.

He joined the queue of people from the local green and cream single decker bus that had dropped them at the entrance, its second scheduled village stop now in the sailing season. The same woman who had been on that day sold him his ticket, and he had it torn by the same old chap waiting at the top of the paddler steamer's gangway.

A short while after that the *Castle*'s steam was up, and the Commander let some of it out on the wheelhouse steam whistle, screaming a triple warning to any latecomers, the sound held like an echo between the hills. A song of summer now in Batch Valley, of fun on the river.

Not that Gareth looked like he was having any, as he searched among the cheerful crowd on board looking for Ffion and the hippie. He had searched the deck several times, the *Castle* round the island and clear of the village, before it occurred to him that he hadn't actually seen them go through the CSC entrance, just assumed it.

He couldn't find them because they weren't there, they hadn't boarded. Leaving him on his way upriver at around the time he should be arriving back at the surgery. His expression suggested that that was something else he intended having words with Ffion Owen about.

When he joined the queue at the galley, he decided he needed something stronger than tea, and ordered a pint of lager, served by Clem, her accent confirming something in him, speaking for the second time that morning of where he really belonged.

Gareth didn't know Lennie either, nor Lennie Gareth, though they had passed each other on deck a few times, both looking for Ffion Owen. While Ffion Owen was first in the engine room, where Tom Parr showed Tim how things worked, and then the wheelhouse, where the Commander made his day by letting him take wheel for a while, keeping the paddler steady against the current.

And when they returned to the deck Lennie, who'd also given up on finding Ffion, bumped into them.

"Wotcha, Ffion," Lennie said, grinning at her.

"Hello, Lennie," Ffion said. "We meet again."

"Yeah, I was wondering if you might be aboard."

"This is Tim."

"Hi, Lennie," Tim said.

"Yeah," Lennie said, dismissing him. Lennie's jeans were held up with a belt in place of braces, and he had slip-on shoes instead of Doc Marten bovver boots, and was trailing Old Spice aftershave, shoplifted yesterday for the occasion and applied with lavish expectation of ending the day with Ffion Owen.

"Fancy a drink then?" he said to Ffion.

Ffion looked at Tim. "Shall we?"

"Just you, I meant," Lennie said, and winked at Tim, a society nicety for Lennie, sharing, chap to chap, what he had in mind, while acknowledging that it was Tim's girl he had it in mind to do it to.

Ffion laughed. "Lennie, I'm with Tim. He's my boyfriend," she explained.

Lennie looked as if he were wondering what that had to do with it. In his world the girl either wanted to go with him or she didn't. Boyfriends didn't come into it. If they didn't like it then it was up to them to do something about it. Lennie so far in his courting career had had no takers.

He tried again. "Come on, just a drink. What's wrong with ya?"

"Lennie!" she snapped. "I am with *Tim.*"

"Yeah, she's with me, Lennie," Tim felt obliged to put in, but added a friendly chuckle to go with it.

"Yeah, well, all right. I only asked," Lennie mumbled then, suddenly feeling out of his depth, out of his world, embarrassed and angry at himself for being embarrassed, or angry at them, or somebody, anybody. And then Gareth turned up.

He spotted Ffion first and came to a surprised halt, his face flushed with lager like last time, but with a different script. "So you *did* get on then?" he said, as if catching her out in a lie.

His gaze scornfully took in Tim, and then moved on to Lennie, another hippie, without long hair but with something about flowers on his T-shirt.

"What do you want, Gareth?" Ffion said.

"What do I want?" he said on an incredulous half laugh, as if, as it concerned him, it should be obvious. "I'll tell you what I want, my girl. I'll tell you what I want," he said heatedly, his accent on its way back to Cardiff. "What I want is an explanation. An explanation and an apology. That's what I bloody well want!"

"Who is this?" Lennie said, frowning.

"You keep out of it," Gareth snapped.

"You what?" Lennie looked both surprised and indignant.

"You heard me. Keep the bloody hell out of it!" Gareth said, and on a surge of temper turned and pushed him hard in the chest, and Gareth paid both for Lennie's embarrassment over Ffion and the push, Lennie's fist catching him on the side of his jaw and sending him sprawling. This was Lennie's world and Lennie was back in it.

The punch seemed to echo in Gareth's eyes as he sat shakily up, and blinked as if to clear them, his expression suggesting someone coming round from more than a blow. The shock of it had been like that of a bucket of cold water dumped suddenly on him. It sobered him, woke him fully, as it were, to where he was, to what had brought him there, and he saw clearly for the first time since the start of this business with Ffion Owen what it could cost him.

He had given in to a weakness, indulged a grievance for purely personal satisfaction, to prove something he realised he no longer needed to prove. An indulgence that landed him back among the losers, on his rear, brawling like some yob in a Saturday night cider house.

It would not happen again.

He got to his feet, to Lennie waiting to carry on. But Gareth had finished. He wasn't afraid, just finished with it. He pointed a finger at Lennie, and then at the other two, his look putting them in what he now considered was their place, before dismissing them with a contemptuous flick of his wrist, and making his way through the small audience of passengers that had gathered.

He spent the rest of the time to Water Lacy, and a bus back Batch Magna, nursing a pain like a botched tooth extraction, and refining a story accounting for it and his lateness back at the surgery. The same story he'd use to explain his face at the party that evening. A story for a different audience, one with Mr Cadwallender in the front row, a light then under which Gareth would modestly shine.

Chapter Twenty-Seven

The following Tuesday Mervyn, unshaven and still in pyjamas and dressing gown in the afternoon, opened his front door to Sidney, and having told him last only yesterday, told him again that, no, there was no word yet of Lennie.

And then sitting at his kitchen table watched Sidney making tea and listened to more of his lies about why he was there.

"… so, you know, just give me a ring, Mervyn, if there's anything I can help you with. Bit of shopping, that sort of thing."

"Yes, thank you, Sidney," Mervyn said, said one thing, his eyes saying another, staring balefully at Sidney's back.

Sidney looked round at him, and Mervyn switched on his councillor's smile, but a weaker-looking version now, a smile that, like Mervyn himself, had been somewhere and hadn't altogether come back.

"You take sugar don't you."

"Yes, one please, Sidney. Avenable Blevins the estate agent dropped in earlier, by the way."

"Oh, yes."

"She didn't make tea. She hadn't come for that. She said she'd never been to bed with a man with his leg in plaster. I told her to try orthopaedics at the hospital."

Sidney laughed a little, carrying the tea mugs to the table, and sat with an expectant air.

Mervyn felt cornered. For the first time since coming up with the idea of the pension pot as a lure he had nothing to say about it. He needed to think straight, and thinking straight, moving on from where he was presently, wasn't something he'd done a lot of since what his hospital notes referred as his DIY accident. He'd spend the time stuck in the past, his recent failures, simmering in a sort of heated vacuum of resentment and frustration. A vacuum at the centre of which sat Sidney, alive and well, and still running the Kingham Prestige Car Service.

And for the first time since plotting to separate him from that business, he had no idea how to do so, no next step. And no reason to give Sidney why, now they were alone, why he couldn't tell him about the pension pot – other than that it didn't actually exist, as Mervyn lately had had a couple of times to remind himself.

Sidney looked to one side of him, and then the other, as if checking there was no one there to hear, and leaning forward opened his mouth to speak, and Mervyn shot a finger up to his own mouth, to his lips, and said, "Thanks for the tea, Sidney. Oh – and while you're here I'll get you that address I promised you," he said, raising a finger again warningly. "Won't be a minute," he added, getting up and leaving Sidney with his mouth still open.

He reached for the crutches leaning against the table, and balanced briefly on his good leg, the other in plaster to a few inches below the knee for a broken foot.

"A fracture of the fore and mid foot, Sidney," he'd told him. "Taking in phalanges, metatarsals, and the tars-metatarsal and transverse joints. And lucky not to have involved the bones of the tibia and fibula, as well. Meaning broken lower leg *and* foot. That was the informed and considered opinion of my orthopaedic man."

"Lucky not to have broken your head," Sidney said.

"Sidney, if the jack had to come down, then let me be the one standing under it when it did so. Let *me* pay for the folly of putting it up there. *That* is the way I see it." He smiled, as if bravely, and was then suddenly solemn, as if not sure which expression was more appropriate.

Mervyn hobbled back a few minutes later and lowered himself onto his chair. He took a folded sheet of paper from a pocket of his dressing gown and held it out.

"The address and phone number, Sidney, of my chiropodist. I too have known the pain of a fungal toenail."

Sidney looked at it, and then at Mervyn, who thrust it at him as if trying to jab him with it, and mimed that he should take it – take it.

Sidney opened it. On it, in hasty capitals, scrawled like graffiti on the polite blue of a page of Basildon Bond writing paper, Mervyn had warned him not to mention the pension pot, that the phone and house may be bugged. He would, he'd added like a signature, contact him later.

Mervyn took it back, gently, considerately, from a stunned-looking Sidney, and smiled at him, a smile with something of the old Mervyn lurking at the corners this time, the old Mervyn pulling strings again.

"Thank you for making the tea, Sidney," he said, looking around and speaking clearly, as if for the benefit of someone else. "It was good of you. It's not so easy getting around on one leg and with crutches."

"Well, that's what friends are for, Mervyn," Sidney said, taking his cue from Mervyn. "I was only glad to be of assistance. Any time you want something done, just – er – you know, just ring. Well, must be going. No peace for the wicked, eh?" he added with an unconvincing chuckle, and leaving his tea untouched pushed back his chair. "I'll – er – I'll be in touch, Mervyn. Don't bother to get up,"

"No, OK, Sidney, thank you." Mervyn watched him leave, brooding that he was able to do so, that he was walking around, still walking around.

He would have to shelve the bigger picture, until, at any rate, he was mobile again. And although it would feel like handing over a piece of himself, he would have to give Odgar Llewellyn-Jenkins his thousand pounds back, with a story about why the hit man couldn't do the job. As he'd told him a story about why it was taking so long. He certainly couldn't spin it out with another story, covering himself until his leg was better. Odgar had been suspicious enough, if not sure of what, when he'd heard the last one.

And remembering that occasion, before his accident, talking together in the car park of the golf club, he saw, as if revealed to him, how he might turn his plaster cast into a weapon and a murder into something else.

If the old Mervyn wasn't altogether back, wasn't altogether thinking straight, he was at least thinking again, his eyes bright with the beginnings of a new dance.

The day after that Lennie was working at the Hall again, there out of a lingering sense of guilt and because he'd had an idea.

Guilt was something else the new Lennie had found himself lumbered with. It was like waking up and discovering he was married, like being followed around the careless ways of the old Lennie by a nagging wife. And what's more, knowing she was right.

No matter how many times he'd argued with himself, telling himself that it was their problem, and, in no mood for logic, that if it wasn't for him they wouldn't be afloat in the first bleeding place, he knew that the punch he'd thrown on Saturday could have meant them losing their licence, and this time for good.

He had spent the rest of that trip in the company of Ffion and Tim, and when the *Castle* had docked at Batch Magna Ffion had checked that no complaint had been made. But he had no way of knowing if one hadn't been made since, which was partly why he was there, on the scaffolding planks again, in the kitchen of the lodge this time, finishing off the ground-floor plastering. That and because he'd had an idea.

Only Shelly had been in the Hall when he'd checked in earlier, and young George, who had arrived too late to go with Humphrey to pick up two guests who'd broken down on the other side of the border, in a village the name of which, when they phoned, they had to spell because they couldn't pronounce it. Shelly, when pumped, had said she'd heard nothing about any sort of trouble and now Lennie was sounding out George, who had volunteered to help him.

George, Lennie had learned with interest, had been working with Humphrey all day yesterday in the galley.

"So, did he say anything about anything, then, Georgie? Humph? When you were with him yesterday?" Lennie said casually. "Anything that might have happened on board, like, know what I mean?"

George, dunking Lennie's trowel in the cleaning bucket, didn't look as if he did.

"Anything about what?"

Lennie shrugged. I dunno. About any trouble, or anything like that."

George shook his head. "No."

"What – and nothing said at the Hall, Georgie, about anything like that?"

"No. Why? What happened, Lennie?"

"No, nothing. It's just that somebody in the pub, the Steamer, said something about a bit of agro somewhere. And I thought the boat was mentioned. And well, they don't want anything like that after the last time, do they."

"No. No, they don't." George's eyes were wide at the thought. "But I'd have heard if there had been." He shook his head. "No. No, it can't have been the boat."

"Well, somebody got it wrong then, obviously," Lennie said, satisfied. He had come to learn that George's ears got everywhere.

"You've made a good job of it, Georgie," he said then, cheerfully, when George handed him up the cleaned trowel. "You can come and help me when I start my business if you like. I could even pay you a few bob."

"What business is that, Lennie?"

"Plastering of course. I'm starting up as a plasterer. A self-employed plasterer."

"Blimey!" George said.

"Yeah," Lennie agreed. "I'll ask Humph for a reference." His hand moved in a flourish." From Sir Humphrey Strange, recommending the work of Leonard W Knowles, Plasterer." He beamed at George.

"What's the W stand for, Lennie?" George wanted to know.

"I dunno. I saw it on a shop front the other day, and thought it looked good."

"Yeah, it does," George agreed.

"Yeah, and then I'll have some fliers printed with that on them and punt them about. And maybe stick an ad in the paper. See, Georgie?"

"Yeah!" Georgie said.

Lennie nodded. "Yeah," he said, and laughed. "Yeah!"

That was Lennie's idea, an idea that had opened up his world and showed him a road out to somewhere else. And in a sense he was already doing it, already working for himself, whistling as he did so, powerful, angled sweeps of the blade as if with a palette knife, an artist of the trowel.

Dewi had taken a day off and had gone to Shrewsbury on the paddle steamer. He hadn't told Sidney he wasn't coming in, and didn't care. Let's see if he likes it! he'd thought, with sudden, vague spite.

Sidney had been even more Sidney lately, even more surly and moody, and Dewi had put it down to the continuing loss of profit to the boat company. It would have been cheaper to travel to Shrewsbury by bus, but the boat trip indulged the holiday feeling he'd started the day with, and the resentment that he'd been harbouring found some satisfaction in adding his share of a return ticket to that loss. A few days ago Sidney had crossed a line.

A few days ago, during a minor disagreement over an accounts entry, a disagreement, to make matters worse, in which he, Dewi, had been in the right, Sidney had showed him what he really thought of him. For the first time in their three years together, he had called him 'Taffy', to his face, deliberately, and slightingly, and without having to think about it. As if, as Dewi had suspected from the very beginning, that was how he had always thought of him, and how he referred to him behind his back.

Another door Sidney had shut on him, leaving him even more to himself, and the little he had there.

And so Dewi was in Shrewsbury, on his way to a chemist's in disguise.

The beard and moustache he had stuck on before leaving were part of a fancy dress set, ordered from the advertising pages of a local newspaper. He had no use for the glasses with Groucho Marx eyebrows, nor the pink plastic nose, which he thought looked more medical than 'hilarious', but the beard and moustache suited his purpose perfectly. He had a false name and address ready in case he had to sign the poison book, and a story of rats under the floorboards, and was sporting a Panama hat to cover the identifying feature of a bald head.

He felt liberated by what he had decided to do, and was wearing a blazer and sporting a cravat to go with the holiday feeling, regretting only that he didn't own a cane. He felt like a different man, and looked it, he considered, finding a long-lost vanity in the plate glass window of a shop, looking, even if he did say so himself, quite debonair, raffish even, the sort of man who winked at women.

He had bought the set because he thought it might be amusing to wear, something to do in the evenings. Perhaps pop in on Edna in the laundrette downstairs with it on, or surprise the other members at teatime in the bowling green clubhouse. At least that's what he had told himself.

He'd told himself another story after that, one about why he was there, in the reference section of Kingham library, swotting up on toxicology.

Studying not the arsenic of his daydreams, the stuff he wasn't spiking Sidney's tea with, but thallium sulphate, colourless, tasteless, readily dissolved in liquid, and highly toxic, the stuff he intended to use. The stuff that came as a compound in a bottle, with a skull and crossbones and a rat's paw up on the label.

And not the impotent chemist shops of his imagination, but one in the real world, the world he was on his way to now, jauntily, down this cobbled side road, Dewi the debonair poisoner.

Chapter Twenty-Eight

Mervyn's new thoughts on Sidney's demise and the bigger picture came with something else that was new – the curious feeling that he wasn't the only one thinking them.

He didn't consider he was being fanciful. He didn't believe as his forebears had, as his father had, that Gwyn ap Nudd, that sovereign of the otherworld, held court among the rocks on Glamorgan's Craig y Ddinas, or that the lights of fairies carousing on the Green Isles of Enchantment lit the darknesses out at sea.

But even when the head of Planning and Strategic Development he was a Celt still, born with a memory much older than most. And in his strained imagination something stirred in the mists of Mabinogi, of Welsh legends, and came to stand with him. And he knew it, without having to think about it, to be tynged amlwg, his destiny. He was no longer alone.

Mervyn drove, or was driven, tynged amlwg at his ear like a backseat driver, to meet Sidney at the golf club on Mortwardine Hill, where the rubble of a 14th century border fortress spoke of the history between two countries, and where now another English prize was to be had.

It was a Sunday morning again, not long after six o'clock, and he had the road, the hill to himself, the sound of larks following him as he climbed in low gear, his eyes in the reflected light from the travelling sun bright with what waited ahead. He was telling himself again, as if primly reminding someone else of it, that he took no pleasure in what he was on his way to do, what had to be done, and was determined that Sidney should not suffer longer than was necessary for him to do so.

And for that he needed to get a good run at him. For that he needed to be in position, hidden in a side lane as Sidney drove past up the hill, and then following him to the second, shorter hill down to the car park and clubhouse as Sidney left his car. As Sidney waited for him when he heard him, a clear target in Mervyn's imagination, standing in the car park, frowning in that Sidney way of his at the speed of the approach, and realising too late that Mervyn wasn't going to stop.

It was an accident, a tragic accident, he would report afterwards, wretched with remorse. And it was my fault – my *fault!* Because I shouldn't have been driving! I thought with my right leg, my good leg, free it would be all right. And then I caught my left foot under the brake pedal, and in confused panic and agony drove the other down on the accelerator. It all happened so *fast*…"

He went on in his imagination to tell them about his friend Sidney. How he'd been concerned about him being housebound after his DIY accident, and had suggested a

256

round of golf. It had been Sidney's idea that they meet that early and on a Sunday, because few members if any were likely to be around to embarrass him. He had protested that he'd simply hold up the game, but Sidney would have none of it.

That was Sidney all over, he thought, feeling quite tearful over the Sidney he'd made up, while waiting in the side lane for the real Sidney to appear, realising then, a few seconds after it had done so, that Sidney's Rover had just gone past.

He switched on and put his own car into gear with a reluctant heart, a man on his way to say goodbye to a good friend, and with the curious feeling that he and Sidney were once more in it together, both going to the same funeral.

On the crest of the hill down to the clubhouse he saw Sidney walk away from his car, having given its polished bodywork his usual suspicious once-over after entrusting it to the public roads. And he saw a second vehicle in the car park, the van of the head groundsman. In early for once, and a witness afterwards to the accident. The helping hand of tynged amlwg.

And in this place of legends other forces moved for him in the mists of Mabinogi. A painted warrior tribe to stand at his back with tynged amlwg, and below them English plunder, the shining fields of plenty. The land of all he had ever desired.

He led the charge with the chorus of 'Bread of Heaven', roaring it like a battle cry. The rush of air through the partly opened windows like the sound of wings gathering strength. He felt he could fly. He felt he *was* flying, sighting up Sidney over the steering wheel, diving like a hawk, death out of a blameless summer's sky, beating time with the words on the car horn then, as if prompted to, something for the groundsman to remember afterwards, his attempt to warn Sidney. Tynged amlwg again.

Sidney, who, as he was supposed to, had stopped and turned in his direction, took it as a greeting, and, frowning at the din, raised his hand vaguely in response.

Mervyn solemnly inclined his head, acknowledging an end they were both about to share.

And then saw him do what Sidney wasn't supposed to do.

Just a few uncertain sidewards steps at first, and then, as if to be on the safe side, casually strolling the rest of the way to his car, and watching from behind it, still frowning, as Mervyn sped past in his.

And for Mervyn it was as if daylight had broken into a dream, bringing with it the logic of the real world, a world in which all Sidney had to do to escape his fate was what he had just done.

A dream from which he awoke, as it were, to find himself on his own, doing the speed he was doing and about to run out of car park.

He panicked and shot his foot out to brake, driving it just under the pedal instead of on it, taking skin off his bare toes and getting the rest, heavy with plaster, stuck.

He screamed when he tugged at it, the pain leaping like flames up his leg.

He screamed again then, at the world as he suddenly found it, a six-foot-high trellis fence blooming with climbing plants rushing up to meet him at the end of the car park. And in the confusion of pain and panic, he did the rest of what he'd intended telling others he'd done after Sidney's demise: he stamped on the accelerator.

The car smashed through the fence between two of its uprights, shedding wood like kindling and taking some of the plants with it as it bounced across a short stretch of lawn outside the clubhouse bar, demolishing a wooden rustic table and a couple of chairs in the outdoor seating area, before ploughing up the summer beds of an ornamental garden beyond it.

He got his foot back then, yanking it free desperately, the pain overridden by what he knew was coming next. He stabbed at the brake, and remembering he had a handbrake used that as well, while trying to steer away from it, the wheel juddering in his other hand, knowing it was too late.

He wailed his way on one long, high-pitched single note across an area of coloured crazy paving around a large fish pond, the car taking off as if trying for the other side, before landing, lily pads and flowering hyacinths riding the waves it sent up, the water brilliant with frantic goldfish.

The engine died and larksong once more was heard on the morning air.

The head groundsman, Mr Hughes, got there first, and looked with awe at the sight.

"It's Councillor Probert," he told himself, peering at the figure inside.

He dropped down and waded to the driver's door.

Mervyn was slumped in his seat with his head on the steering wheel.

Mr Hughes pulled the door open. The pond water rushed in before settling, as if consolingly, around Mervyn's knees.

Mr Hughes touched his shoulder, and then shook it a little

"Are you all right, Mr Probert?"

Mr Hughes was still shaking him, small tentative movements of the hand, as if reluctant to wake someone from a much needed nap, when Sidney turned up panting.

"It's Councillor Probert," Mr Hughes told him.

Sidney, standing on the edge of the pond, catching his breath, nodded. "I know," he said, and indicated the route he'd taken, marked with Mervyn's passing. "I was waiting for him to arrive. I can't make it out. I thought he was going a bit fast. And then he just shot past me. I think he was trying to warn me that something was wrong. Kept sounding his horn."

"Yes, I heard that."

"Is he, er… Is he all right?"

"I dunno. You all right, Mr Probert? Mr Probert?" The groundsman shook him again, putting a bit more into it, and Mervyn stirred and muttered.

"Ah. Well, anyway, he's not – er…"

Mervyn lifted his head and looked at Mr Hughes without seeing him, his eyes elsewhere.

"It was horrible, horrible," he intoned. "And it was all my fault. *My* fault! I should not have been driving. Not with this foot. I got it caught under the brake, you see."

"I wondered if something like that had happened," Sidney put in. "It's in plaster. He broke it."

"It's in plaster," Mervyn said, his head up, as if prompted by words on the air.

"In a DIY accident," Sidney said.

"A trolley jack," Mervyn said.

"Blimey!" Mr Hughes said. "And now this."

"I panicked and stepped on the accelerator for the brake. It all happened so fast. So *fast!*" Mervyn added on a note of anguish, and sunk his head in his hands. "It was an accident," he said into them, his voice choked. "A tragic accident."

"Of course it was," Mr Hughes said soothingly. "And there's no harm done. Well, not much. And don't you worry, Mr Probert. We'll soon have you out of there."

The groundsman looked at Sidney. "But as the club's first aider I'm not happy about trying it without help. Not with his foot and in these conditions. So if you wouldn't mind holding on here, Mr Acton, while I phone."

"No, of course not," Sidney said immediately, fired with the warmth of friendship for a man who, even when in peril himself, had thought to warn him.

"We'll soon have you out of there, Councillor," the groundsman said again, before wading back to the side of the pond.

Mervyn had frozen at the mention of Sidney's name. He turned in his seat, hands still to his face, and slowly spreading his finger peered through them.

"It is you…" he said to himself. "It's *you,*" he said, taking his hands away in disbelief, and as if realising, as if seeing it all then – whatever it was about. The light that dawned in his eyes a confused one, but with Sidney, the answer to it, standing clearly at its centre, gazing at him.

Mervyn read his expression with a sort of wonder. It was, he thought, as if Sidney understood. As if he knew all, from the bullet that had brought down a crow on that same hill to now. Knew and understood all, and forgave all.

And Mervyn, the old Mervyn, because he thought it was expected of him, hid his face over the steering wheel and heaved dry tears of contrition. And then he found he was crying real ones, a weight of them breaking in him, as if all those tears he knew he should have shed in his adult years and hadn't, and now couldn't stop.

"It's shock," Mr Bevan said with crisp authority, standing with Sidney on the edge of the pond, shaking water from his legs. "I'll ring from the office. Won't be a jiffy."

Chapter Twenty-Nine

Sidney had once, in his mind at least, where he waited still to show the world who he really was, promised Mervyn that if he and his boyos didn't do the job he was paying them to do, then he, Mervyn, would learn then to his cost just who he was really dealing with.

It had been an empty threat, made by that other Sidney, the one who had always in his bedtime imagination got the upper hand in the playground, and who always came out best in the world afterwards. It was all that was left of a brief time when the real Sidney, who had to live in that world, had been for once, just for once, briefly, one of its winners. Not in a way that the world could see and applaud, not with looks, or strength, or brains, but behind its back, with cunning, and a patience he savoured, the small victories he won each time, the money, their money, he turned into his.

And it had changed his life, made him into the man he wanted to be, or a good enough copy, if he and others didn't look too closely.

It was his driver, the planted witness to the fight on the boat, who had told him that not only was Lennie back, he had been back for the past few weeks. The driver had been away on holiday, and when he returned found himself having to reconsider his witness statement in an interview at the police station.

Sidney hadn't expected it to happen overnight, but he hadn't even, during what he'd believed was the suspension of the CSC's licence, had an increase in Shrewsbury jobs for his money. He had already said goodbye to the so-called pension pot, to skies and seas the bluest money can buy. Mervyn had been stringing him along about both.

But he had found it in himself, if not to forgive him, if not to fully relinquish another grievance to add to his collection of them, then at least to understand him. After wallowing in it, telling himself that he'd expected little else from life, he had grudgingly allowed that Mervyn had tried to warn him that day in the car park, and was able, in the interests of not looking a complete fool, to put his duplicity down to the first symptoms of the nervous breakdown he was said to have suffered.

Mervyn was presently a patient in the secure Julian Culpepper Observation Ward in Kingham General. Sidney had visited him there soon after he was committed, and found him in his dressing gown and pyjamas leading the day room in 'Shall We Gather at the River?'

Mervyn appeared not to recognise him at first, simply glancing at him without interest as if at a stranger. And Sidney, already unnerved by the world he'd found behind the ward's locked doors, put his offerings of squash and a half pound of grapes down by the side of his chair with relief, and was about to disappear, when Mervyn startled him by suddenly leaning forward and grabbing the skirt of his jacket.

He looked up at him with a sly smile, a smile with some of the old Mervyn in it, and as if acknowledging a secret between them, and assuring Sidney that it was safe with him, shared a wink with him.

And then he returned abruptly to the singing, vigorously conducting it with his hands, rallying those who had faltered when he'd paused, leading the lost and the broken on the road to somewhere else, an outing from themselves.

Sidney joined in briefly, making up the words, covering his retreat to the attendant and the door of the room, the voices followed him into the yard, Mervyn's baritone marching on ahead of them.

He was torn between the feeling that he was leaving a friend behind, and the relief to be out. And he realised then that he was on his own. That for the first time since arriving in Kingham, for the first time since meeting Mervyn, when it came to his business, he now had no one he could talk to. He was on his own.

He was on his own now. When he had won before he had been armed with his knowledge of figures, making them say what others expected them to say. Now he was on his own, armed only with desperation, the fear of going back, stripped of all he had gathered to him since, leaving only the old Sidney.

And out of that desperation had come a plan, a crude affair, a remake of the last incident on the boat, and not without considerable risk. But his will was made and his affairs up to date. And he had, he considered, nothing now to lose. It would literally, as far as he was concerned, be a case of sink or swim.

The American represented far more to him than the loss of Shrewsbury profit. He was a monster who threw long shadows in Sidney's imagination. An ogre from his past when others had had the upper hand, and one who waited for him in the future. An ogre whose greed would leave the wreckage of the Kingham Prestige Car Company, along with that of others, in his wake.

His ambition had to be stopped there, on the river. And he was the one to do it, he told himself again, sitting in his car in Upper Ham, backing it up with another gulp of whisky.

He finished the little that was left, and tossed the half bottle over his shoulder into the back of that normally immaculate car, its seats still wearing their plastic covers from the showroom. He left the Rover, not bothering to lock it, or to run a suspicious eye over the polished dark green paintwork, and walked with a determined, reckless air towards the CSC entrance.

He was on his way to poke, as it were, a stick through the bars of the Burger King's cage, to provoke him to violence. Sidney couldn't fight, but he could swim, and either by the American's hand, or making it look as if it had been, he intended leaving the PS *Batch Castle* the same way Lennie had.

Keeping his passenger licence would be the least of the Yank's problems: let him try getting out of a second attempted murder charge.

Priny was on the phone when Sidney appeared at the booking office window, assuring somebody on the other end that it was something somebody else would grow out of. She smiled at him, and tucking the receiver with a practised movement under her chin, went on talking while ripping a ticket off the roll and giving him change.

On board, Sidney wandered among the other Saturday passengers looking for the American, remembering photographs of him in local newspapers, a big man, in a shirt, smoking a cigar. He thought he'd probably hear him first before he saw him. Like all these big shots who thought they deserved more space in life and to be heard above anyone else. Sidney's anger, fuelled with whisky, simmered.

But he could neither hear nor see him. He joined the small queue at the door of the galley then, when the *Castle* had cleared the island, Batch Magna falling away on her starboard side. When it was his turn to be served he asked, casually, if Sir Humphrey was on board by any chance, as he thought a tourist might, as if the American baronet were some sort of tourist attraction, which he often was, sharing family photograph albums with the Commander and his Mate, Stringbag the collie.

Annie Owen found something to smile at in Sidney, a smile with something of the mother in it. "No, not today he isn't, lovey. It's not his day, see. Tuesday, that's his day, next Tuesday. What can I get you, dear? We've Coney Island special hotdogs, *very* popular, they are. Sandwiches and rolls, Scotch eggs, pork pies, Welsh cakes. And ice-cream of course, in this weather. Homemade, it is. The famous Batch Castle soft ice-cream, a treat for the tongue, it is. Or ice-lollies, Best-Lick-On-A-Stick," she said, pointing one being licked on a wall poster, and then waited, smiling her smile at him again.

Sidney decided he didn't want anything to eat. He was a man who normally drank little, but he felt what his head needed was another drink, something milder than whisky, something to sort out the effects of a half bottle of it.

Had she, he asked, any cider? His wife, Molly, drank cider when out to no apparent effect, in small bottles with a Victorian rustic scene on the label.

"We certainly do. Pint or half?"

"No bottles?" he asked.

"No-oo," Annie said, with a small laugh at the idea, and without enquiring further, picked up a pint glass.

"This is the real stuff, this is. Dotty Snape's. Sheepsnout," she said, drawing it off from the wooden barrel. "Made in the valley here. The best of sweet and dry in one of Dotty's famous mixes. Pure goodness, it is. Nothing but the sun added to it. My husband reckons you ought to be able to get it from the doctor's. Bottles, indeed," she added with another indulgent laugh, handing him the pint, the swill of cider in it lit with a green tinge.

Sidney had relaxed with relief when Annie had confirmed that the American wasn't on board, as if he'd been holding his breath without knowing it. He tried to turn it into a swagger, to tell himself a story about what would have happened if the Burger King had been, and how he hadn't finished with him yet, not by a long chalk, that there was always next week, next Tuesday. But his heart wasn't in it.

He finished his drink standing at the rail, content to watch the paddle wheel leaving white water behind.

Resisting again Annie's attempt to feed him something, he returned to the galley for another pint of Sheepsnout, in a mood for more of the distance it put between him and the world.

And this time found shelter, a refuge from the careless sunlit world of holidaymakers and local day-trippers. The deck saloon was empty, apart from a family picnicking with a furtive air with sandwiches made for the trip, and drinks in thermos flasks, and a young couple who only saw each other.

He tucked himself away in a corner of it, a small, slight figure huddled in misery, sipping his Sheepsnout like medicine.

He knew he wouldn't be back to beard the American. On Tuesday or any other day. He hadn't got it in him. Just *hadn't* got it in him, he admitted to himself, the drink giving him another sort of courage. And he wondered from the same sort of distance, where his gaze saw clearly and did not waver, if it mattered whether he was here or not, to himself or anyone else. If he shouldn't do it without the Yank. Simply slip over the rail and let the river do the rest. Just float off in the white water. Just float away.

It was Tom Parr, doing his usual round of the boat after the passengers had disembarked, who woke him, prodding him to befuddled consciousness with a finger, to say that he might like to know that they had just berthed at Shrewsbury.

Sidney did want to know. He didn't think he could face another three hours on the paddle steamer, the plaything of a multi-millionaire winner, a boat, as he saw it, on which he had surrendered the last of the person he'd told himself and others he was.

He went down the gangway, leaving the *Batch Castle* and the Shrewsbury run behind for the Burger King, leaving the road open for whatever else he wanted to grab – not that it would matter to someone like him, not that he'd notice who or what went under his wheels.

After walking up into town, the irony was not lost on him when, sitting back in the Shrewsbury taxi he'd found, it set off for Batch Magna and his car.

Chapter Thirty

When Sidney arrived home, arrived at the other half of his new life, the neat semi-detached house he'd taken a mortgage out on after starting his business, Molly, the woman who shared that life, was on her way out.

They met in the hall. "Hello, darling!" she said. "I was just nipping out for—"

"Molly," Sidney said firmly, determined to say what he'd carried with him since leaving Shrewsbury, unloading it there, under the chandelier and the line of framed cloth butterflies from Pennington's department store..

"Molly, my name is not Sidney Acton. It is Sidney Thornton. I am a fraud. A fraud and a crook."

"Oh," she said, a small smile ready, uncertain if Sidney, who rarely joked, was attempting to do so now. "Have you been drinking?" she said then, taking a closer look, more amused than anything else. Drinking was something else he rarely did.

"Yes, I have. I – look, let's sit down," he said, and steered her down the hall to the sitting room.

She sat in one of the armchairs, tense now with a mixture of concern and curiosity.

He took the other chair, facing her, and sat straight on it. "I took Acton as a name because that's where I was living before I came here. OK?" he said, as if getting it out of the way.

"Not Kensington? You weren't living in Kensington, then?" Molly said, as if wanting to make sure she had it right.

"No. Not Kensington. And I wasn't running an export/import business. I worked for someone else. A hotel chain. I was an accountant there. A small cog behind a partition in accounts."

"I see," she said alertly.

"I was working on temporary staff invoicing," he went on, and paused, as if that might suggest to her what was coming. It didn't look as if it did.

"I was better than they knew," he went on. "Or cared," he added, and made a sour movement with his lips, looking down at the cream rug, something else, along with the beige three-piece suite, from Pennington's Soft Furnishings.

Then he looked at her. "I stole from them. That's what I did. That's how I became Sidney Acton," he said, and waved a hand in the vague direction of the Kingham Prestige Car Company.

"I see," she said again, nodding slowly.

"I used invoices from fake staffing agencies and opened bank accounts in names similar to those agencies," he told her, not without remembered pride.

"And you were never found out," she said, as if unsure what to say, but feeling she ought to say something.

"I left one jump ahead of the annual auditors. I meant to leave the country, but then…"

"So you weren't touring, then?"

"No. I was on my way to Holyhead, for Ireland. To leave that way. But then, well, I met you."

She smiled. "Yes," she said. And she had surprised herself by falling in love with him, and continued still, at times, to surprise herself.

"Anyway, I—"

"Were you married?" it occurred to her then to ask.

"What?" Sidney said, frowning at the diversion.

"Are you married?" she said on a less conversational note. "Did you leave a family behind when you jumped ahead of the auditors?"

"No. No, there was no one. Well, I was living with a woman at the time, in her council flat there, in Acton. But that was…" He shrugged, his expression suggesting the rest.

"But no children?"

"No, I said."

"And are you still without a father? Or was that also—"

"No, that's true. He did walk out on mum when she was pregnant. And I am an only child. OK? Now, can I—"

"Is she still alive, your mother?"

Sidney sighed. "Yes, she's still alive. The last I knew."

"But not in Kensington, I take it?"

"No. In Islington. Look—"

"On her own?"

"As far as I know, Molly, yes. I send her money," he said defensively. "She doesn't know where I am, I can't risk

273

it, the way she gabs. But I send her money every month. Travel all the way to Bristol and back for the postcode, just in case. She does all right, don't worry. Now, can I get on with it," he said querulously. "This isn't easy for me, you know."

"No, I don't suppose it is. But I'm wondering, Sidney, why you're telling me this now," she said, softening her suspicion with a smile.

"Well, let me finish first," he said, and told her his tale of town hall worthies, bribes and corrupt practices, unlicensed money lending, the Julian Culpepper Observation Ward, and a skinhead called Lennie.

"Mervyn, Councillor Probert, is the chap I usually partner at golf," he added, with a brief return of his elocution lessons.

"Is he?" she said, unimpressed. "And is he still locked up?"

"No, he's out now. Doing much better," Sidney was happy to report. "Be back behind his desk in no time. And as I say, I don't blame him really, it was because of this nervous breakdown."

"Was it?" she said. "Does he know about London?"

Sidney shook his head. "No. Nobody does here, except you. Anyway, today I thought I'll take a hand. Take over where this Lennie left off. Only this time make it stick. I was going to provoke the American into a fight and make sure it ended with me going into the drink. It was sink or swim as far as I was concerned. Do or die. 'Cept he wasn't there," he added lamely.

"And all because you lost money on the Shrewsbury jobs. You could have drowned!"

"There's more to it than the Shrewsbury jobs, Molly! They don't call him the Burger King for nothing."

"Don't they? Because I've heard something completely different."

Sidney shook his head at whatever she'd heard. "This man and his burgers conquered America, Molly," he said, leaning forward with it in the chair. "And now he's started a company here. And when he's bored with the river, what then?"

When she appeared not to know he told her. "The land, that's what, and a new title of Transport King. Think about it. *Think* about it, Molly!" he urged her, hands rigid in the air, emphasising it.

"All right, all right. But why didn't you tell me any of this before? Not your past necessarily, but all this business since. Why? That's what I don't understand."

"I dunno. I just…" He trailed off and shrugged.

"You should have told me, shared it. Brought it home and *shared* it with me. I *love* you," she said indignantly, when he looked as if he didn't understand, glaring at him, eyes as fierce as an owl's.

"I love you, too, Molly," he said, as if startled into it, the true, unguarded voice of Sidney, said like that for perhaps the first time in their relationship, and perhaps for the first time said with hope.

His expression as he looked at her moved her to go to him, but before she could do so, he added wretchedly, as if fearing that it would change everything, "But there's more…"

She sat back carefully in the chair and waited.

"Mervyn suggested," he said after a moment. "I paid him – I paid his boyos, the skinheads, through him to – er – to set fire to my competition, Parry's Taxis. Parry's Taxis, here in town. In Llanshay Road," he elaborated, when she appeared not to know it.

"I know where it is – or was. I just can't believe what I'm listening to."

He scrambled to defend himself. "Yes, yes, I know it sounds bad, but—"

"That's because it is, Sidney. It is bad. It's called arson. You can get—"

"Yes, I know, I know," he said, holding up a hand, not wanting to hear how long he could get for it. "But it was just his taxis they fired, in the garage he had there. Unlike me, Mr Parry owned the cars. But, Molly, no one was hurt and he was insured. And as Mervyn said, he was thinking of retiring anyway, at his age. And we wanted to make it hard for someone to walk in and start up again. Mr and Mrs Parry live in Tenby now. They have a nice little bungalow there, apparently, with sea views," he added, as if chattily passing on news of a neighbour. "Mervyn had a postcard from him. He'd done him a few favours as well in the past."

"Had he? And what if, Sidney, old Mr Parry had been charged with it?"

Although, it occurred to her then, when considering the postcard, that perhaps Mr Parry *should* have been charged. Perhaps Mervyn the salesman had sold both Sidney increased profit and Mr Parry retirement in Tenby.

Sidney smiled a little and shook his head. "The police put it down to a disgruntled driver. Mr Parry was questioned, as I was, as his only business rival. But there was nothing of course to connect him, or me, with it. And he himself had an alibi that night, like I did. The same alibi, as it happens. We were both at a Rotary Club bash, with the mayor and the chief constable, among other guests. That's why Mervyn chose that night."

"Where was I?" Molly wanted to know.

"You weren't here. It was when your dad started to get ill. You stayed with them for a few days."

"Oh, yes," she said, and seemed to be thinking, while he watched her, waiting.

Then she said, "Is there any more to come…? Haven't murdered anyone as well, have you?"

He shook his head, not smiling because she wasn't, and he couldn't be sure if, when she next spoke, he'd have anything to smile about.

"I still don't understand, Sidney, why you're telling me all this now."

"I dunno," he said, after struggling with it. "It's just that I – I dunno, I just wanted not to keep lying to you. That's all."

"A new start?" she said, already having some idea in which direction that would take.

"Yes. Yes, a new start," he agreed, and looked at her as he had before, and this time she went to him.

He put up a hand as if to fend her off. "But please, Molly, no mention of Mervyn or Odgar Llewellyn-Jenkins to anyone. Mervyn, well, Mervyn's Mervyn. And my operating licence is issued by the Public Transport Office in the town hall, which might as well have Odgar

Llewellyn-Jenkins written on the door. Understand?" he said, looking fretfully up at her.

"Yes, of course I do, darling. Don't worry," she said soothingly, and perching on the arm of his chair put an arm around him.

He lent into her and she stroked his hair, with its obstinate bald patch, finding tenderness in his vanity, in the cures he sought for it, as she did in his shoe lifts, something else he had no idea she knew about.

Her strokes were light and loving, but there was nothing loving about her thoughts. They concerned Councillor Probert, who had taken Sidney for a ride, and would doubtless do so again, if allowed to, and Odgar Llewellyn-Jenkins, the man who would be mayor, and who held Sidney's livelihood in his hands.

She was wondering how she might strike at them, while protecting what she held to her now, the foolish and dishonest man who, although he didn't know it yet, would soon, at last, be her husband.

The next morning, after breakfast, Sidney left the house with his golf clubs, to find, as he put it, someone to play with. Molly hadn't been able to have children after her son was born, and there were times, living with Sidney, when she felt she didn't need to.

She listened to the sound of his car until she couldn't hear it, and then picked up the phone.

Chapter Thirty-One

Tim Brown, Ffion Owen's new boyfriend, was Molly's son. She had never really opened up about his father and he had stopped asking. After she had met Sidney, Tim had moved with them to the house from the flat he and Molly had been living in, and for his mother's sake he had put up with the other man for over a year, before moving out to a bedsit in the town.

He thought Sidney a poor thing, unworthy of her, and that she loved him only added, as far as he was concerned, to the mystery of the female sex. But he saw that his mother was happy, that Sidney completed her in some odd way, and that was enough for him.

Her son sounded to Molly as if he had just got out of bed when he answered the phone, and she wondered idly if Ffion was in it.

To her relief he laughed when he heard what Councillor Probert had told Sidney about the American. "The Burger King? What rubbish. Mum, Ffion told you what the situation was there, when we saw you the other day. They're hanging on by their fingertips."

Yes, I know, darling. I just wanted to make sure."

"The only part of what this Probert character told Sid is the bit about Humph having been a short-order cook. I suppose it's because he's an American. Some people's memories are stuck in the last war. He's a really good guy."

"I'm sure he is, but it's not really about the American. It's about bribery and corruption in the town hall – not to mention illegal money lending on the Culpeper Estate," she said, and waited.

"*What...?*" Tim said, fully awake in her ear.

Leaving out the arson part, and Sidney's attempt to perjury himself on the *Castle*, she'd started to tell him when he asked her to hold on while he shot off for a notepad and pen.

It was a story that would see Tim promoted from junior reporter on the *Church Myddle Chronicle* to reporter on the *Kingham News*. A story that had started cautiously with coy hints and suggestions in the inside pages of the *News*, carefully vetted by the paper's solicitors, before making a splash on the front pages of both newspapers when Councillor Probert, spooked by a follow-up report linking a certain department head in the town hall to unlicensed money lending on the Julian Culpepper Estate, fled the town ahead of a police investigation.

Another headline followed shortly after that, when Councillor Odgar Llewellyn-Jenkins, his bank account one thousand pounds lighter, and left to carry the burden of press innuendo and growing public speculation, stood like a Roman on the steps of the town hall and addressed a gathering of local media.

The day was bright with sunlight, but it was winter where Odgar was, his eyes bleak as, quoting Proverbs, he spoke with thunderous righteousness of slanderers and whisperers, and flinging it in the faces of the chief slanderers and whisperers, warned that false witness will not go unpunished.

He paused as if catching his breath and dabbed at his mouth with a handkerchief. And then as if dismissing them, as if disdainfully bowing to the will of the people, said that to those who knew him, professionally and personally, he had no need to distance himself from rumour and insinuation. But he had a duty to the dignity of his office as councillor and the reputation of the town hall, and therefore had decided that the only honourable course open to him was to resign.

Molly poured herself a glass of wine when she heard the news on Border Radio, and toasted the future. She had neutralised two potential enemies to Sidney and the Kingham Prestige Car Service, and so had made a start on a bigger picture of her own.

Chapter Thirty-Two

A few weeks after that Dewi Brice entered Sidney's office without knocking. Knocking first was something else that was now a thing of the past. And the partners' desk, instead of being in front of the window, was lengthways down the centre of the room, and now had two, as it was meant to, seated either side of it. And there was no doubt in Dewi's mind who was the senior partner.

"Welcome, Dewi Brice, with our elevenses," Molly cried dramatically.

"Yes, welcome, Dewi," Sidney echoed, joining in, trying for the same note, taking his cue from Molly and looking happy to do so.

Dewi was carrying a tray with a plate on it of mixed biscuits, coffee for Molly and Earl Grey for Sidney, both the tea and biscuits the real thing.

He had stopped substituting inferior brands after Molly had joined the firm. As he had stopped murdering Sidney in his daydreams, first in deference to her, and then because he no long felt the need to. Sidney no longer entirely being Sidney, or not entirely the Sidney he knew. He was only glad now that he hadn't used the contents of the bottle with the dead rat on the label.

He'd to tried a few times, offering to make the morning drinks, smiling his secret smile at Shirley, while carrying death in his pocket to the cubby hole. Except that the last time he found that he'd forgotten to bring the bottle with him. "Blast!" he'd said, unconvincingly patting his pockets while waiting for the kettle to boil. And the time before he couldn't get the top off, pulling ineffectually at it, sweating and muttering furiously, swearing at it even, and then had to hastily shove it in his pocket when Shirley came to see what the noise was about.

He had celebrated Molly's first day at the office by pouring the stuff down the sink in his flat. He had never met her before – he'd sided with her against Sidney enough times in his imagination, and had an idea *what* she looked like, having pestered him for the details, but had never met her. And then, suddenly one morning, she was there.

And now it was as if she had opened windows in the place and let light in, spreading it between the two offices, her chattiness, the little jokes she made, her giggling with Shirley, and showing an interest in him that when they'd first met that had unnerved him, and then caused him the next day to wear the new shirt he'd been saving in its box for his Christmas visit to his sister's.

"We were just talking again, Dewi, about Prestige Travel," she said, referring an idea she'd had about doing coach trips.

"Well, as I've said, I think it's an excellent idea, Molly. And, you know, the more I think about it, the more convinced I am that there's a gap locally in that market."

Sidney chuckled at the prospect of filling it. "We'll have to look for bigger premises soon, Dewi, the way she's going."

"I would not be at all surprised, Sidney. Not in the *least*," he declared, unloading the elevenses tray.

Shirley, who normally made the drinks, was off for a couple of hours having another wedding dress fitting. Dewi now had two weddings to look forward to, Molly's new engagement ring keeping Shirley's company.

These days, for him, tripping down the stairs from his flat each morning, it was more like going home than going to work, going home to a family.

The steam whistle in the wheelhouse screamed its triple warning to any latecomers, the sound losing itself among the hills of the valley, a song of summer, of fun on the river, and the PS *Batch Castle* pulled away on her last trip of the season.

And from Snails Eye Island the mother otter with her new brood of pups swam out with them in tow to briefly join her, as they did each trip, as if seeing her off, and then welcoming her back, their glistening heads playfully bobbing in her wake.

The End – for *now*…

Preview

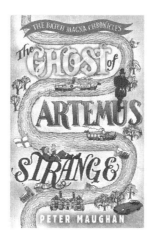

Sir Humphrey has offered to play Father Christmas at the local hospital, but disaster strikes when he realises he won't be able to buy the sack of toys he'd promised the children.

Rupert, a gentleman of the road, is found asleep in an old car in the Hall's coach house. He is scrubbed up and given a room at the Hall, where two guests are already staying: a businessman and his rather young female companion. When money goes missing from their bedroom, Rupert is accused, and Miss Wyndham, the village's amateur sleuth, decides to investigate the matter.

Meanwhile, local author Phineas Cook has come up with the idea of a resident ghost at the Hall to attract paying guests. All goes smoothly until the ghostly actors spend too long in the pub one evening and their performance descends into sword-wielding chaos.

As always in Batch Magna, events somehow manage to turn out all right in the end – but in the most unexpected manner…

The Batch Magna Chronicles, Volume Five

COMING SOON

About the Author

Peter Maughan's early ambition to be a landscape painter ran into a lack of talent – or enough of it to paint to his satisfaction what he saw. He worked on building sites, in wholesale markets, on fairground rides and in a circus. And travelled the West Country, roaming with the freedom of youth, picking fruit, and whatever other work he could get, sleeping wherever he could, before moving on to wherever the next road took him. A journeying out of which came his non-fiction work *Under the Apple Boughs*, when he came to see that he had met on his wanderings the last of a village England. After travelling to Jersey in the Channel Islands to pick potatoes, he found work afterwards in a film studio in its capital, walk-ons and bit parts in the pilot films that were made there, and as a contributing script writer. He studied at the Actor's Workshop in London, and worked as an actor in the UK and Ireland (in the heyday of Ardmore Studios). He founded and ran a fringe theatre in Barnes, London, and living on a converted Thames sailing barge among a small colony of houseboats on the River Medway, wrote pilot film scripts as a freelance deep in the green shades of rural Kent. An idyllic, heedless time in that other world of the river, which later, when he had collected enough rejection letters learning his craft as a novelist, he transported to a river valley in the Welsh Marches, and turned into the Batch Magna novels.

Peter is married and lives currently in Wales. Visit his website at www.batchmagna.com.

Note from the Publisher

If you enjoyed this book, we are delighted to share also
The Famous Cricket Match, a short story play by Peter
Maughan, featuring our hero Sir Humphrey of Batch Hall,
defending the village with both cricket *and* baseball…

To get your **free copy of *The Famous Cricket Match*,**
as well as receive updates on further releases
in the Batch Magna Chronicles series, sign up
at http://farragobooks.com/batch-magna-signup

Printed in Great
Britain
by Amazon